CARNAL
CURIOSITY

A STONE BARRINGTON NOVEL

Stuart Woods

A SIGNET BOOK

SIGNET
Published by the Penguin Group
Penguin Group (USA) LLC, 375 Hudson Street,
New York, New York 10014

USA | Canada | UK | Ireland | Australia | New Zealand | India | South Africa | China
penguin.com
A Penguin Random House Company

Published by Signet, an imprint of New American Library, a division of
Penguin Group (USA). Previously published in a G. P. Putnam's Sons
edition.

First Signet Printing, December 2014

ISBN 978-0-451-46688-4

Printed in the United States of America
10 9 8 7 6 5 4 3 2 1

1

Stone Barrington sat at his desk in the downstairs office of his Turtle Bay town house, poring over documents related to the finances of his new clients, Jack and Hillary Coulter.

Or, perhaps, Hillary and Jack Coulter, since she was the one with all the money, and there was a great deal of it. He added a couple of paragraphs to the memo he was sending to the tax and finance department of his law firm, Woodman & Weld, where his suggestions would be reviewed to keep him out of trouble. His phone buzzed.

"Your five thirty appointment is here," his secretary, Joan, said.

"I have a five thirty?" Stone asked, momentarily baffled.

"The insurance adjuster, Crane Hart, from the Steele company?"

"Oh, of course. Give me three minutes, then send him in." He clicked off before she could respond. He tidied the document on his computer, then e-mailed it, then he shuffled the papers on his desk into a fairly neat stack.

"Much better," a female voice said from the doorway.

"Ah, Mr. Hart," Stone said, not looking up. Then he looked up. "I perceive that you are not a mister," he said.

She was tall, wrapped in a suit too tight and with a skirt too short to be businesslike, and her bright, blond hair was pulled tightly into something at the back of her head. He wondered how she could blink, but she did, and slowly.

Before he could speak, a moment of carnal curiosity flashed between them. "Ah," he said, otherwise speechless. He finally managed speech. "I was expecting an insurance adjuster of the male persuasion."

"Ah," she replied. "A natural assumption, but Steele sends out tall, blond, female adjusters when the loss is great enough."

"I must remember to be robbed at gunpoint more often," he said, waving her toward the sofa instead of toward the chair before his desk.

She took a seat and crossed her legs without

undue exposure, an artful act given the mininess of her skirt.

Stone came and sat at the other end of the sofa.

"Now, about your loss," she said.

"Must we discuss that? I was beginning to think of this meeting as more of a gain."

She placed a briefcase on the sofa between them, unsnapped it, and extracted a file. "You're very kind," she said, "but first, your loss."

"If we must."

"We must." She consulted the file. "It says here that you were robbed of five hundred thousand dollars."

"Five million dollars," he corrected.

Her eyes opened perceptibly wider. "Then you require a taller, blonder adjuster."

"I recovered four and a half million dollars before filing my claim," he replied. "The present adjuster will do nicely."

"Do you have any evidence of this robbery?" she asked.

"I still have a bump on the back of my head," he said, gingerly touching the spot.

"Anything on paper?"

"I have a bank statement showing a five-million-dollar withdrawal, and a redeposit of four and a half million a few days later."

"What happened to the other half million?"

"After I had been relieved of the five

million—at gunpoint, I should add—the person who had taken it exchanged it for four and a half million."

"That seems an extremely unwise transaction," she pointed out.

"Not when you consider that the five million was in tens and twenties, and the exchange sum was in hundreds."

"You mean the villain paid half a million dollars to make it easier to count?"

"Count, transport, carry by hand . . . I believe it's called money laundering."

"Is there a police report covering any of this? Anything at all?"

Stone went to a desk drawer and came back with his bank statement and two documents, one a receipt from the Connecticut State Police and the other a police report from the NYPD on the theft.

"You seem well documented," she said admiringly, "and on this basis I will recommend that your claim be paid immediately."

"Thank you."

"I expect we at Steele were fortunate to get off so light."

"I expect you were."

"Now that we have concluded this matter, do you think you could tell me all of this story, just to satisfy my curiosity?"

"I can certainly do that," Stone said, "but not without inducing a terrible thirst. Would you like a drink?"

"A Belvedere martini, please," she replied without hesitation. "Very dry, straight up, olives."

"For anything more boisterous than brown whiskey over ice, we will have to adjourn to my study upstairs, where the materials for constructing your libation are readily available."

"You talked me into it," she said.

He led her upstairs and into his study, a small but comfortably furnished room with a bar concealed behind the paneling and an ice machine humming discreetly. She sat on the sofa, crossing her legs again, and waited while he assembled her drink, then poured himself a bourbon on the rocks. He handed her the martini glass.

She took a sip. "Perfect," she said. "I missed lunch. Do you have anything to snack on?"

Stone picked up the phone on the coffee table and pressed a button. "Fred," he said, "you have five minutes to put together some canapés for two." He hung up.

"Who's Fred?"

"Frederick Flicker, an English butler who was a gift from a French friend."

"A gift?"

"A year of his services. After that, we negotiate."

"Is he concealed behind the paneling?"

"He's in the kitchen at this time of the day, no doubt canoodling with my cook and house-keeper, Helene."

She suddenly fixed her gaze on a spot across the room, then rose and approached a painting, examining it closely. "Is this one of the Matilda Stones listed on your policy?"

"It is. There's another behind you, a couple more in the living and dining rooms, and, best of all, the four she left me, hanging in the master suite."

"Left you?"

"Matilda Stone was my mother."

"Ahhhh, I should have deduced that. I'm not usually so slow on the uptake." She sat down again.

Fred appeared silently at the door, bearing a silver tray, which he set on the coffee table. "Helene's compliments: some prosciutto, some crumbles of Parmigiano-Reggiano, and a little of her pork ril-lettes," he announced, then he vanished.

"I should keep him on, if I were you," she said.

"I fully intend to."

"May I see the other paintings?" she asked.

"Of course."

"Including the four in the master suite?"

He smiled. "Of course. But let me fix us another drink first."

2

Stone put their drinks on a small tray and led the way to the elevator.

"This is a very handsome house," she said.

"Thank you. How did you come to be named Hart Crane in reverse?"

"My mother had never heard of the poet. Crane was her maiden name, much as your mother's was Stone. Hart was my father's name."

"That makes perfect sense," Stone said.

"Yes, but it doesn't make it any easier to live with. First there's the gender confusion, then the spelling, then the denial of a connection with the author, then, if I'm lucky, people get it right."

"I'll make a note of it," Stone said. The elevator came to a halt, and Stone stepped out and nodded in the direction of the master suite. He followed her in, then set the tray on a bedside table and gave her what was left of her first martini. "Bottoms up," he said. "So to speak."

She laughed.

They tossed off the last sip of their first drinks.

She smiled. "And those are the paintings," she said, traversing the room and standing reverently before the smallish oils. "Ahhhh."

"I'm glad you appreciate them."

"I paint a little, and that makes me appreciate them all the more."

"Your second drink," he said, offering the tray.

"First, I'll bet there's a bathroom in this suite."

"Mine is to your left, yours is to your right."

She chose the one to the right and was back in a flash, accepting and sipping her new martini.

"That was fast," Stone said, sipping his new bourbon.

"It doesn't take long to take off your underwear," she said, as if to herself.

He froze for a moment. "I hope you meant what I think you said," he said.

"I try to speak clearly," she replied, "even after a martini."

He reached tentatively under her skirt and encountered a firm, smooth buttock.

"Mmmm," she said, taking another sip of her martini and facing the paintings again.

He stood behind her and kissed her on an ear. "Perfect hairdo for an available ear," he breathed, and he noticed that his respiration had increased perceptibly.

She reached into her hair and released something, and it fell around her shoulders in thick, glossy waves. "It works both ways," she said, and she sounded a little breathless, too.

He reached around her and cupped a breast in his hand. It felt just wonderful. Emboldened, he undid her top button, reached inside, located a nipple and squeezed.

"You've found the start button," she said, reaching behind her and feeling the front of his trousers.

"So have you."

She found the zipper and pulled it slowly down. "I believe I have," she said, reaching inside and taking him in her hand. "Isn't there a bed somewhere in this room?" She turned to face him and began working on his belt buckle.

His trousers fell to the floor, and he stepped out of them. "The bed is this way," he said, pulling her across the space of six feet. They finished undressing before falling onto the bed, not bothering with the covers.

Half an hour later they lay in each other's arms, breathing deeply.

"I feel well adjusted now," he said.

"Adjustment is my métier," she said. "Are you up to doing it again?" She took him in her hand again to focus his attention. "Yes, I believe you are."

They did it again, this time more slowly.

"I'm hungry," she said a few minutes later.

"What would you like to eat?"

"You mean, in addition to what I've just had?"

"Whatever you want."

"A steak."

"What kind of steak?"

"A prime strip."

"I thought I'd already done that."

"Medium rare," she said.

"Something on the side?"

She laughed. "Green beans and some sort of potatoes."

"Something to start?"

"A Caesar salad."

Stone picked up the phone, reached Fred, and ordered for them. "And a bottle of the Far Niente Cabernet, decanted." He hung up and returned to her.

She snuggled into his shoulder. "I hope you're surprised by all this," she said, "because I certainly am."

"I love a surprise," he replied, stroking her hair.

"There was a moment, when I stood in the door and watched you stacking papers."

"The moment for me came just after that," he said.

"I'm not this way with all my adjustees."

"I should hope not—you'd be continually exhausted."

"I'm not exhausted yet," she said.

"Oh, God."

"You'll be ready again after a steak."

"You could be right."

"When I'm right, I'm right."

Their food arrived on the dumbwaiter. Stone sat up the two electrically operated beds and put the tray between them. Fred had decanted the wine, and Stone poured large glasses.

"So," he said, "how did I get so lucky?"

"Luck of the draw," she said. "I mean, I could have scheduled the old lady whose cat knocked over a candle and set her bedroom on fire. Besides, I'll bet you're lucky a lot."

"Not this lucky."

"I'm surprised you're not married."

"Widowed," he said.

"How long?"

"A while. You?"

"Divorced for three years. Much happier single."

"How did you get into insurance?"

"My ex-husband was a private investigator. I used to help, and I got pretty good at it. After the divorce I applied at Steele, and they found my investigative experience a good fit for sniffing out insurance fraud."

"Did they suspect me of fraud?" Stone asked.

"Oh, no. There was a lull in those cases, and I drew yours."

"Did you know I'm their attorney?"

"Who?"

"Steele."

"You're kidding."

"No, they came to me through Strategic Services, another client."

"I certainly know who *they* are. I'd love to work there."

"Maybe you should meet their CEO, Mike Freeman."

"Love to. Will you introduce me?"

"It's the least I can do after all you've done for me."

She laughed aloud at that. "You're right."

They finished their dinner, sent the tray back downstairs, and made love again.

3

Crane stayed the night, and in the morning Stone put her in a cab. "I had a lovely evening and night," she said.

"Would you like to try for that again this evening? There's a cocktail party, and then we can get some dinner."

"What time?"

"I'll pick you up at seven. Where do you live?"

"Five-seventy Park. How shall I dress?"

"You're a better judge of that than I. I'll wear a suit."

"See you at seven." They kissed, and he closed the door.

"Well," Joan said as he came into his office. "You have a rosy glow. Your insurance adjustment must have gone well."

"My claim will be forwarded with the adjuster's approval."

Joan grinned. "I take it undue influence may have been brought to bear."

"Kindly shut up and go to work," he said. Joan was always interested in his sex life.

"Yes, sir!" She vanished.

Stone sat down and found himself reintroduced to the paperwork of Mrs. and Mr. Jack Coulter. He reread his memo to Tax and Finance and decided he had covered all the bases. "Joan!" he yelled.

She came back into his office. "We have this newfangled thing called a buzzer," she said.

"You need the exercise," he riposted. He scooped up the papers on his desk and handed them to her. Sort these into some sort of sane filings. I'll e-mail you my memo to Tax and Finance, and you can messenger the lot over to them."

She hefted the stack of paper. "Feels like a major new client, if we're starting at this weight."

"I believe that will be the case. Your experience with my file should be of use. You might use that as a template."

"Will do." She vanished, and after a moment, buzzed him. "See? A buzzer! Dino on one."

Stone sighed and picked up the phone. "Good morning, Chief," he said. Dino had been the new chief of detectives of the NYPD for some time now. "You and Viv going to the Strategic Services shindig tonight?"

"It's a free meal, isn't it?"

"Is it? I was thinking just cocktails."

"I can smell a free meal all the way downtown."

"Okay, I have a date. Join us for dinner, whether there or elsewhere."

"If it's free, we're there."

"Then I hope that Mike Freeman provides."

"Who's the date?"

"Somebody new. Her name is Crane Hart." He spelled it.

"How new?"

"Brand spanking new. I think you'll approve."

"I approved of the last one, and she stole five million bucks from you."

"Well, your judgment of women was never that great."

"How about *your* judgment? It wasn't *my* five million she stole."

"My insurance company is making me whole."

"You're a lucky bastard."

"I've been told that recently, without the bastard."

"Shall we pick you up?"

"Okay. Crane will be impressed by my pull with the department. Six forty-five?"

"Yep."

"And use the siren, that always impresses my dates."

"We'll see."

Dino's black departmental SUV rolled to a stop at the awning of 570 Park. Stone went to get Crane, while Dino transferred to the front seat, leaving his wife, Viv, to share the rear with Stone and his date.

Crane came downstairs, glowing in a simple black Armani dress with a black-and-white houndstooth jacket, topped off with a rope of pearls. They exchanged a kiss that would not disturb her lipstick.

Stone helped her into the SUV and made the introductions. "And that's Sergeant Devane at the wheel."

"Ma'am," the sergeant said.

"What have I done to need so much protection?" Crane asked as the vehicle moved off.

"You're with Stone," Dino said. "It's standard operating procedure. The department would never leave you alone in a car with him."

"Then I'm grateful," she said.

The party was held in the executive suite of Strategic Services, which was the world's second-largest security company, with offices and other facilities worldwide. The big double doors between CEO Michael Freeman's office and the large boardroom had been thrown open, and the combination kitchenette and wet bar at one end of the room had been put into use. Stone ordered drinks from a waiter, and they quickly arrived.

Mike Freeman came over and welcomed them, and Stone introduced Crane.

"Crane is an admirer of your company," Stone said.

"That's always nice to hear," Mike replied. "Not many women admire large security enterprises staffed by armed personnel."

"It beats Bergdorf Goodman any day," Crane replied.

"And what do you do, Crane?"

"I'm a fraud investigator and an adjuster in the large-account division of Steele Insurance."

"That's interesting," Mike said. "Why don't you all stay for dinner after the mob leaves, Stone, so that I can talk more with Crane about this."

"We'd be delighted," Stone said, and Mike moved off to greet his other guests.

"Did you say something to him about me?" Crane asked Stone.

"I did not, but you managed to get his attention in about ten seconds, and you got us a dinner invitation."

Stone watched as Crane turned toward the arriving guests, and her face fell just a bit. "Someone you know?" he asked.

"Someone I no longer want to know," she said. "My ex-husband."

Stone looked at the arriving guests. "Which one?"

"The giant," she replied.

There was, indeed, a giant among the group. Stone made him at six-six and 240. The man spotted Crane and started toward her.

Crane turned her back on him and faced Stone. "I don't want to talk to him here," she said.

Stone stepped between them and held out a welcoming hand. "Good evening, I'm Stone Barrington."

The giant grasped Stone's hand in his paw. "And I'm Don Dugan."

Stone tried not to wince and managed to disengage his hand. "How are you, Don?" The man tried to sidestep him, but Stone was too quick for him.

"I'd like a word with my wife," Dugan said.

"I'm afraid she has a bad case of laryngitis."

"Then I'll just whisper in her ear."

"She has an ear infection, too."

"It looks as though I'm going to have to remove you from my path," Dugan said.

"Please reconsider that."

Dugan placed an index finger against Stone's chest and began to push.

Stone took the finger in his hand and bent it backward. Dugan's knees buckled to relieve the pressure, but Stone kept it up. "Come with me," he said. Keeping him with bent knees, Stone led him across the room toward the lobby. "If you make a scene," he said to the man, "I'll break it off and feed it to you." They entered the lobby.

Mike Freeman spotted the pair and fell into step with them. "Going down?" He pressed an elevator button and the door opened.

"Thank you, yes," Stone replied. He walked the giant into the elevator, pressed the button for the ground floor, then, after a final tweak, he let go of the finger and stepped backward off the elevator, keeping an eye on Dugan, and the doors closed.

Mike was already on his cell phone. "A gentleman is coming down on elevator two," he said into it. "Please escort him to the street door and see that he doesn't reenter the building. It's going to take at least two of you."

"Well done," Stone said. "You know that guy?"

"Sort of," Mike said. "He owns an investigative agency. Was he trying to get to Ms. Hart?"

"He's her ex-husband," Stone explained, "and she didn't want to talk to him."

"I was thinking of buying his business," Mike said, "but I just changed my mind."

4

Stone returned to the party and discovered that he had handed his drink to Dino, who returned it.

"Did you and the big guy have a nice conversation?" Dino asked.

"A very brief one. I did all the talking. Where were you when I needed you?"

"Drinking," Dino said, raising his glass. "And you didn't seem to need any help."

"Thank you," Crane said. "That could have turned ugly."

"Is he in denial about the divorce?" Stone asked.

"Well," she said, looking embarrassed, "we're not quite divorced."

"How close are you?"

"We negotiated a property settlement, and now he won't sign it."

"Has your attorney spoken to his lawyer?"

"Yes, but he has been ineffective."

"Who is he?"

Crane told him. "Do you know him?"

"Only by reputation," Stone replied. "He's the sort of attorney who would let the divorce run on, just to up his billable hours."

"I've been getting the bills."

"Tomorrow morning, messenger him a letter firing him and telling him to give your file to the messenger. I'll get this done." He gave her his business card.

"I'll do it first thing," she said, tucking the card into her bra.

Someone was clinking a glass. "Ladies and gentlemen," Mike Freeman called from the other side of the room, next to a giant television screen. "If I may have your attention, an important announcement is about to be made." The TV came to life, framing an empty podium on a dais. "Ladies and gentlemen," a voice said, "the first lady of the United States."

Katherine Lee stepped to a podium and the camera zoomed in for a close-up. "Good evening," she said. "I've asked you here this evening for an announcement. I have decided to enter the race for the Democratic nomination for president of the United States." The friendly crowd burst into applause. She waited for it to die down, then continued. "I realize it's late in the day, but I'm very concerned with the state of the race in the primaries, so tomorrow morning I will file for the New Hampshire primary, and I will be in the race until the convention chooses a candidate." More applause. "I won't be taking questions from the press until tomorrow, but I would like to make one thing perfectly clear: I have not asked the president to support me in the primaries, and he is free to support anyone he likes—sort of free, anyway." Big laugh. "My husband will be releasing his own statement tomorrow morning, but the gist of it will be that he will have no comment on the race until the party has chosen a candidate, and that he expects to support that candidate wholeheartedly . . . whoever she may be." More laughter and applause. "I thank you all for coming tonight, and now members of my staff will pass among you with collection plates." More laughter, more applause, then the camera cut to Chris Matthews and a roundtable of journalists for discussion. The TV went dead.

"Dinner is served," Mike announced, and the group turned to the buffet table.

Later, Stone and Crane said good night to the Bacchettis and entered his house.

"Would you like a drink in the study?" Stone asked.

"Yes, and I think we should talk."

Stone settled her on the sofa, poured them cognacs, then joined her.

"Here's the history in a nutshell," Crane said. "Don and I met a little over three years ago, and I guess he sort of swept me off my feet. He can be very charming when he wants to be. We were married, and he turned out to be a violent drunk. I left him after five months. That was two years ago."

"And nothing has happened since? You didn't file for divorce?"

"No. He was trying to sell his business, and he said any publicity might queer a deal, so I held off. Six or seven months ago I hired the attorney, and negotiations began on the settlement."

"Were you asking for a lot?"

"I wasn't asking for anything—he was. I have some inherited wealth from my father mostly in the form of the house I live in, where I also rent out two apartments. My net worth is not a huge amount, but it's enough to keep me. He wanted half of everything."

"That's outrageous after only a few months of marriage. You shouldn't give him a dime."

"The settlement he agreed to, then refused to sign, gave him a quarter of a million dollars."

"How long ago did he verbally agree?"

"Nearly three months ago."

"This is what I recommend: tomorrow I'll have another attorney at my firm officially represent you and send his attorney a letter withdrawing from the settlement and including a document that, if he signs it, will agree to a no-fault divorce with each party retaining his own assets. We'll tell his attorney that he has until noon the following day to consent, or we'll file for divorce and exercise your right to a jury trial, which he is unlikely to want."

"That will make Don crazy," Crane said, "but I'll follow your advice. Why can't you represent me?"

"Because you and I have formed a relationship, and that would make my representing you awkward from an ethical standpoint. It's better if someone else is the attorney of record."

"I understand."

"I also think it would be better if you didn't sleep here until the matter is settled, though I will certainly miss that."

"I'll miss that, too."

They finished their cognac, then he put her into a cab and sent her home, which had not been his original plan.

5

Stone slept poorly. His dreams seemed to alternate between his extraordinary carnal attraction to Crane Hart and fights with her ex-husband—correct that, husband. He awoke still tired from the day before, and his day was improved only by the newspaper reports of Kate Lee's announcement of the evening before. They were mostly favorable, except from right-wing sources like the editorial page of the *Wall Street Journal*, which questioned the value of being first lady to her qualifications as a candidate. These sources mostly ignored her service as director of Central Intelligence and her foreign policy experience. The more objective sources praised her intelligence and the wit she had displayed in her announcement.

Stone got to his desk late, still feeling fuzzy around the edges from his lack of deep sleep. Joan took one look at him and produced a second mug of coffee, which helped.

He phoned Herb Fisher, his friend and colleague at Woodman & Weld, and asked him to take over Crane's divorce proceedings, then e-mailed him a draft of the letter to Don Dugan's attorney for his consideration.

Joan buzzed him. "I've got to run out for half an hour on some personal business," she said. "Okay?"

"Okay."

"If you don't want to screen your own calls, then let the machine pick up."

"Okay."

She had not been gone for more than five minutes when the phone rang, and he picked it up without thinking. "Stone Barrington."

"This is Don Dugan. I want to talk to you about the damage you're causing to my marriage."

"Hold it right there," Stone said. "First of all, you don't have a marriage, except on paper. Second, since I am not a party to your divorce, I've no intention of discussing anything at all with you. Any contact between you and your former wife should be conducted through your respective attorneys and not through me. Please don't call again. Good day." He hung up.

Another five minutes passed, then the doorbell rang. Joan had left the outside door to the office locked, so he got up and went to answer it. He checked to see who it was through the one-way glass panel and saw a man in a business suit. He opened the door. "Yes?"

"Mr. Stone Barrington?"

"Yes, what can I do for you?"

The man handed him an envelope. "You've been served," he said, then walked away.

Stone closed the door and walked down the hall to his office, tearing open the envelope. Inside was a summons and a copy of a lawsuit against him for alienation of affection, demanding a million dollars. Don Dugan had been busy; it wasn't even lunchtime yet.

He called Herb Fisher.

"Yes, Stone?"

"I've just received a summons. Dugan is suing me for alienation of affection."

Herbie laughed. "Do people still do that? I haven't heard of one of those for years."

"Dugan's just harassing me. He called ten minutes before the server arrived, saying he wanted to talk. I declined to see him, and a few minutes later the server rang the bell. Joan is out."

"So it was all set up before he called?"

"Apparently. I'll fax you the papers. Answer it for me, will you? You can be my attorney of record."

"Sure. What do you want me to say?"

"That they had been married for only a few months, and they separated two years ago, so Ms. Hart's affections had been alienated by her husband long before she met me, which was, as a point of fact, yesterday."

"Did you know she was married?"

"No, I thought she was divorced, until Dugan showed up at a gathering at Strategic Services last evening, tried to make a scene and had to be escorted from the premises."

"Escorted by whom?"

"By me."

"That must have been fun to watch."

"I did it as quietly as I could, in the circumstances."

"No attempt on your part to humiliate him, thus reducing his wife's affection and regard for him?"

"Well, just a little, but as I said before, her affection had been alienated long ago. She had already refused to speak to him."

"Okay, I'll file an answer today. Shall I make it withering?"

"Please do."

"I saw Kate Lee on the *Today* show this morning. She was very good."

"She always is. That's what the gathering was last night: an opportunity to get an advance announcement for a private audience. I gather a lot of money was raised."

"I'll send a check," Herbie said.

"You're a good man, Herbert."

"Don't call me Herbert, it makes me sound like an accountant."

"You remind me of an accountant less than anybody I know," Stone said. "Talk to you later." Stone hung up and faxed him the lawsuit.

Joan returned to the office. "Any calls?"

"Just one, from a jealous husband, followed closely by service of a lawsuit for alienation of affection."

She tried to suppress a giggle. "Not your first, I expect."

"My very first," Stone said.

"Are you guilty?"

"Never ask an attorney that question. Certainly not."

"Is this likely to come to trial?"

"No, but a trial might be fun, in this case."

6

Stone was having a sandwich at his desk when Joan buzzed. "Mrs. Katherine Lee on line one."

Stone picked up the phone. "Good afternoon, Kate!"

"My God, is it afternoon already?"

"You're having a busy day, aren't you?"

"I did all five morning shows, in person, in studio, and I've spent the rest of the morning doing remote interviews with stations in the dozen largest cities. This afternoon I'm doing Washington bureau interviews with every newspaper with a Washington correspondent. And *60 Minutes* on Sunday evening, live."

"Without Will?"

"Of course! Everything from now until the

convention votes is without Will. He won't even whisper advice in my ear when I'm at home."

"Where's home?"

"Good question. I'm headed to Georgia tomorrow morning, where I'm going to speak at Franklin Roosevelt's Little White House, in Warm Springs. Every newspaper editor and TV station in the Southeast will cover it. Then I'm headed back to New York, to the Carlyle. I'll try to avoid visiting the White House for the rest of the campaign. If Will wants to get laid, he'll have to do it in New York!"

Stone laughed. "And how can I help in all this? And I'm not talking about sex."

Kate laughed. "Don't even say the word aloud in my presence, it would end up on Fox News before the day was out!"

"What can I do, Kate?"

"I want you to head up a campaign for votes and contributions directed at every lawyer in New York State."

"That's more than seventy thousand people," Stone pointed out. "Maybe way more."

"That's why I want them on my side."

"Of course, I'll do whatever I can."

"Good. I'm going to send over a staff member of mine, Ann Keaton, who will ask you some standard background questions that we have to ask everyone who joins the campaign. Will you be in your office for the remainder of the day?"

"Yes, I'll be happy to see her."

"I'll put her on the phone."

There was a click, then another click. "Mr. Barrington?"

"Yes."

"This is Ann Keaton, personnel director of the Kate Lee campaign. May I visit you today to conduct a formal interview?"

"Yes, of course. What time?"

"Are you in New York now?"

"Yes, my home and office are in Turtle Bay."

"I'm on the Upper East Side at the moment. Would half an hour from now be convenient?"

"Perfectly." He gave her the street address and hung up.

Twenty minutes later a woman who looked like a college student was seated in his office, very attractive, wearing a business suit and horn-rimmed glasses. "Good afternoon, Mr. Barrington. Are you ready to answer some questions?"

"Yes, I am."

"I warn you, some of these questions may sound intrusive, but it's information we must have in order to employ any person on the campaign."

"I have nothing to hide." Stone wondered for a moment if that was true.

Ms. Keaton took him through his birth, parentage, grand- parentage, education from kindergarten through law school, work history since graduation, current employer, every address where he had ever lived, marriages and divorces, club memberships, military service, or lack of same, foreign travel, and political affiliation. "Have you ever been arrested for anything other than a minor traffic violation?"

"No."

"Ever been arrested for DUI?"

"No."

"Ever been charged with a misdemeanor or felony?"

"No."

"Have you ever associated with criminals?"

"Only when arresting or investigating them as a police officer, or when representing them as an attorney."

"Have you ever been or are you currently a plaintiff or a defendant in a civil lawsuit?"

"No."

"Have you ever been bankrupt?"

"No."

"Have you ever had your wages garnished for nonpayment of a debt?"

"No. Wait a minute."

"Yes, Mr. Barrington? You've had your wages garnished?"

"No. A couple of questions back you asked if I had ever been a plaintiff or a defendant in a civil lawsuit."

"Yes, I did. Do you wish to change your answer?"

"Yes. I was served with a court summons today to answer a lawsuit. It's nothing more than a nuisance suit. I've already instructed an attorney to answer it and to seek its dismissal for lack of grounds."

"What were you sued for?"

"Ah, alienation of affection." He felt himself blushing.

"Is this alienation referring to a woman?"

"It certainly isn't referring to a man."

"Can you tell me, briefly please, about the circumstances surrounding this lawsuit?"

"Yesterday I had a business meeting with a woman."

"Her name, please?"

"Crane Hart."

"Like the poet?"

"The reverse."

"What sort of business were you conducting, and where?"

"She was sent by my insurance company to adjust a claim I had made, and the meeting took place in my office."

"What sort of claim?"

"Someone had stolen a large amount of money

from me, and I had filed a claim. It was all quite straightforward and businesslike."

"And now she's suing you?"

"No, no. She told me she was divorced. Last evening we attended a social event—a fundraiser for Kate Lee—and her former husband was there. It turned out that their divorce was not yet final, but they had been separated for two years. Her former husband—"

"His name, please?"

"Don, presumably Donald, Dugan."

She made a note of it. "Please go on."

"Mr. Dugan attempted to speak with Ms. Hart, and she did not wish to speak to him. He had to be escorted from the premises."

"Did this 'escorting' involve violence?"

"I believe it prevented violence."

"Did he leave voluntarily?"

"Not quite."

"Please, Mr. Barrington."

"He was physically pressed into leaving. No one was hurt."

"And then he filed a lawsuit against you for alienation of affection?"

"Yes, this morning. As I said, they had been separated for two years, so the suit is groundless."

"Was it a documented legal separation?"

"I'm afraid I don't know. I do know that they had conducted negotiations for a settlement."

"Had a settlement been agreed to?"

"Yes, verbally, then Mr. Dugan refused to sign."

"Mr. Barrington, had you and Ms. Hart had sexual relations?"

Stone took a deep breath. "Yes."

"When, may I ask? I mean, time was short."

"Late yesterday afternoon. And later in the evening."

"Did she stay the night in your house?"

"Yes. And may I point out that we were both consenting adults."

"But one of you is married."

"In name only. And at the time I believed her divorce to be final."

"She told you that?"

"I have already said so."

Ms. Keaton closed her notebook. "That concludes the interview," she said. "I must say, Mr. Barrington, I'm impressed by the speed with which you form carnal relationships."

"Thank you, I think."

She regarded him with interest for a long moment. "I'm going to hold on to your answers to my questions, for a while," she said, "instead of submitting them for review. Mrs. Lee is very anxious to have you on board, but I'm going to have to wait until you've successfully dealt with this lawsuit before we can formally ask you to join the campaign."

"I understand. Tell me, Ms. Keaton—"

"Ann, please."

"Ann, are you an attorney?"

"I finished Harvard Law four years ago, and I passed the New York State Bar shortly after that. Then I joined the CIA. When Mrs. Lee left, I went with her as a personal staffer."

"That's very impressive. I'd like you to come and see me about the possibility of joining my law firm, Woodman and Weld, after the campaign is over, of course. Or when you're ready to leave the White House staff."

She stood up and closed her briefcase, then looked at him frankly. "Do I have to wait until then?"

"I think it would probably be best," Stone said. "I'm sure that neither of us would wish to have to answer any awkward questions during another interview like the one you've just conducted."

"That's very prudent, Mr. Barrington. I'll try to contain myself," she said, offering her hand and offering a small smile.

He stood and took her hand. "It's Stone, please."

"Until next time, Stone." She left the office, and Stone collapsed into his chair.

7

Later in the day, Dino called. "Hey."

"Hey."

"Dinner, Patroon, seven? Viv's out of town again."

"You're on."

They both hung up. Stone left his office, went upstairs, undressed and got into a shower, which he made progressively colder. He was having carnal thoughts, and it was a double feature. As he got out of the shower the phone rang. He picked it up while using a towel with the other hand.

"It's Crane."

"Hi there. Nice to hear your voice."

"What are you doing right now?"

"Right now? I just got out of the shower."

"Oh, God."

"Isn't that all right? Being in the shower?"

"It just makes me wish I were in the shower with you."

"I've always found the shower overrated as a venue for sex."

"How about on the bath mat, afterward?"

"Why don't you come over here and we'll negotiate a spot."

"I can't, I have an appointment in ten minutes, and I'm fifteen minutes away from it."

"I'm having dinner with Dino at seven. Like to join us?"

"Are you suggesting a threesome?"

"Certainly not. I'm in no mood to share you."

"I can probably meet you by seven thirty."

"Patroon," he said, and gave her the address.

"Can I stay the night?"

"If we're certain you're not being followed."

"I'll rely on you to help me shake a tail."

Stone laughed. "Anything I can do."

Dino was already halfway through a scotch when Stone arrived and ordered his own drink. "You look rushed," Dino said. "No, not rushed, excited."

"I don't know what's happening to me," Stone said.

"Huh?"

"You know how when you were eighteen you just wanted to screw all the time?"

"I believe I remember being in that state."

"I'm in it now."

"Stone, you've been in that state since the day I met you. This have something to do with Crane?"

"Of course it does, but it's more than that."

"Tell me."

Stone explained about his interview with Ann Keaton. "I don't know what it was, but I was amazingly turned on by the experience, and I think she was, too."

"Stone, it takes a lot less than that to get you turned on."

"By the way, Crane is joining us. She'll be a little late."

"If you start groping each other in this booth, I'm going home."

"You remember her giant husband from last night?"

"He's too big to forget."

"He sued me today for alienation of affection."

Dino burst out laughing. "That's the funniest thing I ever heard."

"I put Herbie on it. He'll scare the guy's lawyer silly."

"I didn't know Herbie was that scary."

"He is when facing opposition." Stone's cell phone went off. "Yes?"

"It's Herb."

"Hey."

"I got the suit tossed."

"How'd you do that? Dugan wasn't represented, was he?"

"His attorney was in court on another case, and I know the guy. I made my case, and Dugan's attorney called his client and got him to back off."

"That's good news."

"Why? You didn't expect it to go to trial, did you?"

"Of course not."

"One more thing: his attorney says he's convinced Dugan to sign the settlement document."

"Too late, we've already withdrawn the offer."

"Get your client to think about it, Stone—she'll have her divorce. Is it worth the money to her, or does she want to roll the dice in court?"

"Do you really think Dugan would get anything from her from a judge or a jury?"

"Given the brevity of the marriage, probably not."

"Then you know what I'll advise her."

"Okay, up to you. You can buy me dinner for my fee."

"You're on." They hung up. "Herbie got the suit withdrawn."

"You lead a charmed life," Dino said.

Stone looked up to see Crane being escorted to their table; he got up and let her into the booth. She pecked Dino on the cheek, then put her hand on Stone's thigh. He removed it. "Later," he said.

Dino rolled his eyes.

After dinner, Stone paid the bill. "Will you do me a favor?" he said to Dino.

"Maybe."

"Will you drop Crane off at my house? I'll get a cab. Give me five minutes."

"Sure, I wouldn't want you shot down on your doorstep."

Stone found a cab outside, went home and let himself into the house. As he arrived upstairs his doorbell was ringing. He buzzed her in.

Crane took the elevator upstairs, and by the time she got to the bedroom she was half undressed.

Stone was already in bed, and he greeted her hungrily.

An hour later they lay beside each other panting.

"Wow," she said.

"Me, too."

"Can we talk now?"

"Do we have to?"

"We can do it again, but not until I've said some things."

"Speak to me."

"Don is dangerous."

"Swell, just what I wanted to hear. How dangerous?"

"He's hit two men he thought were paying too much attention to me, and one of them he put in the hospital. He had to buy the guy off to stay out of jail."

"Does he go around armed?"

"At least some of the time. He's got a carry license."

"I'm sorry to hear that. I was going to shoot him."

"Please try to take this seriously, Stone."

"I *am* taking it seriously. You know, I'm six-two, and I only come up to his collarbone."

"He keeps himself in perfect condition, too, and he was a boxing champion in college."

"Maybe I should just carry a baseball bat everywhere I go."

"It couldn't hurt," she said.

Then they did it again.

8

They awoke at dawn and started all over again, doing everything they could imagine, and they were both inventive. Finally, when they had showered and were having breakfast, Stone changed the subject.

"Dugan has told his lawyer he'll sign the settlement," he said.

She looked at him unsurprised. "It seems to me I've heard that song before."

"It's time to consider what you'll do if he actually signs it."

"What's your advice?"

"It's the easy way out. You get your divorce, and you're free of him."

"But I will have to have paid him a quarter of a million dollars for the privilege of having a life again."

"That's certainly true."

"So what's your advice?"

"The other side of the coin is that you drag him into court and slug it out. You could walk away without paying him anything, but you'd still owe a bunch of attorney's fees. It won't be two hundred and fifty grand, but it could be fifty, even a hundred, depending on how long Dugan drags it out."

"If I win, can I make him pay attorney's fees?"

"Possibly. No guarantee, though. The other thing is, we'll have to wait for a court date, and that could take another year."

She thought about it some more. "All right, tell his attorney that when I get the document with his signature on it, I'll sign it."

"And no alterations to the document."

"Not unless they're in my favor."

"I'll pass that along the food chain, and we'll see what happens."

When Stone got to his desk, albeit a little late, he called Herbie Fisher. "When she gets the signed document, she'll sign it," Stone said, "and we're done with it."

"I'll call his attorney and tell him we need it today without fail."

"Let's say a prayer," Stone said.

Joan buzzed him. "Mike Freeman on two."

Stone picked it up. "Hey, Mike."

"Good morning, Stone. Question for you."

"Shoot."

"What do you think of Crane Hart?"

"Can you be more specific?"

"I don't want to know about your sex life. I want to know if you think she'd make a good employee for us."

Stone thought about it.

"It troubles me that you'd take so long to answer the question," Mike said.

"It's not because I have anything derogatory to say about her, it's just that my business experience with her amounts to a single meeting about my insurance claim."

"Did she handle that efficiently?"

"Very much so," Stone said. "But I don't know anything about her investigative skills, and that's what you're interested in, isn't it?"

"Yes."

"Then I don't know how to help. You can hardly call her ex-husband for a reference, and I don't know how she'd feel about your calling Steele."

"You're right."

"Why don't you ask her in and have some of your people interview her thoroughly?"

"That's my next move. Thanks, Stone." Mike hung up.

Stone had another thought. He called Herbie Fisher. "When you talk with Dugan's attorney, tell him that Crane's acceptance of the deal is contingent on his agreement not to harass her further."

"Too late, I've already called him, and he says that Dugan has already signed the agreement and that I'll have it forthwith."

"Okay." Stone hung up.

Joan was standing in the doorway. "Why do you get involved in these things? Do you need more tsuris in your life, is that it?"

"Your Yiddish is impressive."

"I'm half Jewish, you know."

"I'd forgotten."

"You want me to ask the question again?"

"No."

She went back to her office. She was right, he knew; why didn't he just stay out of it? Too late, he reckoned. He was in it now, until it was resolved, and he had a bad feeling about it.

9

The following day, Stone got a call from Herbie Fisher. "Dugan signed," he said.

"Who says that prayer doesn't work?"

"You can buy me lunch instead of dinner," Herbie said.

"You're on. Today?"

"Good for me."

"The Four Seasons at one o'clock?"

"That's entirely satisfactory."

"See you there." Stone hung up and asked Joan to book the table.

He left the office early and, it being a nice day, decided to walk to the restaurant. On Park Avenue he looked across the street and saw a sign saying KATE LEE FOR PRESIDENT NYC HEADQUARTERS plastered across the windows of what had been an automobile showroom. Curious, he crossed the street and walked in. The first thing he saw was Ann Keaton disappearing into a glassed-in office.

"Can I help you?" a young man at a desk called to him.

"Ms. Keaton," he replied, pointing toward her office and not waiting to be announced. The glass was mirrored on the outside—the room had apparently been the manager's office—but the door was open, and Ann Keaton was at the desk, talking on the phone. She looked up, saw him, and waved him in.

"Look, we're around until election day, and we'll be buying a lot of ad time," she was saying. "You might take that into consideration before you quote me prices like that. I want a volume price." She listened for a moment. "I'll get back to you," she said, then hung up. "Well, look who's here," she said cheerfully. "The lawsuit-bedeviled seeker of a campaign job."

Stone took the chair opposite hers without being asked. "Two things," he said. "First, the lawsuit that was, as you put it, bedeviling me, was withdrawn before yesterday was out, and second, as I recall, the campaign job was seeking me, not the other way around."

"Congratulations and touché," she said. "But I'm afraid the job went to another New York lawyer—campaigns wait for no man."

"I'm delighted to hear it. Spending my days on the phone begging money from recalcitrant upstate lawyers was never my cup of tea."

"What did you have in mind?" she asked.

"Tell you what, I'll give your super PAC another hundred thousand dollars if you don't offer me another job."

"Done!" she crowed.

Stone whipped out his iPhone, called Joan, and told her to mail the check, attention of Ms. Keaton.

"I love a man who acts decisively," Ann said.

"Then you'll join a friend and me for lunch at the Four Seasons right now," he said.

"Let me touch up my lipstick," she said, grabbing her handbag and disappearing into an adjoining powder room.

Stone stood up and stretched, then he turned toward the large open room filled with desks and was stopped in his tracks. Standing not twenty feet from him at a desk, talking to a young woman, was none other than the giant, Don Dugan. Stone was looking through the one-way mirror of the office wall and was invisible to him.

"All ready," Ann said from behind him.

"Close the office door and come here for a moment," Stone said.

She did so. "What is it?"

"See the very large man talking to your campaign worker?"

"How could I miss him?"

"He's the guy who filed the spurious lawsuit against me yesterday, then withdrew it. He's the husband of my client. He's also trouble. A couple of nights ago at an announcement event of Kate's, he made an ass of himself and had to be removed from the premises."

"Just a minute," she said. She went to her desk, picked up the phone, and dialed a number. The young man at the desk next to the one where Dugan stood picked up his phone.

"You see the large gentleman at the desk next to yours?" She listened for a moment. "Take his address and phone number, tell him we'll get back to him, then get rid of him, shred his particulars, and don't, under any circumstances, get back to him." She hung up. "He came in to volunteer," she said to Stone, then she joined him and watched as the volunteer took a business card from him and said good-bye. "Good boy," she muttered under her breath. "Thank you, Stone, for warning us."

Stone watched as Dugan left the premises,

crossed the street, and walked into the Waldorf-Astoria. "I think we can go now," he said.

The headwaiter seated them as soon as they arrived. "We'll be three," Stone said to him, and a waiter came with another place setting and a chair.

"Drink?" he asked her.

"Fizzy water," she said. "Martinis don't mix well with my afternoons."

"A bottle of Pellegrino," Stone said to the waiter. "Tell me, what did you do when you were at the CIA?"

"You know the old joke about if I told you I'd have to kill you?"

"Sure."

"Nothing of the sort. I was an analyst until Kate unearthed me and put me to work for her office. I *would* have to kill you if I told you, if I told you what I did for her."

"And at the White House?"

"Her deputy chief of staff."

"I was around the West Wing from time to time, but I never saw you there."

"I was camped out in the Executive Office Building, working my ass off."

"Ah."

"Today, only the real estate has changed," she said, "but I have more working space—I'm now in a car salesman's office."

"And what do you do for Kate now? Or would you have to kill me if you tell?"

"Whatever she asks," Ann replied. "Officially, I'm a deputy campaign manager."

"You seem to be a deputy a lot."

"It's the deputies who do the dirty work and bury the bodies. The campaign manager just stands in front of TV cameras and denies all knowledge."

"Are you optimistic about Kate's chances in the remaining primaries and the convention?"

"I'd still be at the White House if I weren't. I'd say, just between you and me, that there is a better-than-even chance that your friend Kate is going to be the next POTUS."

"I'm glad to hear it," Stone said. He looked up and saw Herbie making his way across the dining room, stopping here and there to shake a hand.

"Here comes our lunch companion," Stone said. "Now you'll meet someone you might want to hire if you win and work for if you don't."

10

They were on dessert when Ann Keaton looked at her watch. "Uh-oh, gotta get out of here," she said. "Not that you two haven't been wonderful company and a nice break from my particular grind. Herb, very good to meet you. You've got my card, and I'll look for your check later today."

They both stood up and shook her hand.

"Remember your promise," Stone said.

"No job for you," she replied, then she was off.

Stone sat down. "Whew!"

"Brisk, isn't she?" Herbie said. "And this has been the most expensive free lunch I've ever had."

"She fleeced you pretty quickly, didn't she? How would you like a job as New York State campaign coordinator of attorneys?"

"I wouldn't," Herbie said.

"The contribution was a good idea. Make another one after the convention, it will stand you in good stead. After all, you might need the White House on your side someday."

"God, I hope not." Herbie reached into a pocket and came out with an envelope. "Here's a notarized copy of Don Dugan's executed settlement agreement. Get Ms. Hart to sign and have it notarized today, and messenger it back to me. A judge in family court owes me a favor, so we can get this done next week."

"Thank you, Herb," Stone said, pocketing the envelope.

"I talked to somebody who knows Dugan, and I understand he's somebody to be avoided, has a tendency to get into fights and win them."

"A bad combination of character traits."

"It is, if you're, ah, 'seeing' the guy's ex-wife."

"You choose your words well."

"I'd hate to see you get caught in the Dugan meat grinder," Herbie said. "I don't have time for hospital visits or attending funerals."

"I will do my best to avoid both those locales."

Herbie consulted his watch. "I need to get going before the check comes. Get that executed agreement back to me, pronto!" They shook hands, and he left.

Stone called Crane Hart.

"Yes?"

"It's Stone. I have the settlement agreement ready for your signature, and it must be notarized. Can you come by my office right away? We need to get this wrapped up this afternoon, and we can make everything final next week."

"Wow! You really get things done, don't you?"

"Getting things done is what I do. Half an hour?"

"See you there."

Stone signed the bill and left a cash tip; the waiters liked it that way.

Crane signed the document, and Joan notarized it. "So I'll see you in court next week?"

"Nope, you'll see Herb Fisher in court. You'll see me a lot sooner than that. Tonight?"

"Sorry, I've got to visit a policyholder in Greenwich this evening about his claim, and I'll be back late."

"Come over tomorrow night, and I'll cook dinner for you."

"What time?"

"Seven. Bring your toothbrush and a change of socks, and we'll make a weekend of it."

"You're on." She left, and Joan called for a messenger to deliver the document to Herbie.

Stone finished his day and was reading in his study when Fred materialized in the doorway.

His approach was always undetectable; he would just suddenly be there.

"Good evening, Mr. Barrington," Fred said. "May I get you your usual?"

"Good evening, Fred," Stone replied. "You may, and why don't you join me? Let's have a talk."

Fred poured Stone a Knob Creek and found himself a glass of Laphroaig single malt.

"Have a seat," Stone said.

Fred sat.

"You've fit in here very well, Fred," Stone said. "My only difficulty is in finding enough for you to do."

"Oh, I stay busy, Mr. Barrington. Helene always needs my help to polish the silver and the like."

"Well, I certainly don't need a year of your service to know that I'd like you to stay on, and I'm sure Helene and Joan would like that, too."

"I'm very happy here, sir, and happy to know that you'd like me to stay."

Stone made the man an offer. "And that's to include your apartment next door, health care, and a retirement plan."

"I'm very pleased to accept your offer," Fred said. "And there's something else I'd like to raise."

"Of course."

"I've asked Helene to marry me, and she has accepted. We'd like your blessing."

"I'm delighted to give you my blessing, though

it's not necessary. I wish you both every happiness."

"If we may, we'd like to join our two flats into one next door."

"Certainly. Ask Joan to get the builder over. When do you plan to marry?"

"Quite soon, I expect, there's no need to wait."

"Perhaps you'd like to honeymoon at my house in Maine. It's very nice this time of the year, and you can have the guesthouse."

"That sounds wonderful," Fred said. "I'll speak to Helene about it."

"I'll get you flown up and back, as well. There's an airstrip on the island."

"Thank you, Mr. Barrington. I understand we may have an issue around the household."

"What would that be?"

"I believe you've incurred the animus of a rather large and unpredictable gentleman."

"Oh, word has gotten around, has it?"

"Not many secrets in this house. Perhaps you'll recall that I have some expertise with firearms?"

"Pistol champion of the Royal Marines, as I remember."

"Yes, sir."

"Well, I don't believe firearms will be necessary. The issues between the man and his former wife have been resolved."

"Oh, I'm very good with a blackjack, too," Fred replied. "Though, strictly speaking, that was not an authorized weapon in my service."

"Keep it handy, Fred," Stone said. "You never know."

Fred polished off his drink and stood up. "Is there anything else I can do for you, sir?"

"Ask Helene to fix me something for dinner and send it up in the dumbwaiter around seven, will you?"

"Of course, Mr. Barrington. And I bid you a good evening."

Stone turned on the evening news and was greeted with a report of a fistfight at the Waldorf-Astoria at lunchtime. "No," he said to himself, "it can't be."

11

Stone awoke very early and reached for the other side of the bed. Empty, and would be until tonight. He had an itch that needed scratching, and the only option available was exercise. Normally, he accomplished that in his downstairs home gym, but it was such a beautiful day outside he decided to take advantage of it.

He checked the temperature on his iPhone and decided he wouldn't need a jacket or sweatpants. He got into shorts and a T-shirt, tied a light cotton sweater around his shoulders, just in case, put some money and his wallet into a pocket—again, just in case—and let himself out of the house.

It was six thirty a.m. on a Saturday morning, and New York City traffic was very light. He started jogging up his street and heard a vehicle start up behind him, but ignored it. He ran up to Park Avenue and headed uptown toward Central Park, feeling good. The air was clear and fresher than usual, without the taint of carbon monoxide. He stopped for a light, jogging in place to stay warm, and a dark blue van pulled up beside him, idling in the crosswalk. He heard a door slide open, then the light changed and he began to run again.

On little more than a whim, he caught a red light and ran across Park Avenue, then continued up the west side of the street. The dark blue van kept pace with him, occasionally stopping for a moment, so as not to outrun him. He felt a threat, but he was happy to have it confined to the opposite side of the four-lane street.

At Fifty-seventh Street he turned and ran toward Fifth Avenue, and the van followed. He could see its reflection in shopwindows without turning his head. At Fifth he crossed the street, turned right, and thus lost the van, since Fifth Avenue was one-way downtown. He ran up to Fifty-ninth Street, then, just before entering the park, he saw the van racing toward him on Central Park West. Then he was on a footpath and hidden by trees. He had lost the tail.

The few people out at this time of day were either other joggers or dog owners taking advantage of the no-leash rule before nine a.m. He ran through the zoo and into the Sheep Meadow, where dogs were happily chasing sticks and rolling in the grass with each other, enjoying a morning's freedom from their collars, then he headed north for the running track that circumnavigated the reservoir. As he approached West Eighty-sixth Street, he saw the van waiting for him, and two burly men got out. They might have been brothers, about six-two or -three and well over two hundred pounds. He put on a little speed and beat them to the other side of Eighty-sixth and ran toward the track.

Then he turned and ran back for a few steps and saw them running toward him. "Hey, want to do a few laps? Follow me!" He ran quickly for a few seconds, then looked over his shoulder and saw them standing on the track, hands on hips, huffing and puffing. "See you around the other side!" he yelled, pointing.

He ran easily three-quarters of the way around the track, and then he saw something inviting. In a clearing a few yards away a man was hitting baseball grounders to half a dozen kids with baseball gloves. There was a bag on the ground holding three or four bats, and a pile of balls at his feet. "Good morning," he said to the man.

"Good morning," the man replied.

Stone, jogging in place, dug into his pocket and

came up with a hundred-dollar bill. "I'll give you a hundred bucks for one of your bats. Your worst one."

The man stopped hitting balls. "What do you want it for?"

"There are two large men waiting for me at Eighty-sixth Street, and I think I might need it. They seem to be up to no good."

"Take your pick," the man said. "No charge."

Stone selected a badly scarred softball bat and dropped the C-note into the bag. "Buy some new balls on me."

"No problem," the man shouted. "Smack one of them for me!"

Stone went on his way, bat in hand. As Eighty-sixth Street hove into view, he saw the two men standing in the middle of the track, waiting for him. He pulled up five yards short of them. "Okay, fellas," he said, swinging the bat back and forth, "who's first? Or do you want to try it together?"

The man to his right came at him with a rush; Stone sidestepped and caught him smartly on the back of a knee. The man yelled and went down onto the cinder track like a bag of potatoes. Stone didn't hesitate going after the other one, but the man pulled a Glock from his waistband, pointed it, and started backing away.

"Go ahead," Stone said, "take a shot at me, and let's find out how long it will take the cops to get here. I've already called them." He hadn't even brought his cell phone.

The man started toward him, the gun out ahead.

Stone swung and caught the gun and part of a hand. The weapon spun away into the grass, while the man held on to his injured hand and swore.

"Now," Stone said, "you want to get out of here before the cops come, or shall I try a few head swings?"

"Awright, awright," the man said, making to look for his pistol.

"Forget the gun, or I'll scatter your brains."

The other man struggled to his feet and made for the van, limping badly. "Come on, Skip!" he yelled. "Let's get outta here!" The two made it back to the van and drove quickly away.

Stone turned to look for the gun and found the hitter behind him, his bat in one hand, a cell phone in the other. "You want me to call the cops?" he asked.

"I guess not," Stone said, looking through the grass for the gun and finding it. "They're gone."

"Were they muggers?"

"Maybe," Stone said, popping the magazine from the gun and racking the slide to eject one in the chamber. "I didn't ask them." He drew back and threw the gun as far as he could into the reservoir, then followed it with the magazine. "I don't think they'll be back, though." He handed his bat over. "Please return that to your collection, and thanks for your help."

He ran on before the man could respond. On Eighty-sixth Street, there was no sign of the van, nor was there when Stone popped out of the park at Central Park South.

He ran over to Madison, which was one-way uptown, then down to his street before turning left and heading for home.

There was no sign of the van on his block as he let himself into the house.

He wasn't sure what he had accomplished by dealing with the two men, but at least Don Dugan would know that he wasn't going to sit still for a beating.

He went upstairs and got into a hot shower. He supposed that he should start packing a weapon, until this was over.

12

Crane turned up on time and rang his bell.

Stone picked up the phone. "I'm downstairs, in the kitchen." He buzzed her in.

"On my way!" she yelled back, and he heard the door close.

She came into the kitchen wearing a short black sleeveless dress and gave him a big kiss. "Smells good," she said. "What is it?"

"Osso buco," he replied, then went to the bar, got her a drink, and replenished his own. He clinked her glass, and they sipped. "I'll need your help in just a minute," he said.

"Sure."

He poured some olive oil into his copper risotto pan with a chunk of butter and some salt and added a dozen ounces of arborio rice and some salt, then took a wooden spoon and stirred while it took on a sheen. "Okay, now," he said, handing Crane the spoon, "you add some chicken stock, like this"—he poured it from a carton—"and keep stirring. As soon as it's absorbed by the rice, add some more."

"For how long?"

"Until all the stock is absorbed—about twenty, twenty-five minutes."

Crane began to stir. Twenty-five minutes and a downed glass of whiskey later, Stone mixed in a couple of fistfuls of Parmigiano-Reggiano, then added half a carton of crème fraîche. "Stir a little more," he said, and while she did he arranged the already-cooked chunks of veal calf's shank on a platter, added the sautéed haricots verts, then set it on the set table. He found a trivet for the risotto pan, then set that on the table, too, where an uncorked bottle of Far Niente Cabernet waited, breathing. He poured two glasses, then pulled the table out so she could slide behind it.

Crane tasted the meat. "Yum!"

"It's Elaine's recipe," Stone said. "Did you know Elaine's?"

"I was there a couple of times years ago. Don didn't like it, because she wouldn't give him her best table." She tried the risotto. "This is terrific. Is it her recipe, too?"

"No, I got that out of the *New York Times Magazine* years ago."

They dug in. "How was your day?" she asked.

"Good. In your absence I went up to the park and ran off my sexual anxiety."

"Don't worry, you won't be anxious long," she said.

"Tell me, do you know some acquaintances of Dugan who look like brothers, dark hair, six-two or -three, over two hundred pounds, one of them named Skip?"

"The Drago brothers," she said, looking alarmed. "Don uses them for collection work. It's a big part of his business. Where have you seen them?"

"They were waiting for me in a van when I left the house this morning. I suspect they had spent the night there, hoping to catch me with you. They followed me to the park."

"What did they have to say?"

"Hardly anything. I borrowed a softball bat from a nearby citizen and persuaded them to go away. One of them left a Glock in his wake, which I deposited in the Central Park Reservoir. Your drinking water may taste a little like gun oil for a few days."

"This is not good news," she said.

"I didn't view it as such. I hope I don't have to shoot them on some future occasion."

"I don't know what to do about this," she said.

"Leave it with me. I think we can resolve it at your Wednesday morning hearing."

"I could speak to Don."

"You don't need to do that—in fact, you shouldn't."

She leaned over and kissed him under an ear. "I wouldn't want anything to happen to you, but I'll trust you to handle it."

"Shouldn't be a problem."

They finished dinner and left the dishes for Helene to take care of later.

Stone explored a little and discovered that she wasn't wearing underwear under the short dress. He cupped a cheek in one hand and pulled her to him. "You can dress this way anytime you like."

"I do it all the time, when I'm not working," she said. "Can we go upstairs and fuck now?"

"Oh, yes," Stone said, leading her toward the elevator.

She was, if anything, even more avid than the last time they had been together, and he was incredibly excited to have her back in his bed. It was eleven o'clock before they could leave each other alone for a while.

"Can we watch the news?" she asked.

"Sure," he said, switching it on.

"Someone told me that Don got into an argument with someone in the restaurant at the Waldorf yesterday. I want to see if there's any follow-up."

There wasn't. "Does he do this sort of thing often?" Stone asked.

"He's always getting into fights, and at the slightest excuse. Road rage is a problem, too."

"I think we need to get you a protection order on Wednesday," he said.

"I don't think it will stop him," she said.

"It will let you put him in jail if he bothers you again."

"I did that once before—it just made him angrier. Can I borrow a gun from you?"

"You'd need a license just to have it in your home," Stone said, "and that takes time. I can arrange some protection for you for a couple of weeks, until things cool down."

"What about protection for you?"

"You really think he'll continue to come after me?"

"Yes, I do. I'm sorry I got you mixed up in this. If we hadn't run into him at that party, he wouldn't even know about you."

"It's not your fault, Crane."

"Maybe not, but I still feel guilty."

Stone switched off the TV and pulled her to him. "Let me see what I can do to help you forget about it," he said, burying his face in her lap.

She stayed until Monday morning, and he walked her out the back way, through Turtle Bay

Gardens. A gate led out to Second Avenue, and he put her in a cab there.

She kissed him. "You be careful," she said.

"I'll have somebody call you at your office later this morning about security arrangements," he said, helping her into the cab.

He went to his office and called Bob Cantor, whom he sometimes used for help with security.

"What can I do for you?" Bob asked.

"I need a team of two men, armed, to keep a woman safe from her estranged husband, a large and angry man."

"You have anything to do with the estrangement, Stone?"

"Nope, they were estranged for two years before I met her. She has a divorce hearing in family court Wednesday morning."

"You want them armed?"

"Yes, indeed." Stone gave Bob the number. "Have them pick her up at work when she leaves the office today."

"I'm on it," Bob replied.

13

On Wednesday morning Stone went down to the courthouse and took a seat at the rear of the Family Court hearing room. Crane and Herbie Fisher were already seated at their table, and an attorney was at the other table, but no sign of Don Dugan.

The judge, a woman in her late thirties, entered the courtroom, and everyone stood, then sat.

"Case of Dugan v. Dugan," the judge said. "Are both parties present?"

Dugan's attorney stood up. "Bob Harvey for Mr. Dugan. Judge, my client seems to have been detained, and I can't reach him on his cell phone. I move to continue the hearing at a later date."

Herbie was on his feet. "Your Honor, Herbert Fisher for Mrs. Dugan. This is the third occasion on which Mr. Dugan has failed to appear after giving assurances. He has repeatedly delayed proceedings, settlement conferences, and other meetings for a period of two years. The parties have agreed on a property settlement, notarized copies are before you, and we move for an immediate final decree."

Don Dugan strode into the courtroom and down the center aisle, joining his attorney. "Sorry about that, Judge. Traffic was bad."

The judge glared at him. "It's always bad and no excuse for a late appearance. In your absence, Mr. Dugan, I have a motion from Mrs. Dugan's attorney for the immediate issuance of a final decree."

"Well, I think we need to talk about this some more," Dugan said.

His attorney whispered something in his ear, and he whispered back.

"Well?" the judge asked.

"We are ready to proceed, Judge," Dugan's attorney said.

"That's very kind of you, Mr. Harvey. Mr. Dugan, have you read the settlement agreement?"

"Well, not all the way through," Dugan said. "My attorney told me to sign it, so I did, but I don't want a divorce."

Stone looked at Herbie, who was saying nothing, apparently, allowing Dugan all the rope he needed to hang himself.

"Mr. Dugan," the judge said, "I assume you agree with the settlement amount—two hundred and fifty thousand dollars, in your favor."

"Oh, yes, Judge. I figure she owes me that. I had a lot of expenses."

"I see that you cohabited for something less than six months. Is that correct?"

"Yes, Judge."

"What extraordinary expenses associated with the marriage did you incur in that brief period?"

Dugan looked at her blankly. "Uh, I'm not sure what you mean."

"For instance," the judge said, "did Mrs. Dugan come to the marriage with a burden of debt that you paid off?"

"I'm not sure I remember," Dugan said. His attorney remained mute.

"I'm waiting for you to explain why you believe your wife owes you a quarter of a million dollars," the judge said.

"Because she agreed to it," Dugan replied.

"I see. Mrs. Dugan?"

Crane rose. "Yes, Your Honor?"

"Why are you giving your husband all this money? Do you figure you owe him this?"

"No, Your Honor. I agreed to pay him so that I could finally bring an end to the farce of our marriage."

"Did you bring debts to the marriage?"

"No, Your Honor," Crane replied. "In fact, I paid off more than a hundred thousand dollars of his credit card debt."

"Mr. Dugan, is that true?"

"I don't remember anything like that," Dugan replied.

Herbie was on his feet, with a sheaf of papers in his hand. "Your Honor, I have copies of the bills right here." He handed them to the bailiff, who took them to the judge.

She looked them over for a long couple of minutes. "I see here that you had a great deal of debt before your marriage, Mr. Dugan, and that it was all paid off the week before your marriage date. Is that consistent with the facts?"

"Ah, I guess so, Judge."

"Mr. Dugan," she said, "it appears to me that you are using this divorce to extort money from your wife. Is there anything you wish to say to the contrary?"

Dugan and his lawyer conducted another whispered exchange. "My client doesn't wish to argue the point, Your Honor," Harvey said.

"I didn't think so," she said. "Mr. Fisher, your motion for a decree is granted, but the settlement agreement is vacated."

"What?" Dugan shouted. His attorney grabbed him by a lapel and whispered something.

"Your Honor," Herbie said, "I have prepared a

decree which restores Mrs. Dugan's maiden name, and also have a motion for a protection order, requiring Mr. Dugan to remain at a distance of at least one hundred yards." He handed the documents to the bailiff. "Please note that the order is drawn to also protect my colleague, Mr. Stone Barrington, who is associated with this case."

The judge took the document from the bailiff and read it quickly. "Why is Mr. Barrington included?"

"Your Honor, this past Saturday, Mr. Barrington was accosted in Central Park by two employees of Mr. Dugan, two brothers named Drago, one of whom was armed with a handgun. Mr. Barrington managed to discourage and disarm them, but we would not like a recurrence of such an event."

"Anything, Mr. Harvey?"

"Nothing, Your Honor."

"Granted," the judge said, signing the documents with a flourish and returning them to Herbie. "Anything else?"

"We request attorney's fees in the amount of fifty thousand dollars," Herbie said.

"Mr. Harvey?"

"Nothing, Your Honor."

"Mr. Dugan is ordered to pay attorney's fees in the amount of fifty thousand dollars," she said. "Forthwith."

Dugan opened his mouth to speak, but his attorney beat him to it. "Nothing, Your Honor."

"Then this case is concluded. Next case?"

Stone's car, with Fred Flicker at the wheel, awaited them outside the courthouse, and the three of them piled into the rear seat.

"I'm not sure I understand," Crane said. "When is the new hearing?"

"We're done, Crane," Herbie said. "You are a free woman, you have back your name, and you and Stone both have a protection order against Dugan. I'll press Harvey for the attorney's fees."

"I'm flabbergasted," she said. "A week ago I was in the middle of an unsolvable divorce, and now . . ."

"Now it's over," Stone said. "Herb, who was that judge?"

"She's new to Family Court, but I've known her for years. I knew that she had strong opinions about women and settlements."

"Fred, get us out of here," Stone said.

As they drove away, Stone saw Dugan and his attorney standing on the courthouse steps, shouting at each other.

14

Fred dropped Stone at his house first. "Dinner tonight?" he asked Crane.

"If you don't mind, I think I need a night off."

"Of course."

"And I think you can call off the security, since I have the protection order now."

"Okay, if you think so." He got out of the car, and Fred drove off to deliver Herbie and Crane to their offices.

Joan was waiting for him with a fistful of messages. "Where have you been?"

"In court."

"For what? You don't have any cases at trial."

"I sat in on Crane's hearing. She's now a free woman."

"Bill Eggers has called you three times. You'd better get back to him first."

"All right. Please call Bob Cantor and tell him Crane doesn't need protection anymore. He can call off his men." Stone went into his office and called Eggers. "Hi, Bill."

"I had a call this morning from Jeb Barnes at Steele Insurance," Eggers said.

"How is Jeb?"

"Mad as hell."

"About what?"

"He says you robbed him of one of his favorite employees."

"And who would that be?"

"Somebody called either Hart Crane or Crane Hart, I can't remember which. Who is the gentleman?"

"Crane Hart, and it's a lady."

"And how did you engineer her departure from Steele? Did you get Mike Freeman to hire her away?"

"I certainly did not. I took her to an event at Strategic Services—you were there, you saw her."

"The dishy blonde?"

"If you say so."

"And did you ask Mike to hire her?"

"I did not. He called and asked me what I thought, and I told him I had no knowledge of her professional qualifications, except for a single meeting we had when she was adjusting my insurance claim."

"This sounds fishy to me."

"I stayed out of any business Mike had with Crane, I promise you."

"Then I think you'd better call Jeb Barnes and tell him that."

"I will, if you like."

"I like." Eggers hung up.

Stone buzzed Joan. "Get me Jeb Barnes at Steele Insurance."

Barnes was shortly on the line. He was not Stone's favorite insurance executive. Fortunately, he was not the client, his boss was.

"Jeb, I hear you've lost an employee and you're blaming me."

"I damn well do," Barnes replied.

"Well, you're wrong."

"You got Mike Freeman to hire her, didn't you?"

"I did not. I took her to an event at Mike's office, but that was it. In fact, I was in court with her this morning, and she didn't mention changing jobs."

"In court? What for?"

"She was getting a divorce."

"How did you know that?"

"I recommended an attorney to represent her."

"She sent me her resignation in the interoffice mail this morning."

"Perhaps you can make her a counteroffer," Stone suggested.

"She just got a raise ten days ago."

"Money works wonders, Jeb."

"That woman was the best piece of . . ." Barnes didn't finish the statement.

"What?"

"Never mind. Good-bye."

Stone tried to imagine Crane in bed with Jeb Barnes, but he couldn't, fortunately.

Stone began returning his other calls, but the thing with Crane ate at him all day. His last call of the day was to Viv Bacchetti.

"Hey, Stone."

"Hey, Viv, sorry to take so long to get back to you. I was in court."

"How long since you've been in court, Stone?"

"Long time."

"You free for dinner tonight? Dino has a big cop dinner, and I'm at loose ends."

"Sure."

"Meet me at P.J. Clarke's at seven thirty, then."

"Will do."

Viv was already at the table when he got there, sipping a scotch.

"Am I late?"

"No, I'm early. I had to take a dress back to Bloomingdale's, so I just walked down here after that."

A waiter brought Stone a Knob Creek.

"Tell me," Viv said, "did your being in court today have anything to do with Crane Hart?"

"Yes, Herb Fisher was handling her divorce hearing, and I spectated."

"How did it go?"

"Herb handled it brilliantly."

"I'm so glad," she said.

The waiter took their orders.

"Something you're not telling me, Viv?"

"Did Mike Freeman call you about Crane going to work for him?"

"Yes."

"Did you recommend her?"

"No, I told him I didn't know her qualifications well enough to do that, and I suggested he have some other people in his office interview her."

"Did he do that?"

"I don't know, but . . ."

"She got the job, didn't she?"

"Yes. I spoke to her boss—her ex-boss—about that. He was pretty upset."

"Is his name Jeb Barnes?"

"Yes. What's going on, Viv? Do you know something about all this that I don't?"

"Did she tell you she got a job with Mike?"

"No."

"Does that strike you as odd?"

"Well, sort of. She had the opportunity to tell me but didn't. I asked her to dinner, but she said she needed a day off."

"I see."

"What do you know about Crane that you're not telling me?"

"I heard from a girlfriend that Crane got the job with Mike."

"Seems everybody knew it but me."

"I saw her at Bloomingdale's half an hour ago. She was getting out of a cab with Don Dugan."

Stone's jaw dropped. "Herb just got her a protection order today."

"She apparently doesn't need it anymore."

"I guess not." Stone thought Viv knew more, but he couldn't get anything else out of her.

15

S tone got to his desk the following morning feeling tired and grumpy. He had gone to bed angry about Crane's not telling him about her new job and, especially, about Viv's report of sighting her with her, now officially, ex-husband.

Joan brought him a mug of coffee and some mail. "Uh-oh," she said, looking at his face.

"Uh-oh what?"

"That is not a good face."

"My face? It's the only one available, at the moment. I didn't sleep well."

"That's because you're unaccustomed to sleeping alone."

"And smart-ass remarks will not improve my mood."

"There's a check for fifty thousand in the mail. Maybe that will improve it."

"From whom?"

"A lawyer named Robert Harvey."

Stone riffled through the mail and found the check: it was made out to him and Woodman & Weld. "Well, I don't know why it was sent to me. Messenger it over to Herbie."

"And I was so looking forward to depositing it," Joan said, and flounced out with the check.

Stone went through the mail, which was inconsequential, except for a dinner invitation from Mr. and Mrs. John Coulter. He scribbled *Yes* on it and put it in the pile to go back to Joan. He'd invite Crane, he thought.

Joan buzzed. "Mike Freeman on one."

Stone pressed the button. "Hey, Mike."

"You don't sound so good this morning, Stone. Something wrong?"

"No, I just didn't sleep well."

"I thought you'd like to know I hired Crane Hart."

"I heard, though I seem to be the last to hear. She didn't mention it when I saw her yesterday, but I sure heard from Jeb Barnes at Steele. He was royally pissed off."

"He'll get over it," Mike said.

"When did this happen?"

"On Tuesday. She had interviews last week. Didn't she mention it?"

"Not a word."

"She starts next Monday."

"I hope you'll be very happy together."

"We're not getting married, Stone, she's just coming to work for me."

"Where? In New York?"

"Yes."

"Don't you have an Alaska office?"

"Stone, you really got up on the wrong side of the bed this morning. I'm sorry I didn't tell you sooner, but she only accepted yesterday. I was going to invite you to lunch, by way of thanking you."

"Not today, Mike," Stone said. "I'd be poor company, I think."

"I'll call you again, then. Take care." Mike hung up.

Stone finished the snail mail, then turned to his e-mail. He worked through the list for twenty minutes or so, then he came to the last one: it was from Crane.

> *Dear Stone,*
>   *I want to thank you again for referring me to Herb Fisher, who did such a brilliant job. Also, Michael*

*Freeman has offered me a job at
Strategic Services, and I've accepted.
A good week for me!*

*Something else: Don and I had
dinner together last night. He was
very sweet and apologetic about his
behavior. We managed to clear the
air, and we're back together again.
In an odd way, I have you to thank
for that. Of course, this means that
you and I can't see each other
anymore, but things have all worked
out for the best.*

*Affectionately,
Crane*

Stone's jaw very nearly hit his desktop. He
stared at the screen, uncomprehending, for a
long moment, then he typed a reply:

*Congratulations on the new job.
As to your personal life, I knew you
were smart, but I didn't know you
were crazy.*

Joan came back in and took the mail, then she
regarded him closely. "Now what? You look as

though you've been poleaxed." Stone's phone rang, and she picked it up. "Hi, Dino. Yes, he's here, hang." She handed the receiver to Stone.

"Hey, Dino."

"You sound hungover."

"No, just tired. I didn't sleep well."

"Had to do it alone, huh?"

"Don't start."

"Well, I called to tell you that I'm going to shoot you on sight for sneaking out to dinner with my wife last night, but I don't want to add to your woes."

"Thanks so much."

"I hear the lovely Crane has a new job."

Stone sighed. "I heard that, too."

"Yeah, Viv interviewed her and recommended her to Mike."

"Funny, Viv didn't mention that."

"She also said she saw Crane with that psycho, Don Dugan."

"Yeah, I had an e-mail from her this morning— they're a happy couple again."

"You're shitting me."

"I shit you not."

"Maybe I should just assign a couple of homicide detectives to her now, instead of waiting until he offs her."

"That might be a good move."

"You think you can get your head together by dinnertime? Viv's working."

"Sure, why not? Where?"

"Well, you were at Clarke's last night, so let's make it Patroon. I never get tired of Ken's Caesar salad. Seven thirty?"

"Yeah, good." They both hung up.

Joan buzzed. "Ann Keaton on two."

Stone immediately felt better and pressed the button. "Good morning."

"And the same to you. You remember the giant guy you warned me about the other day? I read on Page Six that he got into a fight at the Waldorf right after he left our offices."

"I heard something about that."

"Thanks again for the advice."

"Listen, would you like to go to a dinner party Saturday night?"

"Sure. How am I dressing?"

"It's black tie, so dress to kill."

"I'll get my grandmother's jewelry out of the safe, then."

"Good idea."

"Who's our host?"

"A couple named Jack and Hillary Coulter— she's Hillary Foote Coulter, if that rings a bell."

"It does. She's high up on our contributor list."

"Then you can thank her in person. Drinks at seven thirty. Where do you live?"

"Park and Sixty-third, number five-seventy."

"My ex-partner and his wife live there."

"Who are they?"

"Dino and Vivian Bacchetti."

"Oh, I've met them. I'm on the co-op board, and we interviewed them when they were buying."

"I'll pick you up at seven thirty, then."

"Looking forward."

"So am I." He hung up feeling much, much better.

16

Stone and Dino arrived at Patroon and walked into the restaurant together. The owner, Ken Aretzky, shook their hands and showed them to a booth. Their drinks arrived without ordering.

"Nothing like being predictable," Dino said to the waiter.

"We like it that way," the man replied.

Dino took his first sip. "You look better than I expected," he said to Stone. "Are you over the lovely Crane already?"

"There wasn't much to be over," Stone said. "A couple of rolls in the hay."

"Well, at least you and the giant ex-husband didn't get into it again."

"The night is young," Stone said, nodding toward the door.

Dino followed his gaze to the front door, where Ken was greeting the newly happy couple.

"How'd they even find out about this place?" Dino asked. "I thought it was our secret."

"I brought her here," Stone said.

"Doesn't she understand anything about the male restaurant prerogative?" Dino asked. "She can't go with another guy to a place you took her to."

"Have the rules committee drop her a note, will you?" Stone said.

"I'm on it."

"They look perfectly normal," Stone said. "Not like a couple with a protection order between them."

"If she has a protection order against him, then I can have him arrested," Dino said. "Just say the word."

"I'm thinking about it," Stone replied. "The idea of seeing him dragged out of here in cuffs is a very attractive one."

"Then you could ask her to join us. You could even take her home."

"What would we talk about?" Stone asked.

"What do you usually talk about?"

"What a rotten ex-husband she has."

A waiter stopped at Crane's table, then came over to Stone and Dino. "Mr. Dugan would like to buy you a drink," he said.

"Two large, expensive cognacs," Stone said.

"Tell him to pour them in his lap and set fire to them."

"Ah, I'll tell him you said you already have a drink," the waiter said.

"Good idea," Dino chipped in. The waiter left. "Let's not start anything."

The waiter delivered the message. "Ignore them," Stone said to Dino. Ignoring them turned out to be hard, but Stone managed.

"Look, they're leaving," Dino said.

"I'm not looking. Tell me what they're doing."

"Dugan threw some money on the table and escorted Crane out. They're gone."

"Smart move on Dugan's part," Stone said.

Ken Aretzky came over and Stone asked him to join them for a drink.

"Didn't I see you in here last week with that blonde?" Ken asked.

"I apologize for bringing her here," Stone said.

"Don't apologize, she's very decorative. I hear from the waiter that you and the guy don't do business."

"That's an accurate report," Stone said. "He and the woman weren't doing business as recently as yesterday, when they were divorced."

"And he's taking her out to dinner the next night?"

"I'm sorry if I've cost you a customer."

"You'll just have to come twice as often, to make it up to me," Ken replied. "I'll tell my reservationist not to seat the two of you on the same night."

"A very good idea," Stone said, "unless you want a brawl for a floor show."

"My china and crystal are too expensive to bear that," Ken said. "Though it might be entertaining to watch."

"It might not be so entertaining," Dino said. "You saw the size of the guy."

"Tell me, Stone," Ken said, "what's the secret to handling a guy that big?"

"You have to throw the first punch," Stone said. "And aim low."

"And it had better count," Dino added. "You don't want him getting on his feet again."

"I think if I were you," Ken said, "I'd carry a blackjack."

"Good idea," Stone said. "I've got one somewhere. I'll dig it out."

"Do cops still carry blackjacks?" Ken asked Dino.

"It's optional. It's against policy to hit somebody in the head or the spine with it, except in aggravated circumstances or to save a life."

"How about a nightstick?"

"Uniformed cops still carry them. They can be very useful. You hold a guy by the wrist and stick it in his armpit, he'll come along, and on tiptoe, too. Or you can strike the common peroneal nerve, just above the inside of the knee, and he'll temporarily lose control of the leg."

"I did that with a softball bat recently," Stone said. "Worked like a charm. I cherish the memory."

Ken waved over a waiter. "Bring these gentlemen red meat on the house," he said.

17

Stone arrived at Ann Keaton's apartment building on Park Avenue with Fred Flicker at the wheel, having persuaded Fred not to wear a chauffeur's cap.

The doorman took his name, then buzzed Ann. Shortly, she was installed in the rear seat of the Bentley.

"Where is our dinner party?" she asked.

"A few blocks from your building—many more from my house. I like your grandmother's jewelry, both the diamond necklace and the matching bracelet."

"Thank you. The old girl had excellent taste, and she lived in a time when the family was truly rich, instead of just comfortable. Tell me," she said, "you mentioned that you and Dino Bacchetti had been partners. Were you once a policeman?"

"For the first fourteen years of my statutory adulthood, I was. Dino and I met as young detectives, when we were made partners. It was a good relationship, and we have remained close friends since that time. Dino stuck it out and is now chief of detectives."

"Why did you leave the department?"

"A knee injury was given as the reason for retiring me, but popular demand among my superiors had much to do with it."

"How so?"

"I had a tendency to buck the system and to hold opinions about cases that were not shared by my lieutenant or captain. I did that once too often."

"Then you went to law school?"

"No, I had finished law school before joining the force but had not taken the bar exam. Bill Eggers, whom you know, I believe, suggested that I cram for the exam and, when I had passed it, join Woodman and Weld—specifically to handle cases that the firm would rather not be seen to be handling."

"Sounds interesting. What sort of cases?"

"Oh, client's wife gets a DUI after an accident, client's son is accused of date rape. Like that. Things that a police background might be helpful in dealing with."

"You were a fixer."

"That term is inappropriate—I did not 'fix' cases, I resolved them. This is the second time you have cross-examined me—it will be my turn soon."

The car glided to a halt in front of their hosts' apartment building on Fifth Avenue, and after a short examination by a receptionist, stopping just short of being frisked, they were elevated to the top floor of the building.

"My building only has a doorman," Ann said. "Your friends' building has a receptionist."

"And one with a bulge under his left arm," Stone said.

"Do you think we're in danger here?"

"I very much doubt it. The 'receptionist' is supposed to see to that, I believe."

The elevator door opened directly into a large foyer, and after being checked off a list by a butler, they moved through double doors into a very large living room, one that contained a couple of dozen other guests without seeming crowded. A pianist was playing Rodgers & Hart. Their hosts separated themselves from a knot of others and greeted Stone and Ann, while Stone made the introductions.

"You'll be happy to know," Hillary said, "that we both signed our wills today."

"I'm relieved to hear it," Stone said. "Now nothing can possibly happen to you."

Jack laughed heartily. "I hope you're right." He beckoned a waiter and left them in his hands while he turned to other guests.

Stone ordered and asked the waiter to bring their drinks to the terrace. He guided Ann across the room and out a pair of French doors to take in the view of Central Park just after sunset. They stood by the railing and watched the lights come on along Central Park West.

"And how do you know the Coulters?" Ann asked.

"They are my recently gained clients," Stone replied.

"And do you 'fix'—pardon me, resolve for them?"

"They are the sort of people who don't require much resolving, just a management of their affairs and a tax and wealth strategy."

"Did you draw their wills?"

"No, the firm has specialists for that."

"Do you manage their money?"

"They have their own investment counselor and accountant."

"Then you just strategize for them?"

"That's as good a description as any of what I do for them. When they signed on, I produced a strategy document that my firm used to get their lives properly organized."

"Perhaps you should organize my life," Ann said. "Somebody should, anyway."

"Are you so disorganized?"

"I'm afraid so. I'm so busy with the campaign that I have a hard time even writing checks for my monthly bills."

"Then what you need is half a Joan."

"Half a Joan?"

"Like my Joan, only you probably need her only part-time. If you can find a really excellent Joan, you will be astonished at how much more smoothly your life proceeds."

"What a good idea. Can you recommend someone?"

"No, but my Joan probably can. Shall I ask her to?"

"Yes, please. My apartment has an unused maid's room that could be an office."

Their drinks arrived, and they turned their attention back to the falling of night upon the city. Then, quite unexpectedly, Stone heard an all-too-familiar sound. The pianist stopped playing. He took Ann by the elbow and guided— half dragged—her across the terrace to the wall between two sets of French doors and pressed her against it, glancing into the living room as they proceeded.

"This is so sudden," she said. "What the hell are you doing?"

"Not to alarm you unduly," he half whispered, "but there is at least one man in the living room wearing a mask and a shotgun."

"And what are you going to do about it?"

"Absolutely nothing."

"But you're a former police officer."

"Correction: I am an *unarmed* former police officer, and as such, I do not argue with shotguns. Now, be quiet and give me your necklace and bracelet."

She quickly took them off and handed them to him, and he put them into a hip pocket. Then he looked to his left and saw a barrel, supported by a gloved hand, protruding from the living room. A man dressed in black, wearing a black mask, stepped onto the terrace and looked at them, bringing the shotgun to bear.

"Give me your jewelry," he said to Ann.

"I don't wear jewelry," she replied.

"Give me your wristwatch," he said to Stone.

"I'm happy to, but you should know that my name is engraved on the back, and it would get you caught. I have less than a hundred dollars in my pocket that you are welcome to." He moved a hand toward his pocket but was stopped by a negative noise from behind the mask.

"If you don't mind, we'll just stand here quietly

and finish our drinks while you do what you came here to do," Stone said. "Please don't harm anyone. That would greatly increase your chances of getting caught and doing some very serious time."

"Ah, a lawyer," the man said. "Don't move." He went back into the living room, where there was some shouting going on.

"What are we going to do?" Ann asked.

"We're going to stand here quietly and finish our drinks," Stone said, reaching for his cell phone.

18

The phone rang twice before being answered. "What is it, Stone? I'm in the middle of dinner, and I plan to let my wife seduce me when we're done. Call back after ten o'clock."

"Hold it, Dino. I'm at the home of Mr. and Mrs. Jack Coulter with thirty other people, and there's an armed robbery in progress." He recited the address. "There are at least two men with shotguns, and somebody has probably disabled the doorman and the downstairs receptionist."

"Shit," Dino said. "And this is a very good steak."

"You don't have to come yourself, remember? You have a large force of detectives. And don't wait to call backup, send it now. And for God's sake, tell them not to use sirens, the doors to the terrace are open."

"I'm on it." Dino hung up.

Stone turned back to Ann. "That was very quick of you—about not wearing jewelry."

"It was the only thing I could think of to say."

He placed a hand on her cheek and kissed her. She responded nicely.

"What was that for?"

"For the fun of it. Also, we're less likely to be disturbed by men with shotguns if we're canoodling."

This time she kissed him. "I prefer this to men with shotguns," she said. They kissed some more. "How long do we need to do this?" she asked.

"Until the police break down the door," Stone said. "Maybe longer."

Perhaps three minutes later Stone heard the sound of doors slamming, and he peeked into the living room. People were lying on the floor in disarray, and some of them were getting up. Jack Coulter was the first to get to his feet.

"It's all right now," Coulter was saying. "I'm very sorry for the interruption. I assure you this was not the evening's entertainment. I'll call the police now."

Stone stepped into the living room. "I've already called them," he said.

"My friends," Coulter said, "I think this is as

good a time as any to announce dinner. Please take a few deep breaths, calm yourselves, then proceed to the dining room for the buffet, and we can talk to the police while we eat. You can wait until tomorrow to call your insurance agents."

The pianist began to play again, and people began to make their way into the dining room. It was almost as if nothing had happened. Stone heard a woman say to her husband that it was their most exciting evening in years.

Another two minutes passed before men with body armor and automatic weapons burst into the living room, followed closely by Dino, his weapon drawn.

"They went thataway," Stone said, pointing toward the elevators. "Didn't you pass them on the way up?"

"No, they must have taken the service elevator," Dino replied.

Jack Coulter walked over, and Stone introduced Dino. "There's a back exit from the garage in the basement," Jack said, "and an alleyway to the north."

Dino spoke some words into a handheld radio, then directed the armored men to take the service elevator. "Now," he said to the crowd, "was anybody hurt?"

There were negative murmurs from the crowd, some of whom were already seated and eating.

"It seems to have been for the jewelry," Stone said. "There was quite a lot of it."

"That reminds me," Ann said, "may I have mine back?"

Stone dug it out of a pocket and gave it to her.

"Smart move," Dino said.

"It was Stone's idea."

"Ladies and gentlemen," Dino barked to the crowd, "detectives are going to interview you individually. Please give them your cooperation."

Stone tapped him on the shoulder. "Dino, I think I know one of the men, possibly two."

"You want to share their names?"

"Two brothers named Drago. I had an encounter with them a few days ago in Central Park, and I think I recognized the voice of the one who spoke to us."

"First names?"

"Crane told me, but I've forgotten."

"Crane knows them?"

"She said that Don Dugan employs them as debt collectors."

Jack Coulter spoke up. "What was that name?"

"Drago."

"No, the other one."

"Don Dugan?"

"He's the man who sold us our security system. It was installed less than a week ago."

Stone smiled and spread his hands. "There you go," he said to Dino.

"Dugan is in the security business, too?" Dino asked.

"Incontrovertibly," Stone said. "Are the doorman and receptionist downstairs all right?"

"They were both wearing a lot of duct tape and shut in a closet," Dino said, "but they're okay."

"The receptionist was armed," Stone said.

"That's what he told us. We didn't find his gun, but he was wearing a shoulder holster." He turned to Jack. "Now we have to question your guests," he said. "Where may we talk to them one at a time?"

"In my study, there," Jack said, pointing. "My wife's study is beyond that, if you want to talk to them two at a time."

"Thank you," Dino said. He turned and instructed the other detectives. "Start with the ones who've finished eating," he said. "Stone, where were you when this went down?"

"Ann and I were on the terrace," he said. He introduced them. "You've met before, when you were interviewed by your co-op board."

"Ah," Dino said. "That's why you look familiar. Let's have a look at the terrace." He led the way outside; Stone, Ann, and Jack followed. "Where were you when this happened?"

"Standing at the railing," Stone said. "I heard a shotgun being racked, and we moved over there." He pointed. "Pretty quickly. One guy came out. Ann's jewelry was in my pocket by then. He asked about my wristwatch, but I told him it had my name engraved on the back, and he let it go. He left us and went back inside."

"How many of them were there?"

"Four," Jack said. "They were all dressed in black suits and wore masks and gloves. One of them had a small valise, also black, and they put all the jewelry into that."

"They were pros," Stone said. "The one I talked to was very calm."

"You think he recognized you?" Dino asked.

"Maybe not. Last time we met I was wearing sweats instead of a tuxedo. He knew I was a lawyer, though."

"How'd he know that?"

"I told him it would go better for him if he didn't hurt anybody, and he said, 'Ah, a lawyer.'"

"Does he know your name?"

"He does, if he remembered me from the park. If not, no."

"Detective, would you and your men like some dinner?" Jack asked.

"Thank you, no, they're working, and I've

already eaten, sort of." He looked at his watch. "Stone, do you know where Dugan lives?"

"No, but he could be at Crane's place." He gave Dino the address.

"I think I'll take a couple of guys, and we'll have a chat with him."

"Kiss him for me," Stone said.

19

Stone and Ann lined up for the buffet and perched on a sofa to eat.

"They're all so cheerful," Ann said, looking around at their fellow diners.

"They're relieved," Stone said. "If somebody had been hurt it would be different, but they're all happy that they got through it."

"They lost their jewelry, though."

"If it wasn't handed down from a grandmother, their insurance companies will replace it. They're no worse off than when they arrived for dinner."

"Do you think they'll get any of it back?"

"That depends on the professionalism of the robbers, or whoever sent them. If they start trying to fence it tomorrow, they'll get caught and at least some of the jewelry will be recovered. But if the robbery was as well planned as it seemed to be, then they'll have, in advance, acquired a fence—that's somebody who receives and resells stolen goods."

"Thank you, I got that from a thousand cop shows on TV."

"If they're really smart and not too greedy, then they've already got an expert removing the stones from the settings, grading them by size and clarity, and tomorrow they'll be on a plane to Amsterdam, where there are so many diamond merchants they'll be untraceable. Then, in a couple of weeks, the robbers will get their money."

"And Don Dugan?"

"Right. I wouldn't be stunned to hear that he planned the robbery. It will be interesting when Dino gets his client list and starts finding out how many of them have been robbed."

"But how would Dugan know there'd be a dinner party here tonight, and that the guests would be wearing so much jewelry?"

"I'm only guessing, but I'd say that his installers, when they were here doing their work, might have overheard something from the Coulters or one of their servants. Maybe they even got a look at the invitation on Jack's desk. Any dinner party here would attract a lot of jewelry, but 'black tie' on the invitation means all the women will be wearing their best stuff. And I'll bet there were more than a few Patek Philippe wristwatches among the gentlemen."

"Those would be easier to trace, wouldn't they?"

"Yes, but not so much in Hong Kong or Mumbai."

They finished dinner, then said their good nights.

"I'm sorry the party got so exciting," Hillary Coulter said to them.

"I managed to hang on to my jewelry," Ann replied.

"I'm happy for you," Hillary said. "Stone, so you imagine this will make the newspapers?"

"I expect the type is being set as we speak," Stone replied. "You may not want to answer the phone tomorrow."

"We have an unlisted number."

"That won't slow them down. Just have a maid answer and take messages."

They took the elevator downstairs and found the receptionist back at his desk and the doorman getting cabs for people. Fred and the Bentley awaited at the curb.

They were getting out of the car at Ann's building when Dino's car stopped, and he got out.

"You're still up?" Stone asked.

"I've done all I can do."

"Did you find Dugan?"

"One of the tenants in the building said that Dugan and Crane had gone to the country for the weekend."

"That's what I would do, if I had planned a robbery in the city," Stone said. "Is somebody looking for him?"

"Our source didn't say where in the country. We'll visit him Monday morning."

"Best to Viv," Stone said, and Dino walked off toward his elevator.

"I'm on the other elevator bank," Ann said. "Like a nightcap? I'm still wide-awake."

"Sure," Stone said, and they rode up to her floor.

Her apartment was smaller than Dino's, but beautifully furnished, with good pictures. "Looks as though your grandmother left you more than jewelry," he said, looking around.

"Yes, this place is furnished almost entirely with things she left. I had a chance to cherry-pick the furniture and pictures before her house was sold."

She poured them a cognac, and they sat on the living room sofa. "I fully expect you to make a major pass at some point," Ann said, "and I'd be disappointed if you didn't, but please, not tonight. I'm still awake, but I'm tired."

"Would you normally be in bed by this time?"

"Yes, but with a book or, more likely, some campaign document. I have to be in the office by nine, but I sleep only about six hours. How about you?"

"More like eight—after all, my office is in the house."

"I remember, I was there."

"Of course. Would you like to come to dinner tomorrow night? I promise we won't be visited by men with shotguns."

"Sure."

"Come at seven, then."

"All right."

Stone polished off his cognac and said good night.

Fred was waiting. "Did you have a good evening, Mr. Barrington?"

"An interesting one, Fred. The dinner guests were robbed of their jewelry at gunpoint."

"I saw the police arrive, but I didn't know they were headed for your floor. I didn't see anyone arrive or leave who looked like a robber."

"They probably came in through the basement garage," Stone said. "Apparently, it's accessible via an alley."

"I did notice that the doorman disappeared. I thought he had gone home for the night, but then he turned up again later. I guess he was having his dinner."

"No, he was locked in a closet with the receptionist, until the police freed them."

"Well, you never know, do you?"

"No, you never know."

20

Stone had finished breakfast and the Sunday *New York Times* and was watching *The Chris Matthews Show* on television while idly working on the *Times* crossword when the phone rang.

"Hello?"

"Stone Barrington?"

"Speaking."

"This is Don Dugan."

Stone was stunned into silence. Why would this jerk be calling him? "Yes?" he said finally.

"I know that you and I got off on the wrong foot, and I'm sorry about that. Why don't we have lunch one day next week and talk? I'm really not such a bad guy."

"That remains to be seen," Stone said.

"I know that Crane probably said some things

about me that weren't entirely true—that's the way a relationship can go when it's on the rocks. I think you and I might have more in common than you think."

"I can't imagine what," Stone said. "I'm not interested in having lunch with you. Anything else?"

"Now, don't be that way. Let's talk, see if we can get along."

"Let me set you straight once and for all, Mr. Dugan: since the first moment I laid eyes on you I haven't seen or heard a single good thing about you, not one. On the other hand, I've heard a lot of bad things about you, enough to make me believe that you are someone I want nothing to do with. Crane is a big girl, but she seems to have trouble learning from experience. I expect that she will soon regret becoming reacquainted with you, and when she does I hope no harm will come to her, because if that happened I would start to take a much deeper interest in you and your affairs than you might find comfortable."

"That sounds like a threat," Dugan said.

"Then you're more perceptive than I thought. Don't contact me again." Stone hung up. He was too angry to concentrate on either the television program or the crossword. He needed a change, and he called Ann at home.

"Hello?"

"So you're not working?"

"I'm reading the *Times*, that's work for me."

"I had a thought. It's a beautiful day, and I have a pretty little house in the upper left-hand corner of Connecticut. Why don't we drive up there, have dinner in a very good restaurant, and stay the night. I'll have you at your office by noon tomorrow."

"You know, I just had a call canceling a meeting for tomorrow morning, so I'll hardly know what to do with myself. You're on."

"Then I'll pick you up in an hour. Bring a toothbrush and a change of socks."

She laughed. "I'll be downstairs in an hour."

Stone showered and shaved, got dressed, threw some things into a valise, put on his best tweed jacket, and left a voice mail message for Joan. "I have disappeared from your life until midday tomorrow. Don't try to find me."

Stone went down to the garage, pulled the cover off the Blaise, the French sports car he had bought a year before, and backed it out of the garage. Ann was standing under the awning of her building with a couple of small bags when he arrived. He pressed the trunk button, and the doorman set her luggage inside, then he pressed the button that opened the gullwing door on the passenger side, and she got in. And offered him a kiss.

"Good God, what is this machine?"

"It's a Blaise."

"Aha! I read about it in the *Times* last year. It made quite a splash at the auto show."

"It did. I bought it from my friend Marcel duBois, who is its builder."

"Is he the same friend who gave you Fred?"

"He is." Stone drove up Madison, took a left on East Sixty-sixth Street, crossed Central Park, and soon they were across the Harlem River Bridge and on the Sawmill River Parkway. He tuned in some jazz on the satellite radio and pressed the map button on the huge glass display screen and selected the address of the Connecticut house. The route appeared on the screen. "That's where we're going," he said.

"Washington? I've heard about it, but I've never been."

"It's the prettiest village in Connecticut, bar none." He pressed a button on the steering wheel and said, "Set the temperature at sixty-eight degrees and the fan on auto." The number appeared on the screen, and cool air came into the cabin.

"Does it drive itself?" she asked.

"Almost. If there's an obstruction in the road, like a deer or a wreck, it will stop us faster and more smoothly than I could, but otherwise, it leaves the driving to me, which is more fun."

There was the sound of a cell phone ringing, and Ann dug it out of her purse. "Hello? Hi, boss."

"Hi, Kate," Stone shouted.

"Yes, he's driving us up to Connecticut. I'll be in the office by noon tomorrow." She covered the phone. "She says hi back. Yes, I have. I'll e-mail my draft to you, and you can send back your changes and I'll incorporate them and send you a final draft. We'll do our best to have a good time. Bye." She hung up and pressed some keys to send the e-mail.

"I guess I should have expected that," Stone said.

"I'm away, but I'm not out of touch. I'll try to keep it to a minimum."

"Do what you have to do, I'll adapt."

"That's sweet of you, but it would be nice if I didn't have to talk to anybody from the campaign, even Kate, for a few hours."

"Then switch off your phone."

"I can't do that. I'd run the risk of seeing something about the campaign on TV that I don't already know."

"God forbid."

"That's how you operate in these circumstances. You have to know everything before some reporter asks you about it." Her phone rang. "Hello, Chris. I'm taking the day off, can it wait until tomorrow? And I'll want to know who else is on. You're sweet." She hung up. "Chris Matthews. He wants me on his Sunday show next week."

"I haven't seen you on TV yet."

"I try not to appear too often. I wait until I have something important to say."

"A good policy. What will you say next weekend? Has something important happened?"

"Something will. And just about everything is important at this stage of the game."

An hour and a half later they pulled into Stone's driveway and came to a stop in front of the cottage.

"It's beautiful," she said.

"Thank you." He took their bags inside and upstairs, and she followed.

"How about a nap before dinner?" she asked, kissing him.

"You talked me into it," Stone replied, working on his buttons.

They dined at the West Street Grill, in Litchfield, and they both saw people they knew.

"So we're an item now," Ann said.

"Willy-nilly."

"Okay by me," she said.

Then they went home and took another nap.

21

Early light was filtering through the blinds in Stone's Connecticut bedroom when, suddenly, "The Stars and Stripes Forever" filled the room at high volume.

Stone sat up in bed, his hands over his ears. Ann Keaton slept soundly beside him, undisturbed. He shook her. "Ann, turn off your cell phone."

"Huh?" she said sleepily, then she sat up and looked at him dumbly. "What?"

Stone pointed at the bedside table. "Your cell phone!"

Ann took some serious-looking plugs from her ears. "Oh!" She picked up the phone. "Hello?"

Stone collapsed onto the bed, his ears ringing.

"What? Who the fuck is this?" She listened

some more. "Where? Do you have any idea what time it is on the East Coast?" She listened again, and her face furrowed into a deep frown. "Neither the candidate nor I have any comment to make." Finally, she hung up. "What time is it?" she asked.

Stone checked the bedside clock. "A little after five."

"What time would it be on the West Coast?"

"Three hours earlier—a little after two a.m. Listen, next time we sleep together, I get the earplugs, okay?"

"I'm sorry about that. I'm hard to wake up."

"Not even John Philip Sousa does it for you?"

"Not while I'm wearing earplugs."

"That doesn't make any sense at all."

"I have to go back to New York," she said.

"I'll have you back by noon, as promised. Now, please go back to sleep."

"You don't understand, everything has changed."

"What could happen in California at two a.m. that would change everything?" He was wide-awake now.

"The vice president," she said, as if that were an explanation.

"Has he been assassinated?"

"Worse. He's been caught in bed with a woman not his wife."

"Doesn't he have Secret Service protection?"

"Yes, but he smuggled her into his house in

La Jolla, and the press were alerted. The woman has a husband, apparently, and he has some connections in the news media. Last month, a Secret Service agent was summarily kicked off the VP's detail, and he got mad enough to call the husband. At least, he thinks that's what happened."

"Who thinks?"

"The West Coast bureau chief for the AP. That's who called."

"Why would he call you?"

"For comment."

"Comment?"

"Don't you get it? Kate's biggest opponent just got caught with his pants down. Literally."

"Oh. I guess that could affect the race, huh?"

"Oh, yeah."

"How?"

"I don't know. She picked up her cell phone and pressed a speed-dial button. "Jeff," she said, "it's Ann. Marty Stanton has been caught with a woman at his house in La Jolla. No, not his wife. Get your ass out of bed and get a breakfast-time poll started. This will be all over the morning shows, and we have to know how Stanton's supporters break when they get the news. I'll be back in the office by nine a.m." She hung up.

"What are your expectations?"

"It won't matter to some of his supporters. White males will stick with him, women of all races won't. We just can't predict how many will support Kate and how many support others in the race."

"You've got the New Hampshire primary coming up pretty soon. That ought to be a pretty good poll."

"Yes, but in New Hampshire—we can't wait for that. This will affect where and how we spend advertising dollars. Kate will probably have to spend a lot more time in California before New Hampshire. Before, we had pretty much conceded the state to Stanton, since he's a very popular former California governor. Now there are delegates to be picked up. Let's get out of here."

Stone got his feet on the floor. "Not without a shower and some breakfast."

Ann got out of bed and began looking for clothes. Stone got into and out of a shower. "You're next. You don't want to get to the office looking like that."

Ann turned and looked in the full-length mirror on the wall. "Oh, God."

"I'll fix some breakfast while you fix you."

They were nearly to Danbury before Ann could get a cell phone signal. Stone had a mini cell at his house, but the local area had only spotty service.

"Betty," Ann was saying, "call our California campaign manager and get him to set up a phone bank to poll the convention delegates out there and see where we stand. I'll be at the office by nine. Call me there."

"You'll be at the office by seven thirty," Stone said. "I hope you have a key to the place."

"I do."

"Do you think Stanton will drop out of the race?"

"He won't if he's smart, and he's pretty smart. His people are already doing what we're doing, testing the waters."

"There've been rumors about his sex life for years," Stone said.

"Yes, and most of them are true. Will extracted a promise from him when he put him on the ticket that he'd keep it in his pants, but the cock famously doesn't have a brain."

"I really don't see how he can pull it out—you should excuse the expression—and stay in the race."

"It's good that people saw us together at the restaurant last night. Two of them were either news reporters or producers."

"Why is that good?" Stone asked. "Not that I mind our being seen together."

"Because that makes you my boyfriend, whether you like it or not."

"I'm okay with the characterization," Stone said, "but what the hell does that have to do with the race?"

"It will help with the rumors," Ann said. Her phone rang. "Yes? How many have we talked to? What's the split? Shit! I thought we'd do better." She hung up. "It looks like Marty Stanton's delegates are pretty much sticking with him."

"What rumors?"

"Huh?"

"You said that our being seen together would help with the rumors."

"You haven't heard?"

"Heard what?" Stone was mystified.

"About you and Kate."

"What about Kate and me?"

"The rumor is that the two of you are having an affair, and right under Will Lee's nose."

22

Stone turned onto I-684 and accelerated. "What are you talking about?"

"Is it true?" Ann asked. "If it's over, then I don't care."

"Of course it's over! I mean, it never was over! I mean, we were never having an affair! Where did that come from?"

"Some blogger mentioned it, and when we tried to trace him, it seemed to have come from somebody in California. We think the original source could be Marty Stanton."

"Why would he do that?"

"Insurance—in case something happened like what just happened. You shouldn't be surprised if it comes up again."

"Surprised? I'll be shocked and outraged!"

"Stone, it's just politics—don't worry about it."

"What is Will going to say? They're both my friends."

"Will won't believe it. Tell me, how many times have you had dinner with Kate—lately, I mean."

"I had dinner with both Will and Kate twice, and on one occasion she called me when she didn't have anything to do and invited me up to the Carlyle for dinner."

"Just the two of you?"

"Just the two of us, plus a butler, a waiter, and a full complement of Secret Service agents. It certainly wasn't an assignation."

"If some reporter asks you about it, don't lie. Say what you just said to me."

"I've never been alone with Kate at any time. There have always been others present, usually Will."

"That's a good line—use it. Now, the other thing is, you can't let anyone say that I'm a beard for you and Kate."

"Certainly not! What do I have to do, tell them I fucked you last night?"

"I hope you won't phrase it exactly that way, but I won't be insulted if you intimate it—and, by the way, you fucked me twice last night."

"I have a very clear memory of that."

She laughed. "So do I, and a fond memory."

"For me, too."

Ann's phone rang and continued to ring right up until they pulled up in front of the campaign headquarters. Stone pressed the button that opened the trunk, then he got out, handed Ann her bags, and kissed her. A strobe light began to flash rapidly.

"Don't worry about it," Ann said, nodding toward the door. A photographer stood there, still shooting. "It can't hurt."

Stone drove into his garage and put the cover back on the Blaise, then he went to his office and turned on the TV to *Morning Joe*, which had been recorded. A reporter was standing outside a house overlooking the sea.

"This is the La Jolla, California, home of Vice President Martin Stanton," the reporter was saying, "where in the wee hours of this morning a jealous husband showed up and demanded to see the vice president. He was questioned by the Secret Service, and while they were talking to him a garage door opened and a car driven by a woman left the premises. The husband, a local attorney and Democratic committeeman, identified the driver as his wife. He was not detained by the Secret Service. A spokesperson for the vice president said she had no knowledge of the event and declined any comment. A spokesperson for first lady and presidential candidate Katherine Lee also had no comment. We have not heard from the White House."

Joan came into the office. "What on earth are you doing here?" she asked. "You should still be in bed."

"I drove up to Connecticut yesterday and came back early this morning."

"Have you had breakfast?"

"Yes, thanks."

"Did you see that thing about the vice president?"

"Yes, I did."

Joan went to her office and came back with the *Times* and the *Daily News*. "Here's the woman," she said, handing Stone the *News*.

Stone looked at the photograph of an attractive woman who appeared to be in her thirties. Her name was Laura Grayson, and her husband was Carl Grayson. He looked up at the TV again and saw Martin Stanton leaving his house and getting into a black SUV. Reporters were shouting questions at him. He stopped for a moment. "It was entirely innocent," he said. "We were watching an old movie on TV, and it ran late. It was entirely innocent." He got into the car and was driven away, as the reporters continued to shout questions at the car.

"You think he can get away with that?" Joan asked.

"That remains to be seen. By the way, I've been told that some blogger put out a report that Kate Lee and I are having an affair."

"*What?*"

"That was pretty much my reaction, too."

"Are you?"

"Of course not. I've never even been alone with her."

"Oh, I'm so relieved to hear that," Joan said, clasping a hand to her bosom.

"We may get some calls about it. I just wanted to warn you. For the record, I'm seeing a deputy campaign manager of Kate's. Her name is Ann Keaton."

"Oh, yes, she came here to interview you."

"Right."

"Was she in Connecticut with you?"

"Yes."

"Are you having an affair with her? Not that I need to ask. I would be astonished if you weren't."

"Joan, you're forgetting yourself."

She went off to her office. The phone rang, and Joan buzzed him. "A gentleman from Page Six at the *Post*."

Stone picked up the phone. "Stone Barrington."

"Mr. Barrington, Henry Jacobs at Page Six. We have a report that you're having an affair with Kate Lee. Any truth to that?"

"Certainly not. That's preposterous."

"We have a report."

"It's a lie. Don't believe everything you read on the Internet. I've never so much as been alone with Mrs. Lee." He hung up.

Joan buzzed again. "*People* magazine on line two."

"Oh, shit," Stone muttered, and picked up the phone.

23

The morning wore on, and the calls from the press kept coming. Stone answered every one and delivered the same message. He declined television interviews.

Joan buzzed again. "This time it's only Dino."

"Dino? How are you?"

"Question is, how are you? The Internet is alive with stories of you and Kate Lee."

"I know, I've been answering calls and issuing denials all morning."

"Relax, it'll calm down before the day is over. I know that, in spite of how horny you always are, you're too smart to get involved with a woman who is married to the president and, simultaneously, running for president. Our vice president, however, is not all that smart."

"Yeah, Ann Keaton and I were in Connecticut last night, and she started getting calls about Stanton around sunup."

"Well, put it out of your mind, and let it die of its own accord. Now, would you like to hear how the investigation of your dinner party robbery on Saturday night is going?"

"Yes, please."

"My lead investigator finally reached Don Dugan this morning and questioned him. Apparently, he was in the Hamptons all weekend, and your former girlfriend and others have alibied him solidly. His story is, he fired the Dragos after your encounter with them in Central Park."

"Yeah, sure. Have you talked to the Dragos?"

"We can't find them. They haven't been seen by anybody who knows them for a week."

"I'm telling you, they're your guys, and if you nail them, they'll implicate Dugan."

"I don't doubt it."

"By the way, Dugan called me yesterday and made nice."

"How nice?"

"He actually told me that he's a nice guy and we should be friends."

"And you reacted how?"

"I pretty much told him to go fuck himself."

"Well, you're such an authoritative voice that I'm sure he's trying to do that right now."

"Anything on the jewelry?"

"Nah, and I didn't expect there to be. This was a pretty slick robbery, and I'm sure they had disposal all worked out ahead of time."

"That's what I think, too. Anything on who the other two guys were?"

"Now that you mention it, two first cousins of the Dragos are missing in action, too—disappeared about the same time the brothers did."

"Sounds like you're ahead of the game, Dino."

"Only in my own mind. We don't have any witnesses who can identify anybody, except this one guy who's sure he recognized a voice. We don't have any jewelry, either."

"Once you find the Dragos, it will start to come together. You know the type—they'll fall apart."

"Gee, let's hope so. I'd really like this to go like a one-hour TV cop show, all wrapped up after forty-three minutes, plus commercials."

"Of course, they could lawyer up and make you prove everything, and then you're fucked."

"Don't say that, it's not nice. Anyway, we have techniques other than beating confessions out of perps."

"Yeah, I'm sure they sprayed DNA all over the scene. Were the doorman and receptionist any use at all?"

"None."

"I'd be willing to bet that one of them has been bought."

"Or both. We're running that down."

"Dinner this week?"

"You name it."

"Tomorrow night?"

"Sure, Viv will be here. You bring what's-her-name."

"Kate Lee?"

"The other one."

"Ann Keaton."

"That one."

"I'll do my best. See ya."

They both hung up.

Joan buzzed. "Ann Keaton on hold for you."

Stone pressed the button. "Good morning."

"Afternoon," she said.

"Sorry to keep you waiting. I didn't get enough of you last night—can we do it again?"

"Careful, I'm on an office line, and it gets recorded."

"Oops."

"I'll call you back on my cell in a minute."

Stone hung up and waited for the phone to ring. It rang. "Now can we arrange an assignation?"

"Stone, have you gone nuts?" It was Kate Lee.

"Kate, I'm so sorry. I thought it was going to be Ann."

"I'm sure it will be soon. How are you faring with the media?"

"I'm telling them the truth," he said.

"Good, that's all you need to do. Hang in there, and this will blow over."

"How about Martin Stanton's case? Will that blow over?"

"I can only hope not," she said, laughing. "He should get what he deserves. Bye-bye."

"Bye." Stone hung up, and the phone rang again. "Yes?"

"It's Ann."

"I just had a call from Kate, and I thought it was you."

"Oh, God, I hope you didn't say anything compromising."

"Almost, but not quite."

"Where were we?"

"I was saying I didn't get enough of you last night."

"Ah, yes, I remember now."

"Any chance of dinner tonight?"

"Unlikely. Can I call you, if I can bust loose?"

"Sure. Tomorrow night I'm having dinner with the Bacchettis. You're invited."

"That's much more likely. I hope you can understand how hard it is for me to make plans."

"Sure I do. Did you get any poll results on Stanton?"

"Yes, and he's holding remarkably well. This thing hasn't played out yet, though. If the woman talks to a tabloid or if her husband is mad enough to press the issue, that could change. I wouldn't want to be in Stanton's shoes."

"How about his delegates?"

"They're holding, almost to a man, so to speak. How are you doing with the press?"

"Just telling them the truth."

"That'll work. Hey, you didn't tell me you took Kate to dinner at a restaurant. I had to read it in the *Post*."

"God, I forgot about that. We still weren't alone, though—the Secret Service delivered her and took her away when it was over."

"Good. I'll call you later." She hung up.

Stone contented himself for the rest of the day with memories of the night before.

24

Five o'clock was approaching, and Stone still hadn't heard from Ann. Joan buzzed. "Mike Freeman on one."

He pressed the button. "Hi, Mike."

"Good afternoon, Stone."

"You sound like you're on a satphone."

"That I am—somewhere over Kansas, from the appearance of the landscape out the window."

"Watch out for tornadoes."

"Will do. I'm having dinner with your friend Teddy Fay, and I'll be giving him your message."

"Thank you, Mike. Tell him I wish I could present it myself."

"I'll do that. Everything else all right?"

"Well, let's see, I was at a dinner party on

Saturday night when four men with shotguns arrived and took all the available jewelry."

"How interesting for you. Has the crime been solved?"

"Dino and I think Don Dugan is the mastermind. His company installed the security system."

"Interesting. He didn't strike me as the criminal type."

"He did me. Dino, too."

"Well, you see, I've never been a policeman. I don't have your finely tuned perceptions where criminals are concerned."

"You need a year on the NYPD. Maybe Dino can get you a detective's badge."

"I'm afraid I don't have the qualifications. Gotta run."

"Take care, and thanks again for the delivery."

Mike Freeman walked into the garden restaurant at The Arrington, in Bel-Air, and looked around at the tables. He spotted Billy Burnett, aka Teddy Fay, entering from the other side, and they met in the center, where the headwaiter seated them. There was a bottle of champagne in an ice bucket and a special vase of flowers on the table. The two men shook hands and sat down, and a waiter appeared and opened the champagne bottle.

"Would you like a glass, Billy? This is an occasion for celebration."

The waiter poured the wine, then disappeared. Mike picked up his glass. Billy didn't.

"I'm sorry, Mike, I would be drinking this under false pretenses."

"What do you mean?"

"I've thought about your very kind and generous offer, and I've decided not to accept."

"I'm sorry to hear that, Billy."

"May I explain?"

"Of course."

"I've been working for Peter Barrington and Ben Bacchetti at Centurion Studios for some months. So has Betsy, for that matter. At first I couldn't imagine what I'd be doing there, except providing some security that I thought was no longer necessary, but as it's turned out, I'm loving being in and around the film business, and so is Betsy. I started just doing odd jobs for them, but I've taken on more and more responsibility to the point where I'm working as an associate producer, and the boys have intimated that I might be producing my own films at some time in the near future. Betsy has taken over their travel and public relations department, and she's very good at it."

"Well, I'm happy for you both, Billy," Mike said, "though I'm sorry you won't be joining Strategic Services."

"Thank you, Mike."

"But there's another cause for celebration."

Mike took an envelope from his pocket and held on to it for a moment. "This is a gift from Stone Barrington. He is very grateful to you for protecting Peter and for your friendship." Mike handed over the envelope, but Billy didn't open it.

"That's very kind of him, Mike, but entirely unnecessary. Accepting money for what I did would lessen the good feeling I got from doing it."

"It's not money, Billy. Please open the envelope."

Billy turned it over and looked at it, then he saw the rear flap. THE WHITE HOUSE, WASHINGTON, D.C. was printed on it. He opened the envelope and unfolded the certificate, signed by the president. Unexpectedly for both of them, Billy's eyes welled with tears. "How is this possible?" he finally managed to ask.

"It's possible because Stone Barrington is a very good friend of Will and Kate Lee," Mike said.

"I feel very strange," Billy said.

"Perhaps a little celebratory champagne will settle you." He raised his glass again. "The future," he said.

Billy raised his glass and sipped. "Suddenly, I feel that I have one. For a long time now, I've expected the life I'm leading to come to a sudden end at any moment."

"The pardon brings with it the deletion of every mention of your name from every law enforcement database. You're now a free man in every sense of the word. You can go back to calling yourself Teddy Fay, if you wish."

Billy smiled. "I don't think that name has been deleted from *every* database," he said.

"There won't be any public announcement," Mike said. "The president issued the pardon under seal, because of your past association with the CIA. You can go right on being Billy Burnett, if you like, but don't flash that pardon to anyone, except in extreme circumstances."

"Well, I've devoted considerable time to building my identity," Billy said. "I've got a valid birth certificate, a genuine passport and driver's license and Social Security number, credit cards, bank accounts, the works. It would be a great deal of trouble to change my name again, so I think I'll just stick with William James Burnett. I've come to rather like the guy."

They drank more champagne, then had a good lunch.

That evening, Billy took Betsy to dinner at Michael's, in Santa Monica, their favorite restaurant, and broke the news to her.

Betsy blinked. "You mean I won't be Mrs. Burnett anymore? I'll be Mrs. Fay?"

"No, we're going to stick with Mr. and Mrs. Burnett," Billy said. "Teddy Fay is still an infamous name in some quarters, even though the pardon removes it from all the federal and state law enforcement databases. I think we'll let Mr. Fay rest in peace."

"I'm so happy for you, Billy," Betsy said. They finished their dinner, then went back to the apartment in Peter Barrington's hangar at Santa Monica Airport.

As they crawled into bed, Billy said, "How would you like to live in a real house? We can go shopping for one tomorrow."

"Oh, Billy," she said, "in my whole life I've never lived in anything but furnished rooms, public housing, motels, and apartments. I would just love living in my own house."

"Consider it done," Billy said.

25

At midmorning the following day, at the building near Washington, D.C., called Black Rock, which housed the National Security Agency, Deputy Director Scott Hipp sat, with a stack of files on his desk, doing personnel reviews. There was a soft knock at his open door, and he looked up to see Kathy Dorr, a young woman who was one of his brighter minions, standing there.

"Got just a moment, sir?"

"Sure, Kathy, come in and take a seat."

She sat down and came directly to the point. "In conducting the daily review of the past twenty-four hours of our computer communications data scan, something interesting popped up." Dorr handed the sheet of paper in her hand to Hipp.

Hipp looked at it. "Teddy Fay? That rings a bell, doesn't it?"

"Yessir. Fay is a former long-term CIA employee who went rogue in a rather spectacular way some years back. Most of the story was suppressed, but he's suspected, without much in the way of actual evidence, of a couple of high-level murders, namely a speaker of the House and a Supreme Court justice, and he's been a fugitive in all the years since."

"As I recall, the evidence was mostly just speculation," Hipp said.

"Nevertheless, sir, he's been on a CIA watch list ever since."

"Where did this data capture come from?"

"From a satphone call, probably from a corporate jet, somewhere in the Midwest. Present capabilities don't make a tighter identification possible, but the call was made to the office of a New York City attorney named Stone Barrington."

"Ah," Hipp said. "Stone Barrington of the Arrington hotel incident of some time back."

"Yes, sir."

"As I recall, we picked up the name The Arrington on a scan much like this one, and that led to a successful resolution of a very serious situation."

"Yes, sir."

"What is the protocol for handling the interception of a name on the CIA watch list?" He wanted to see if she knew.

"Well, it would range—depending on the urgency—from an e-mail from you to the deputy director for operations, or someone on his staff, up to a director-to-director phone call."

"Well, let's not involve the directors on this one," Hipp said. "I'll deal with it myself. Thanks for bringing it to my attention, Kathy."

"No further action required on my part?" Dorr asked.

"Nope. This one is probably less than it seems. Let's not get the Agency's bowels in an uproar."

"As you wish, sir." Dorr got up and left.

Hipp read the brief report again. Sometimes of a mischievous bent, he thought of sending it directly to the director of Central Intelligence, Lance Cabot, who would then distribute it, causing excitement or, perhaps, consternation up and down the Agency's chain of command. He sighed. No, he didn't want to get involved in that. Still, he had a bureaucratic responsibility to bring the matter to the attention of the CIA at a sufficiently high level that would allow him to wash his hands of it.

Hipp went to his Agency contacts list on his computer and found just the right person to hand it off to. He typed a short note and clicked on the SEND button. There, he thought; no longer my problem.

At an anonymous building on the Upper East Side of New York, Assistant Director Holly Barker, the CIA's New York station chief, sat at her desk listening, as attentively as she could manage, to a man who was trying to convince her that he deserved immediate promotion to a higher GS level. A soft ping sounded and she flicked her eyes to her computer monitor screen just long enough to see the words "Teddy Fay" appear in a box, then slowly fade away.

"Here's how it goes," she said, cutting off the man, while he paused to take a rare breath. "A quarterly review of all personnel is conducted by supervisory staff, who make recommendations to me based on rather rigid criteria determined by the Civil Service. If you wish your name to float to the top of that process, begin by impressing your immediate supervisor sufficiently to affect his opinion of your commitment, experience, and skills. Coming to me is a blatant violation of the chain of command. Is that perfectly clear?"

The man reddened. "Yes, ma'am."

"You've been at this long enough to know that," she said. "You shouldn't inject our personal relationship into the process. Now go do good work." God, she thought, she had worked with the guy for a while, but it wasn't as though they were sleeping together.

The man made his escape, and Holly turned

to her computer and opened her e-mail account.
There it was: and the subject was *Teddy Fay*. She
hesitated: opening this e-mail might very well be
opening a large and unattractive can of worms.
After a protracted period of unsuccessfully hunting Teddy, he and Kate Lee had made a kind of
truce, to which Holly was a party. Simply put: if
Teddy would permanently vanish and stay vanished, they would stop looking for him. With the
greatest reluctance, she opened the e-mail.

> *To: Holly Barker*
> *Assistant Director of Central*
> *Intelligence*
>
> 1. *A computer scan this day of the*
>   *previous day's volume of cellular*
>   *and satellite traffic produced the*
>   *name "Teddy Fay" in a satphone*
>   *conversation between an*
>   *unidentified aircraft somewhere in*
>   *the United States and an attorney*
>   *named Stone Barrington, in New*
>   *York, New York.*
>
> 2. *Since the name "Teddy Fay"*
>   *appears on a CIA watch list,*
>   *interagency protocol requires that*
>   *this office notify an official of your*

Agency's operations directorate of the existence of this conversation.

3. This transmission meets that requirement.

4. Any further action, such as extracting the relevant conversation, would require the involvement of the FBI, who would then be required to seek a federal search warrant before reviewing the contents of the phone call.

5. Please acknowledge this transmission.

Scott Hipp
Deputy Director
National Security Agency

"Shit!" Holly said aloud and with feeling. She wished she had simply deleted the e-mail, but she had not. She had received the handoff of a hot potato, and if she wasn't careful, she could get her fingers burned. She made a mental note: next Christmas, send Scott Hipp a festively gift-wrapped cyanide capsule.

She picked up her phone and dialed a number.

"Stone Barrington."

"Are you free for lunch today?"

"I believe I am," he said. "Who's buying?"

"You are."

"In that case, the Four Seasons at twelve thirty."

"Done." She hung up. This thing better not be something, she thought.

26

Stone directed Joan, when making the reservation, to request a corner table. CIA people did not converse in a relaxed manner in restaurants when civilians were seated on all sides of them.

He found Holly waiting at the top of the stairs by the bar. She was unusually prompt, and this made him suspicious. Instead of offering a cheek for a peck, she offered a hand. Uh-oh.

The headwaiter seated them at a corner table. "You're looking well," Stone said, offering a small smile.

"Mmmmf," Holly replied.

"Well, sweetheart, what deep trouble are you in today?"

"I'm in no trouble at all," she replied.

"Well, let's review: you were prompt and on time, and you declined a kiss in favor of a handshake. These are not characteristics of the hotly sexual and wildly wanton woman I know so well. What's up?"

She started to speak, but the waiter arrived to take their drink order. He raised his eyebrows in her direction.

"Just some wine," she said.

"A bottle of the Cakebread Chardonnay," he told the man.

He turned back to Holly. "Now."

The waiter returned with the wine before she could speak. "Does he keep it in his pocket?" she asked.

"Nearby. It's a popular wine." He tasted, nodded, and the waiter poured them both a generous glass. "Now," he said again.

"I have received," she said, "in an alarmingly official manner, information that the words"—she looked around to see if anyone could overhear, then whispered—"'Teddy Fay' have recently passed your lips."

Stone tried to remember. "Possibly," he said at last, "they passed the lips of someone I was listening to at the time. Tell me, has your Agency, in fear and desperation, begun stooping to the level of recording the privileged conversations between attorney and client?"

"No," she said, "the National Security Agency has been charged with the task of stooping to that level. From time to time, they like to remind us that they know how to do it."

Menus came, and Stone waved them away. "Dover sole, new potatoes, and haricots verts for two." The waiter dematerialized. "It saves time," Stone said to Holly, "and I know how you love Dover sole."

"Quite," she said. "Now to the business at hand."

"This is business we're discussing?"

"Not yet, but if this conversation doesn't go well, then we will descend rapidly into that ring of hell called business."

"You know how anxious I always am to make the lives of those who protect our country and the world easier and more pleasant. How can I help?"

"You can relate your conversation of yesterday, the one that included the mention of the forbidden words."

"Ah, yes." Stone took a sip of his wine. "No."

"Stone . . ." And there was threat in her voice.

"Attorney-client privilege, sweetheart. You're familiar, aren't you?"

"Stone, I don't give a fuck about your legal business or your privileged conversations with clients. I'd just like to know the context in which the name occurred."

"All right," Stone said, "in passing."

"What?"

"It occurred in passing. It was not the subject of our conversation, it just came up."

"Does either of you know where . . . what's-his-name is?"

"The geography of our conversation covered parts of Kansas and New York City. To the best of my knowledge, what's-his-name is not in either place. And if you put a pistol to my head, I couldn't put my finger on him. Now, Holly, why don't you just relax, have some wine, and tell me what the fuck is going on here."

"You know I can't do that."

"And you know I can't do it, either. But perhaps with a little wine and a little goodwill we can discuss this and then forget about it, to the extent that our conversation never took place."

Holly took a large swig of her wine, which was instantly replaced by the waiter. "It's like this: what's-his-name's name appears on a CIA watch list. Do you understand now?"

"Ah, yes. An NSA computer caught someone mentioning his name."

"Exactly. Now I've shown you mine, you show me yours."

"Love to. Oh, I'm sorry, not that."

"No. Not right now."

"Later, then. All right, a friend of mine, in a privileged conversation, mentioned that he might, in the course of his wide travels, bump into what's-his-name somewhere or other. I suggested that if such a bumping-into occurred, he might convey my warm good wishes to what's-his-name."

"And why are you so warmly disposed toward what's-his-name?"

"Well, to begin with, unlike the Agency, I have never thought of what's-his-name as a villain, a threat to national security, a mortal enemy, or even a bad person."

"Come on, there's more."

"Beyond that you and I will have to rise to that level of confidentiality that surpasses even Agency security or attorney-client privilege. Agreed?"

"All right, agreed."

Their Dover sole arrived, was presented, boned, and served.

Stone took a bite and savored it. "I owe what's-his-name a great debt of gratitude for saving the lives of my son, his best friend, his girlfriend . . . and his father," he said finally.

Holly stared at him, mute.

"I kid you not."

"And how did this heroic benevolence occur?"

"Ah, now we're straying into the realm of 'need to know.' And you do not *need* to know."

Holly chewed a chunk of sole thoughtfully. "But I *want* to know," she said.

"Tell you what," Stone said, "when we're old and gray—all right, older and grayer—and when your Agency and my privilege are no longer chips in the game, and when we are far from recording devices and vulture computers, I will tell you all. After, of course, extracting your promise of eternal silence."

"I have to wait that long, do I?"

"You do. I will, however, offer you some very genuine and very serious advice, based on solid fact and sound truth. Are you interested?"

"Always."

"If I were you, serving in your post, I would contact the official at the NSA who sent you this message, and I would tell him to remove what's-his-name's name from the CIA watch list, and from any other watch list with which he is acquainted."

"That would be really, really sticking my neck out," she said.

"No, it would not. I can tell you that, to the contrary, you would be shielding yourself from further tsuris connected with what's-his-name."

"How do you know this?"

"I can't tell you, but I'll give you a tip: when you return to your warren on the Upper East Side, sit down at your computer and search every law enforcement database at your disposal and use key words corresponding to what's-his-name's name. But, since I know how busy you are, I'll save you the time and tell you what results you may expect: a big fat zero."

"That is absolutely impossible," she said. Then she screwed up her forehead. "Unless . . ."

"Well, yes," Stone said. "Let's leave it at 'unless.'"

"But how did you . . . ?"

Stone held up a warning finger. "Ah, ah."

"Oh, all right!"

And they parted the best of friends.

Holly went back to her office and sent the following e-mail:

> *To: Scott Hipp*
> *Deputy Director*
> *National Security Agency*
>
> *1. Your transmission of this date is acknowledged.*
>
> *2. Please permanently delete the subject name from any and all watch lists, including the one in question.*

3. *Please acknowledge having done so.*

Holly Barker
Assistant Director of Central
Intelligence

She clicked on the SEND button and hoped
that was the end of it.

27

Kate Lee's helicopter, on loan from a wealthy supporter, landed on the White House pad, and a Marine helped her down the stairs and escorted her to the nearest entrance. Three minutes later, she was in the family quarters and stripping down for a shower. She was fully soaped when the shower door opened and the president of the United States, appropriately dressed for a shower, entered and pressed her against the tile wall, holding her head by the hair and kissing her ravenously.

When they had had their way with each other and were sufficiently unsoaped, they repaired to the living room, both dressed in terry robes, and Will poured them both a stiff bourbon on the rocks.

"What's this horseshit I hear about you fucking Stone Barrington?" he asked with a straight face.

"It's horseshit," she replied, clinking her glass against his. "What's this I hear about you fucking the deputy press secretary?"

"What?" he demanded, then his face softened. "All right, I deserved that."

"You certainly did, Bubba. I hope the Stone thing has faded from the bubble memory of the media by this time. Some blogger, no doubt spurred on by Marty Stanton, circulated it. Probably Marty thought it was a shot across my bows. What are you going to do about him?"

"Do? What can I do? He's already been caught in flagrante delicto."

"Well, not quite."

"As near as, dammit—nothing I can do about it now, except haul him in and treat him like a schoolboy."

"That would make a nice story, as soon as we could get it leaked."

"I'm not going to do it, though. I'm going to ignore the event and ignore Marty, too. He won't be invited to any more intelligence briefings, and I've already ignored two of his phone calls."

"Ah, the freeze."

"The deep freeze. He hates that."

"And that man is a heartbeat from the presidency."

"So are you, come to that. Closer."

"But it ain't in the Constitution."

"I don't think we have time to get an amendment ratified before the convention."

"Pity."

"How's it going, baby?"

"I think it's going about as well as can be expected."

"Any signs in your polling of support for Marty cracking?"

"In Nebraska, maybe, not in sunny California."

"Pity about all those delegates."

"Damn straight. I had thought we might peel off enough of them to get us to a second ballot at the convention."

"I can see how you might have thought that, but I can see how it might not happen, too. Californians are accustomed to, if not inured to, Marty's sexual escapades. It's what they've come to expect of him."

"Whatever happened to the Bible Belt?" Kate asked. "Why don't they rise up against him?"

"Because they're voting at the Republican convention, instead of ours. Well, all right, they're voting at ours, too, but they're not as easily shocked as they once were. I think it's Hollywood movies, *People* magazine, and the supermarket tabloids."

"No doubt," Kate agreed.

"Now, if Marty would be kind enough to make a couple of other great big mistakes, you might be able to rub them all together and start a fire."

"I wish I could count on him to do that, but he's not as stupid about other things as he is about sex."

The house phone rang, and Kate picked it up. "Yes?" She covered the phone and looked at Will. "The kitchen wants to know what we'd like for dinner."

"Something plain—meat loaf?"

"Can you rustle up some meat loaf?" Kate asked. "Good."

She hung up. "Be here at half past seven."

"I'm going to miss being able to order anything I want," Will said.

"Well," Kate pointed out, "with a little luck, we may not have to move out of here."

They clinked glasses again.

"From your lips to God's ear," Will said.

"Oh," she said, "I've got gossip."

"Lay it on me."

"Ann Keaton is fucking Stone Barrington."

"How do you know?"

"Well, she's seeing him—can sex be far behind?"

"Lucky guy."

Kate laughed. "Lucky girl!"

They had another drink.

28

Scott Hipp gazed at Holly Barker's e-mail, then, with his finger on the DELETE button, he paused. Why not have some fun with this? He pressed the FORWARD button and typed in Lance Cabot's private e-mail address, then he added a bit of text to the message: *The name in question is that of Teddy Fay.* He pressed SEND and chuckled to himself.

Holly got on her computer and began visiting law enforcement Web sites, beginning with the FBI's. She typed in "Fay, Teddy" and got an immediate response. "No match found." She moved on to other databases and got the same response from each one. Then she went to the CIA mainframe and tried again. "No match found." She was stunned.

Her hotline to Langley went off, and she picked up the phone. "Holly Barker."

"It's Lance."

"Good afternoon, Lance. How are you?"

"Very well, thank you."

"I'm glad to hear it."

"I've had an e-mail from you, forwarded from Scott Hipp at NSA."

"Ah," she said.

"Ah, what?"

"Ah, Scott is trying to make trouble."

"May I ask on what authority have you made this request to him?"

"My own authority. Or does the director have to approve every such action?"

"Not necessarily. Why don't you tell me the background to all this."

"Lance, I'm sorry, but I can't do that on the phone or in an e-mail."

"Not even on *this* phone?"

"Especially not on this phone. You're coming to New York tomorrow, why don't we discuss this off-campus at that time?"

"I'm coming to New York this afternoon," Lance said. "Meet me at the East Side Teleport at four o'clock."

"Certainly. See you then."

But Lance had already hung up.

Holly stood next to her car and watched the chopper from Langley descend through the overcast, make its approach, then set softly down on the pad, shiny with drizzle. Holly's driver removed a bag from the helicopter's luggage compartment, then opened the rear door. Lance got out and, ducking unnecessarily under the spinning rotors, went over to where Holly stood waiting. Holly shook his hand and waited until her driver had put the bag into her car and gotten back behind the wheel.

"Let's walk," Holly said.

"You don't even want to talk in your own car?"

"No, and not even with my own driver."

They watched Lance's chopper lift off, head downriver, and climb into the overcast, then they walked around the edge of the pad and stood overlooking the East River.

"All right," Lance said. "Why do you want Teddy Fay's name removed from the Agency watch list?"

"Because it's already been removed from every law enforcement database and, although I haven't checked, probably from every other government and media database, as well. Google him, and you'll get nothing."

"On your authority again?" He looked hard at her. "Think before you answer."

"Not mine. On what authority do you think such an action could be effected?"

Lance thought about that for a moment. "Possibly the national security adviser," he said finally, but not with any conviction.

"If you were director of the FBI and you got such a request from the national security adviser, what would you do?"

"Raise hell, probably. The director of national intelligence could do it."

"But would he? On his own authority?"

"Probably not."

"If he tried, the FBI and others would be demanding to know who ordered it."

"Certainly I would."

"Did you get an order for Teddy's files to be scrubbed from our database?"

"No, I did not."

"Then the files should still be there, shouldn't they?"

"They should be," Lance agreed.

"But they're not," Holly said. "I checked."

As usual, Lance's face betrayed nothing, but Holly knew him well enough to know that he was as amazed as she had been.

"The only authority that could have effected this is—"

"Yes," she said, cutting him off. "You wanted background—here it is. Maybe eighteen months ago, Teddy surfaced in an e-mail to me. I took it to Kate. After some discussion she proposed that we reach a truce with Teddy: if he would stop misbehaving, we would stop hunting him. I passed that on to Teddy, and he agreed. We've heard nothing from or of him since."

"Did Kate say anything about scrubbing Teddy's name from multiple databases?"

"No, and I don't think that would have entered her mind."

"Did you do anything to effect this?"

"Only my e-mail to Scott Hipp."

"But Scott contacted you first?"

"Yes. Teddy's name surfaced in a computer scan of satphone and cell phone transmissions. Apparently, the authority who ordered his name scrubbed forgot about our standing watch list."

"In what context did Teddy's name turn up?"

"In a satphone conversation between someone aboard an aircraft in the middle west and a New York City landline."

"Who was on the airplane?"

"Undetermined. I don't think they have that capability, or they would have found out."

"Who was on the landline?"

"Lance, please believe me when I tell you, you don't want to know."

"Was it Kate?"

"No, Kate had nothing to do with the conversation. But that's all I can tell you."

"You mean, it's all you *will* tell me."

"If you like."

"Holly . . ."

"Please don't press me on this, Lance."

Lance squinted at the Pepsi-Cola sign across the river. "Do they still make Pepsi-Cola?" he asked. He was not thinking about Pepsi-Cola.

"They do."

"Holly, has Teddy Fay received a presidential pardon?"

"I have no information to that effect."

"Why would Will Lee do that?"

"I have no information to indicate that he has."

"If it hasn't been made public, then he must have done it under seal."

"I have *no such information*," Holly repeated.

"Where would a sealed pardon be housed?"

"Lance, stop this. Will Lee is still your boss, and there's at least an even chance that when he leaves office, Kate will be your boss once again. As of this moment, neither you, nor I, nor Scott Hipp has any evidence that such an event has taken place. If such a notion were published or broadcast, a firestorm of speculation would ensue, and that might change the outcome of a presidential election. If something to that effect should appear, then the only possible source would be you or me. And it's not going to be me."

"I don't like this."

"Frankly, I don't care if you don't like it. I'm not going to allow this to be aired publicly, not even from you."

"Let me get this straight," Lance said. "*You* are not going to allow *me* to do something?"

"You've got it straight," Holly said. "Tell me, who would you like to be the next president of the United States?"

Lance didn't reply.

"Lance, I have worked for you for many years, and I am very grateful to you for the confidence you have placed in me during those years. But I have worked for Kate Lee, and I'm grateful to her, too. I tell you this: I would do *anything* to prevent *anyone* causing damage to Kate's presidential ambitions. *Anything it takes.* And if I were unable to prevent that happening, then I would do whatever I possibly could to destroy the person or persons responsible for it. Now tell me you fully understand what I just said to you."

Lance's shoulders sagged a tiny bit. "I understand you, Holly." He looked at her. "And you're right. I fully concur in your instruction to Scott Hipp to remove Teddy Fay's name from our watch list. I will do nothing to interfere with Kate's campaign. You have my word."

During all the time Holly had worked for

Lance, she had never heard him use those last words. And she believed him.

"Can I give you a lift to the office?" she asked.

"Yes, thanks."

They walked back to her car.

29

Stone and Ann got to Patroon first and ordered drinks. They clinked glasses.

"How's it going?" Stone asked.

"I think you mean, how is Marty Stanton's libido playing in the polls?"

"That's what I mean."

"Marty has developed a chink in his otherwise impressive armor."

"Is this incident going to make a difference?"

"Not unless somebody decides to openly criticize him for it, and I don't think that will happen. No Democrat is going to raise the issue."

"How about Republicans in the primaries?"

"It could come up in, say, a Republican debate, but it's problematical for them. They know it could either help or hurt them, but they don't know which. If you don't hear about it in a debate, then it means they've all agreed ahead of time not to bring it up."

"But in the general election?"

"If Marty is the nominee, he will be fair game for Republicans. Even if their candidate doesn't raise it, some super PAC or other will. There'll be commercials, and they'll be to the point."

"And could it cost Democrats the election?"

"In a tight race, it could."

Stone looked up to see Dino and Viv enter the restaurant, and he got up to greet them, then made the introductions. Scotch was set before them, and the subject changed.

"We got a lead on the Dragos," Dino said. "It's being run down now."

"How good a lead?"

"I'll let you know before dinner is over," Dino said.

"These are the guys you think were among the robbers?" Ann asked.

"Two and the same," Stone replied.

"Will they implicate Don Dugan?"

"That's our hope."

"I wish Dugan was a Republican," Ann said.

Everybody laughed.

"Dino," Stone said, "have you checked to see if any other of Dugan's security system clients have been robbed?"

"Yeah, but he's new to the alarm business, and there are fewer than a dozen of them. Mostly, he's installing new equipment on existing wiring. That was true of the Coulters' installation."

"It would be stupid of him to raid other clients' homes right now," Stone said. "I think the Coulter robbery must have been an opportunistic thing—Dugan heard about the party, maybe even saw the guest list."

"That's a very good theory," Dino said. "You were always good at theory, Stone. But practice? Well . . ."

"I practiced as well as you did, pal."

"Now, boys," Viv interjected. "Stop being boys."

Menus were brought and food ordered. A perfect Caesar salad was whipped up tableside.

Dino's phone rang, and he answered it. "Bacchetti. Yeah? Good work! Well, that was to have been expected. Get hold of an ADA and work up something to offer them. I'm here if you need me." He hung up. "We bagged the Dragos, both of them."

"Hoorah!" Stone half yelled. "Let me guess: they lawyered up."

"Sure they did, but that won't prevent us offering them a deal they might not be able to refuse."

"Are you willing to let them walk to get Dugan?"

"That's not my call—the DA makes that one, thank God."

"Are you going to press for it?"

"I may have to, seeing that we don't have a hell of a lot of evidence against them. It's not like they were arrested holding a suitcase full of jewelry."

"Why don't you bring in Dugan?" Stone asked.

"What for? Unless the Dragos fold, we don't have a damned thing on him."

"Walk him through the precinct, let him see the Dragos and vice versa. Worry him, and worry them even more."

"You think squad room theater is the way to go?"

"It couldn't hurt."

"It might. I'd wager that Dugan already knows about the bust, if he's any good at all, so he'll be ready for us, lawyer standing by. In fact, I don't think he'd even lawyer up. I think he'd brazen it through and enjoy making asses of us. I don't want to give him that pleasure."

"You could be right," Stone admitted.

"The robbery was beautifully planned, and it went off without a hitch. I've got to think that he planned for a bust, too, and that everybody has already learned their parts."

"You think he's that smart?"

"So far, I don't have any reason to think he's stupid," Dino said.

"Where did you find the Dragos?"

"In Brooklyn, sleeping at their mother's apartment." Dino's phone went off again, and he answered it. "Bacchetti." He listened for a minute or two. "Then why did they run?" He laughed a little. "Has the ADA showed? All right, keep me posted." He hung up. "Their lawyer told them to answer questions, so they did—denied everything, of course."

"Why were they at their mother's apartment, then?"

"They said their place is being painted."

Everybody laughed.

"Is it?"

"We're checking. If it is, then the planning is very, very good."

30

Stone and Ann spent much of their night making love, sleeping, then waking and doing it again.

"You have a lot of pent-up sexual energy," Stone said to her at one point.

"Not anymore," she replied. "I'm good for another year of celibacy."

"Don't count on it," Stone said.

When Stone reached his desk a little later than usual, Joan buzzed him.

"Yes, ma'am?"

"Lance Cabot called and invited you to lunch. You didn't have anything on your calendar, so I made the date."

"And where did you decide we should lunch?"

"At the Harvard Club, twelve thirty, Lance's idea."

Stone arrived at the august club on time, and asked for Lance. He was directed to the main dining room, an impossibly high-ceilinged chamber worthy of a cathedral. Lance greeted him politely—Lance was always polite, never warm. There was a bottle of Meursault in a bucket beside the table, and Lance already had a glass. He poured Stone one.

"How is your life these days, Stone?" Lance asked.

"It could hardly be better," Stone replied truthfully.

"I hear you're seeing one of Kate's girls."

"Really, Lance, is the Agency troubling itself with my social life these days?"

"Not really, but a lot of gossip comes my way. I understand, too, that you've been seeing a lot of Will and Kate Lee—especially Kate."

"Don't believe everything you read on the Internet, Lance. I hear Martin Stanton is behind that rumor—anything to take the eye of the press off his own ball."

"That would not surprise me, knowing what I do of Stanton."

"And what do you know of Stanton, Lance?"

"*Everything,*" Lance replied, almost with relish. "The man's a swordsman: he's fucked his way from one end of California to the other, not missing much along the way."

"Is he really that bad?"

"Oh, I hear he's very good, thus, his success."

"Do I hear a note of admiration in your voice?"

"That was contempt—please don't confuse the two."

"How do you feel about the possibility of having Kate as your boss again?"

"Kate and I always got along very well," Lance said. "I expect we would again. She's smarter than Will, you know."

"That's what Will always says," Stone chuckled. "I think Will's the better politician, though."

"Will's better with Congress and the various governors. Kate is better on policy."

"Defense policy, you mean."

"All sorts of policy: defense, foreign, even domestic. I'll bet you didn't know that about her."

"No, I didn't, and it's an interesting observation."

"Will has never put any policy forward that he didn't run by Kate first. And she has often reworked things before they were announced or went to Congress."

"How do you know these things, Lance?"

"Never ask me how I know things, Stone, just believe I do."

"I expect that's good advice."

"The best thing about being in my position," Lance said, "is that I know almost everything there is to know. And if I don't know something, I know who does and I know how to find out." Lance saw a waiter approaching and glanced at the menu. "I'll have the halibut," he said.

"So will I," Stone said without looking at the menu. The waiter departed.

"Teddy Fay's presidential pardon, for instance," Lance said.

Stone was caught off guard but tried not to show it.

"Who?"

"That fellow you helped Holly chase all over the island of Saint Marks," Lance said. "That fellow who took out Yuri Majorov last year. Very nicely done it was, too."

"Oh, that fellow. How could he possibly get a pardon out of Will Lee?"

"Teddy knows people," Lance said. "He knows you, for instance. And you owe him."

"I can't deny that," Stone said, "and I'm grateful to him. But that does not translate into a presidential pardon."

"You haven't denied it yet, Stone."

"Denied what?"

"That you got Will Lee to pardon Teddy."

"Well, just so you won't interpret silence as

confirmation, I deny having anything to do with any such thing as a presidential pardon. I deny asking Will to issue one. Is there anything else you'd like me to deny, Lance? Just tell me what, I'm in a denying mood today."

Lance actually laughed, something Stone had almost never seen him do. "Thank you for that confirmation, Stone."

Stone shook his head.

"There are other things I know," Lance said. "Things that you should know."

"I'm listening." Their halibut arrived.

"Your troubles with Majorov are not over," Lance said.

"What, did someone forget to drive a stake through his heart?"

"Yuri is a member of a clan, Stone. In particular, he has a brother named Yevgeny, who has recently been chosen to replace his brother at the top of his organization."

"I'm sorry to hear it," Stone said.

"That position has been likened to the Pope, chosen by a corrupt and dangerous college of cardinals who have their tentacles into just about everything criminal these days. Please forgive the mixed metaphor."

"You're forgiven," Stone said, making the sign of the cross. "Now tell me what I have to worry about."

"Nothing immediate," Lance said, "but that hotel your group is building in Paris with Marcel duBois is going to be very tempting to Majorov's organization."

"Well, Yuri certainly wanted The Arrington badly enough. You think Yevgeny will follow in his footsteps?"

"I would not be in the least surprised," Lance said. "Our man in Paris, Rick LaRose, who you know, is keeping a close watch on developments. If he should perceive a threat, Rick will be in touch."

"I like Rick," Stone said.

"He will soon be our station chief in Paris," Lance said, "after a little prep work to shape him up. He will be our youngest station chief."

"Please congratulate him for me."

"Wait a couple of weeks, then send him a congratulatory note."

"I'll do that," Stone said.

The rest of their lunch passed in idle chat. Lance had done his probing, and Stone had received his warning.

31

Stone was back at his desk, drowsy from the wine, when Dino called. "Hey."

"Hey, yourself."

"Both of us liked your girl," Dino said.

"You always like my girls."

"This one was especially nice. Viv and I both like smart."

"Now that you mention it, so do I. Stay in touch with her, she could turn out to be someone important at the White House."

"If Kate wins."

"If Kate doesn't win, she'll just be a political consultant or a lawyer. I'm favoring the latter."

"Has Eggers met her?"

"I don't know—not when I was around, but

Bill has a very wide acquaintance, so I wouldn't be surprised."

"He does, doesn't he. You're turning out to have a wide acquaintance, too."

"Oh? Who are we talking about."

"We're not talking about him—I don't think you'd want to."

"Come on, Dino, give."

"One of my detectives says he recognized an old acquaintance at your robbery scene of last week."

"By 'old acquaintance,' do you mean old perp?"

"That's it."

"And who might that be?"

"Your friend Coulter."

"Coulter is an old perp? You're kidding. The man is a model of upper-class respectability."

"My guy says he's an ex-con named Fratelli. That name ring a bell?"

Stone ran a lot of images of John Fratelli and Jack Coulter across the inside of his eyelids. "The name makes a dull thud, but that guy ain't Coulter."

"My guy says the two are one and the same."

"The only thing they've got in common is height," Stone said. "In every single other way they are very different."

"My guy says he's used the money to remake himself."

Stone knew exactly what money Dino was talking about. "What money?"

"The money from that heist out at Kennedy airport years ago. Eddie Buono was the mastermind."

"Oh, yeah, I remember that."

"We talked about Fratelli, remember?"

"No recollection," Stone replied. The slide show in his frontal lobe was stuck on one image: a three-quarter shot of Coulter's face, featuring a nose very much like that of Fratelli. Was it possible?

"My guy wanted to fingerprint Coulter—that would end the discussion, one way or another."

"Is Fratelli wanted for something?"

"Not that I know of."

"Then your guy has no cause to print him. Dino, Coulter is my client."

"So was Fratelli."

"Sort of. I talked to him a couple of times. But Coulter is my signed-up client, and I'm not going to let him be put through the gossip mill because some stupid detective thinks he looks like somebody from twenty-odd years ago."

"He's not a stupid detective."

"Then call him in and tell him not to behave stupidly. You think Woodman and Weld takes on clients without checking them out?"

"I wouldn't think so."

Stone had not done any checking out at all; his only information about either of the Coulters came from Joan, who knew of Hillary Coulter from the society pages. "Then let this be the end of it, Dino."

"I'll pass on your message to my guy," Dino said. "But he kind of has a point."

"Oh?"

"If Coulter is Fratelli, then he has the kind of past populated with people who might be a part of that robbery—heist guys, for instance, maybe fences."

"I don't buy it for a minute, Dino."

"Well, what about this? Another one of the Coulters' guests got hit at home."

Stone didn't like the sound of that. "Yeah?"

"This victim had an elaborate security system— not Dugan-installed—which included an alarm sensor on a concealed cupboard that held a rather large personal safe. The system was somehow breached and the safe cracked either by a very good safecracker or just by someone who had the combination. His wife's jewelry was taken, but what really upset him was that he had a stash of bearer bonds and a few pounds of gold bars, just in case the world ended tomorrow."

"And there's no Dugan connection?"

"No, but there's a connection to your client Coulter."

"I'm telling you, Dino, even if Coulter is Fratelli, what would his motive be? He's happily married to a very rich woman, and I happen to know—don't quote me on this—that their finances are very well blended. A couple of robberies—even big ones—wouldn't come to a drop in their bucket, so there's no motive."

"Okay, I'll yield to you on that one, but how about the insurance connection? The victim's insurance company: your client Steele. They also insured about half of what was taken at the dinner party."

Something clicked very loudly in Stone's head. "There's another connection," he said.

"I'd like to hear about it."

"Crane Hart."

"Yeah, but she works for Mike Freeman at Strategic Services."

"Her most recent employer before Mike was Steele. That's how I met her—she was the adjuster on my claim."

"Now, why didn't I know that?" Dino wondered.

"It never came up, I guess. But it's just possible that when she was with Steele, she had access to the files on clients. Maybe when she left she took some files with her. You can put a lot of information on a computer thumb drive, and that would be a treasure trove for a gang of thieves."

"Stone, I take back my disparaging remark of last night about your detective skills."

"Thank you kindly."

"I think we'll have a chat with Crane Hart."

"Don't do that yet."

"You got a better idea?"

"Yes. Talk to her boss at Steele. He'll know what files she had access to." Stone looked up the number and gave it to Dino.

"I'll talk to the guy myself," Dino said.

"Let's not bring Mike into this—not until you've got something solid. I introduced him to Crane."

"And you don't want him to think you're fingering her because she dumped you?"

"Something like that. And I'd hate to get her fired, if she's not involved."

"Okay, I'll tread softly."

"When you talk to the guy at Steele, don't make it about Crane, just ask who over there might have had access to customer files. See if he brings up the name spontaneously. He was very upset when she left him for Mike, and it wouldn't surprise me if he held a grudge, so don't dangle her name in front of him."

"I'll do that, pal, and I'll let you know how this plays."

"Good luck, Dino." Stone hung up, hoping he was wrong.

32

Stone had closed his office for the day and was sitting in his study with Dino, who had dropped by on the way home. Stone had just poured the drinks when his phone rang.

"Hello?"

"Stone, it's Jack Coulter."

"Good to hear from you," Stone said, not wanting to mention his name in Dino's presence.

"I wonder if you're free for lunch tomorrow?"

"Certainly."

"May we meet at the Brook, the club on East Fifty-fourth? You know it?"

"Yes, that will be fine."

"Twelve thirty. See you then." Jack hung up.

"Sorry," Stone said, taking his seat, "a client wants to have our annual lunch."

"Does that happen a lot?" Dino asked.

"A fair amount. I think they just want to know I haven't forgotten them. Tell me, how's the commissioner's run for mayor next year looking?"

"All I know is what I hear on the local TV news. Everybody seems to think he's running."

"Are you among them?"

"It wouldn't surprise me. If he didn't run and somebody got elected who isn't his pal and who wanted to appoint his own commissioner, he could find himself on the sidewalk."

"Not for long," Stone said. "A law firm or a security outfit like Strategic Services would snap him up."

"I can't see him wanting to run the city. Do you have any kind of idea what sort of horseshit the mayor of New York has to put up with?"

"Only a fair idea. If he runs, and if he's elected, he's going to appoint you commissioner to replace him."

Dino nearly choked on his drink. "Why do you say that?"

"Because you're the only member of the police hierarchy he likes. He hates everybody else. One of the reasons he appointed you chief of detectives was to piss off the half dozen other top captains who wanted the job. Most of them quit when you got it, which must have delighted the commissioner."

"Yeah, well, it was nice to see them go."

"And if he appoints you commissioner, a whole bunch of other guys will walk, and you'll get to replace them with your people, which is to say, the commissioner's people."

"I admire your logical thinking," Dino said, "but we're a long way from that happening."

"Maybe not as long as you think," Stone said. "When he announces for mayor, he'll have to resign as commissioner."

"Right, and he doesn't get to appoint his successor, not until he's mayor."

"But the commissioner and our current mayor are pretty tight, aren't they?"

"They certainly are."

"What's the matter with his asking the mayor to appoint you? Anybody else he appointed would just be a chair warmer until the commissioner is elected."

"You think the commissioner would do that?"

"I do."

"And you think our present mayor would appoint me?"

"If the commissioner asked him nicely, yes."

"It's hard for me to get my head around the big job," Dino said.

"It was hard for you to get your head around being chief of detectives, too, but you did it."

"I guess I did, at that. What's more, I've gotten to love it."

"You can't love doing something unless you're good at it, Dino."

"You sound a lot like Viv."

"You think she'd like to be the wife of the commissioner?"

"She'd love it, as long as she could keep her job at Strategic Services. Being the commissioner's wife doesn't pay, you know, and Viv has done very well with Mike. I think if a condition of being the commissioner's wife was that she'd have to quit her job, she'd divorce me!"

"But she wouldn't move out," Stone said.

Dino laughed. "We're getting way ahead of ourselves."

"Ahead of ourselves is somewhere we have to be," Stone said.

"Okay, with that in mind, what if Kate gets elected president?"

"I think that would be great."

"Suppose she wanted to appoint you attorney general?"

Stone laughed. "That is entirely outside the realm of possibility. I'm completely unqualified, and the Senate would never confirm me, and even if they did, I wouldn't want all the tsuris."

"Okay, how about deputy attorney general for criminal investigations? No Senate confirmation required."

"No, I'm way too happy right here in this house. You know what's much more likely to happen?"

"What?"

"Kate appoints you deputy director of the FBI."

"Holy shit!"

"If you were commissioner she would make you director, but you'd make a great deputy director."

"I'm getting dizzy here," Dino said. "Let's talk about something real. If Kate gets elected, then Ann Keaton is going to work in the White House. How will you ever get laid again?"

"Ouch! What a thought."

"You might have to move to Washington, pal, or at least get a place there."

"I guess she's not going to commute to the White House from New York," Stone admitted. "So if I want to see a lot of her, I'll have to do something like that."

"You're way too comfortable here," Dino said. "It would be good for you to make a move for a few years. You might even like it down there."

"I've liked it when we've been there," Stone admitted. "And I know a few people."

"With Ann in the White House, you'd know everybody in about fifteen minutes. Have you talked to her about any of this?"

"It seems premature. Kate doesn't even have

the nomination yet, and Ann and I are just getting started."

"I think you need to live in the future a little, like you said. You don't want all this to fall on you when you haven't thought about it, planned for it."

"Okay, I'll think about it. If you'll think about being commissioner."

"You got yourself a deal, pal. Maybe we can still improve our lot in life!"

33

Jack Coulter received Stone in a handsome sitting room at the Brook. It was an old club, and one of the few that had managed to stay all male. He wondered how they had managed that under city law. The mayor had had to resign from the club when he ran for the office.

"How are you, Stone?"

"I'm very well, Jack, and you?"

"Better every day."

"We had a very interesting evening with you last week."

"A little too interesting, I think. Shall we go in?"

Stone followed Jack to the dining room, and they were seated and ordered lunch.

"Something I've wanted to talk to you about," Jack said. He looked uncomfortable for a moment, then sighed. "You and I have met before, you know. Last year."

"That was something that hadn't crossed my mind until yesterday, when it was mentioned to me."

"It was the detective, wasn't it? O'Brien?"

"Is that his name?"

"He arrested me once, twenty-five years ago, but he couldn't make it stick. He has a long memory."

"I'm impressed, Jack. How have you managed this transformation? I never twigged, until Dino brought it up. His detective had mentioned it to him."

"I've always been a good mimic," Jack said. "You should hear my Jimmy Stewart."

Stone laughed.

"I was living at the Breakers, in Palm Beach, when I met Hillary and her brother, Winston, and his wife. Before I knew it, I was talking and behaving like them. After a little of that, I managed to fit in. Then Hillary and I fell in love, and here we are."

"And a member of the Brook, too!"

"Winston engineered that. He's very much an insider here. There's no formal admission process—one day you get an invitation, and that's it."

"Saves a lot of letter writing, I guess."

"Stone, I'm concerned about this thing with the detective. He thinks, naturally enough, that with my background I might have some connection to the robbers. I don't. A couple of decades' separation from that life, and when you get back, everybody is either dead or in prison."

"Dino and I had this conversation yesterday, and I think I convinced him that you weren't involved."

"Well, it's a relief to hear that."

"I'm glad I could be of help."

Lunch arrived, and they tucked in.

"It occurs to me," Jack said, "that I might be helpful in this matter, but I don't want to become directly involved, for obvious reasons."

"I understand."

"In thinking about the robbery, I remembered that I once knew a very smart fence. His name is Jacob Sutton—born Schwartz, I think. He had—probably still has—one of those stalls in the diamond market, over in the West Forties."

"I know the place."

"In a robbery like the one at our place, it would be smart to get the proceeds out of the country quickly—remove the stones and ship them, then melt down the gold and platinum. But Jake worked another way. He'd remove the stones, sometimes recut the larger ones, reset them, retail what he could and sell the rest to the trade. He'd get double what he would have gotten in Amsterdam or Tel Aviv, but it took patience, something most criminals don't seem to have much of. Everybody wants to get paid now, you know?"

"That's very interesting. Is Jake known to the police?"

"When I knew him, he had never once been arrested. He was a pillar of the Hasidic community in Brooklyn and something of a philanthropist. He worked his stall every day. Everybody knew him, trusted him."

"I'll see that he's looked into."

"Something else: we recently had our security system updated. We were having a lot of false alarms with the old equipment, and on the recommendation of our insurers, it was replaced by a man named Dugan. I mentioned this to the detectives."

"Between you and me, Don Dugan is a prime suspect," Stone said. "Believe me, no stone will be left unturned where he's concerned."

"I'm glad to hear that, and I'd like to know what comes of the investigation."

"I understand that one of your dinner guests had his own home robbed."

"Robert Quincy," Jack said. "I talked to him yesterday. He had no connection with Dugan, though. His most important loss was a number of gold bars—he wouldn't say how many, but my impression was that it was considerable. That would be very easy to dispose of—melted down and recast in one of a number of ways."

"I've heard about that case. You're right, Dugan didn't sell him his security system. What connects your robbery with his is that you are both insured by Steele. They're my clients, and believe me, they're going to be all over this. The total of the claims is going to be enormous."

"I would imagine so. They've already been to the apartment and investigated. We're fortunate in having photographs of and receipts for most of Hillary's things, and what we don't have, Harry Winston or Tiffany or Cartier will have in their files."

"I hope your guests were as smart as that."

"The insurance company insists on it when they're covering big-ticket items. Nobody is going to get burned, except the insurance company."

"I'm glad to see you land on your feet, Jack. I hope this business is not going to make life difficult for you."

"I hope that, too. That's why I want to do whatever I can to help the police break this—but with you as an intermediary."

"Dino Bacchetti, whom you met, is chief of detectives and my closest friend. I'll do everything I can to see that undue attention isn't directed at you."

"Thank you, Stone."

The two men chatted about other things, finished lunch, and said good-bye.

As soon as he got back to his office, Stone called Dino and told him about the conversation with Jack Coulter.

"He really wants to help, Dino. He's not involved in this."

"I've never heard of this guy Sutton," Dino said. "But I'll see that he's thoroughly checked out."

"I'd appreciate it if you'd do what you can to keep your people away from Jack. Anything you want to know, I'll ask him for you."

"Okay, we'll work it that way. I understand the guy's position, and I don't want to expose him. I'll keep O'Brien off his back. I know how to do that."

34

Stone was about to call it a day when Joan buzzed him. "Jeb Barnes, from Steele, is here to see you. He didn't call for an appointment."

"Send him in."

Jeb Barnes came into Stone's office looking as though he had bad news.

"Come in, Jeb, and have a seat." Stone directed him to the sofa. "It's late in the day. Can I get you a drink?"

"Thank you, yes. Scotch, any kind, rocks."

Stone poured the scotch and handed it to Barnes, then poured himself a bourbon and sat down. "What can I do for you, Jeb?"

Barnes knocked back half the scotch and took a couple of deep breaths before speaking. "I'm in a terrible jam, Stone, and I don't know who else to go to."

"Tell me about it."

"I know you and I haven't had the best relationship, but you're the only person I know who understands these things."

"It's all right, Jeb. Just tell me what's happened."

"I had a visit from the police this afternoon." He stopped as though that would explain everything.

"Go on."

"As you know, since you were there, there was a big jewelry robbery at the home of Jack and Hillary Coulter. We insured the bulk of the things taken from the guests. About seven million dollars' worth."

"I know. Is the company blaming you for insuring those people?"

"Of course not. We're delighted to have that sort of business. It's unusual, though, for so many clients to be hit in one robbery."

"I imagine so. You still haven't told me what the problem is."

"The police asked me who among our employees would have access to customers' files, files that would hold information that might be used to put together that kind of robbery."

"Did you give them names?"

"Yes, of course—half a dozen of them. There was one name I didn't give them."

"Why not?"

"No longer an employee. That doesn't matter, though. I'm talking about Crane Hart."

"That's right, she left Steele. Did she have that sort of access to client records before she left?"

"Yes, she did."

"Then why didn't you give her name to the police?"

"Because when she was still an employee, she and I were having an affair."

Stone took a couple of deep breaths himself. "But she would have still had access to the records if you weren't involved with her, wouldn't she?"

"No, she wouldn't have. You see, the most sensitive of our records, the files of our richest and most heavily insured clients, are kept in a room adjacent to my office. Nobody gets to them, except through me."

"I see, except I don't see, really."

"Our affair, such as it was—it was only sex, without much romance—was conducted mostly in my office. There are times when I have to pull all-nighters or work weekends, so there's a Murphy bed and a bathroom in my office suite. That's where most of the, ah, screwing went on."

"And how did that give her access to your customer files?"

"I'm a heavy sleeper, and sex pretty much renders me unconscious. A number of times I would wake up in the night to go to the bathroom, and Crane would be gone. This would be three, four a.m. I don't know how long she stayed after I fell asleep or what she did during that time."

"And you think she may have used those opportunities to rifle your files?"

"Possibly. Obviously, I couldn't tell the police about the affair. Knowledge of it within the company could get me fired, and, incidentally, I do have a wife, if not much of a marriage."

"I understand."

"Crane was the aggressor. She could be very seductive, wanton, even. It was the best sex I'd ever had in my life. I couldn't believe my luck."

Stone nodded; he knew exactly what Barnes meant.

"Stone, I know you have contacts in the police department. Could you speak to somebody there about this? I want them to have the information, I just don't want it to get back to the company."

"I can do that, of course, Jeb, but you must understand: if Crane had any involvement in the robbery, and she's caught, she could be tried, and you may then have to testify. Not necessarily, but very possibly."

"At that point, there would be nothing else I could do but testify. Would it have to be in open court?"

"If it came to that, yes."

"Then I'll have to let the chips fall where they may."

"Jeb, there's something you could do that might help the police and make them grateful to you."

"Name it."

"Put together a list of the names of your customers who might be candidates for a robbery. I can ask them that the names be kept in confidence."

"So if others were robbed, they might establish a connection to Crane?"

"Yes."

"I don't want to get her in trouble, if she's innocent in all this."

"I can understand that, but if she's innocent, they're not going to make a fuss about it. They'll just have a chat with her."

"All right. If you like, I can write down a list of likely clients right now, from memory."

Stone went to his desk, retrieved pen and paper, and set them on the coffee table before Barnes. He picked up the pen and began to write. Finally, he handed two sheets of paper to Stone. "You'll keep these in confidence, won't you? I mean, you won't let anyone see this, except the police?"

"Of course, Jeb." He took the sheets and put them into a file folder.

"I also wrote down the approximate sum each of them is insured for. There are some quite large numbers there."

"Good. I'll get right on this, Jeb, and I'll let you know if the police have any further questions. I'll ask them not to return to your office, unless it's absolutely necessary."

Barnes stood up, looking relieved. "Thank you, Stone," he said, offering his hand. "I'm very grateful for your help."

"I'm happy to help, Jeb. Good night." He opened his office door and saw him to the street door.

"Wasn't that guy not your favorite client?" Joan asked as he passed her office.

"Maybe not, but now I'm his favorite attorney."

35

Stone and Dino met for drinks and dinner at P.J. Clarke's. The bar was jammed, as usual, so they took their drinks to a table.

"Okay," Dino said, "who goes first?"

"I will. You already know about my lunch with Jack Coulter, but late in the afternoon Jeb Barnes, from Steele, turned up at my office, very worried."

"That's the one my guys talked to at Steele?"

"That's the one. He was upset because he hadn't told you everything you wanted to know."

"What did we want to know?"

"You wanted a list of names of people in his office who could have had access to customers' files, who might have used the information contained therein to choose robbery victims."

"We got that, as I recall."

"No, there was a name missing: Crane Hart."

"And why didn't he want to give us her name?"

"Because he was fucking her—or rather, vice versa. She was the aggressor, he says."

"The lady gets around where beds are concerned."

"Seems that way. Jeb says the files of the richest clients are housed in a room off his office, and nobody has access without his permission."

"And he gave Crane that permission?"

"No. He has a bedroom and bath there, and when he woke up in the night, she'd be gone. He says he's a heavy sleeper, and she would have had the opportunity to get at the files."

"Weren't the file cabinets locked?"

"He didn't say, but apparently not."

"That's all very interesting."

"There's more. In my conversation at lunch with Jack, he told me that his insurers—Steele—recommended Don Dugan for the replacement of his security system."

"And the person at Steele recommending Dugan could either be Crane or someone she could influence, like Barnes."

"Right. If I'd thought of this earlier, I'd have asked him. Also, I remember when I switched my household insurance to Steele, after they became my clients, they sent a representative over who went through my house with a fine-toothed comb, making lists of items to insure and commenting on my security arrangements. The other Steele client, who was robbed of his bearer bonds and gold, would have had a similar visit. That could be how the safecracker found the safe concealed behind a panel."

"I wonder who's going to be robbed next?" Dino asked.

Stone took Jeb Barnes's notes from a pocket and handed them to Dino. "This is a list Jeb made of his richest clients, the ones with the most insurance. It would be interesting to know about their experience with Steele, if the company recommended Dugan for security system work and who from Steele surveyed their apartments or houses."

"It certainly would," Dino said, tucking the list into his own pocket. "I'll have each of them interviewed by a detective."

"Barnes is worried about Crane's being interviewed by detectives," Stone said. "He believes she might be innocent in all this, and he doesn't want her unnecessarily disturbed."

"Let's see if her name comes up in these next interviews," Dino said. "If it does, we'll be talking to Crane whether Barnes likes it or not."

"Jeb's greatest fear is that his company will find out he was fucking Crane and fire him. I told him I'd ask you to be discreet in your investigation."

"Sure, we'll be discreet—up to a point. Anything else?"

"Nope. Your turn."

"I talked with a detective who's our top jewelry theft investigator and dropped the name of Jacob Sutton. He actually knows Sutton, because he's spent a lot of time at the diamond center investigating cases, but he had no idea that the guy was a fence. I've authorized him to have a team look into the man and his business thoroughly. If he's been fencing for as long as Coulter says he has, he's probably connected to a lot of robbery cases over the years. We're concentrating on the ones that the statute of limitations hasn't run out on."

"Sounds good."

"Everybody's excited about Jake Sutton. Nailing him would be a very big win for the department."

"And for you, since your predecessors never nabbed him."

"Yeah, well."

They ordered steaks and fries and wine and began to enjoy themselves.

After dinner, Dino said, "Viv tells me that Crane is impressing people at her new job."

"Good for her."

"Makes me wonder, though."

"Wonder what?"

"Who is Crane fucking at Strategic Services?"

36

Stone arrived home and went to his study to check his phone messages. Nothing. That was a relief. He turned the lights off and went upstairs to his bedroom. On the way up in the elevator, he had the odd feeling that something had been amiss in his study, but in thinking about it, he couldn't imagine what.

He undressed in his dressing room and got into a nightshirt, then he adjusted the bed to point him at the TV and turned on the late news. Again, he had the feeling that something was wrong with the room, but it took him a couple of minutes to grasp what it was. He sat bolt upright in the bed and stared at the bedroom wall facing him. His mother's four paintings, which normally hung there, were gone.

He got out of bed, raced downstairs, and turned on the living room and study lights. Two more paintings in the study and five from the living and dining room were gone. He had a terrible feeling in the pit of his stomach, and he had to take a few deep breaths before he could call Dino.

"Bacchetti."

"It's Stone."

"You think of something else I should know?"

"Yes. The next robbery has occurred. All of my mother's paintings, eleven of them, are missing."

"Holy shit, Stone, those are irreplaceable!"

"I know."

"I'll get the art squad on this right away. Are you available now?"

"Yes."

"How did they get into the house?"

"I don't know. They must have come in while you and I were at dinner."

"Any suspects?"

"The first time Crane was in the house she commented on the paintings, paid a lot of attention to them. She knew my mother's work."

"Now we interview Crane," Dino said.

"Okay with me, and you needn't be gentle."

"We're on it." Dino hung up.

Stone got dressed and poured himself a brandy; he needed it. Presently, the doorbell rang, and two detectives came into the house.

"I'm Jim Connor, this is my partner, Aaron Cohn," the older of the two men said. "I understand you've had a burglary."

Stone went to his computer and printed out color photographs of the eleven paintings, then he handed them to Connor. "That's the lot," he said.

"Do you have any idea of their value?" Connor asked.

"There was an auction at Sotheby's last month," Stone said. "A smallish painting of hers went for a million nine. It wasn't her best work. My collection was the cream of her career."

"I know Matilda Stone's work well," Connor said, "and I feel for you. Are they insured?"

"Yes, with Steele, who are my law clients, too. I also serve on their board of directors."

"Did you buy all the paintings?"

"My mother left me four. The others I've collected over the years, the most recent acquisition late last year."

"I understand you feel that a Ms. Crane Hart may have been involved in the theft?"

"Until recently, she was with Steele. We met when she came to adjust a claim I had made. She knew my mother's work, and made a point of admiring the pictures. I assume Dino has briefed you on her possible involvement in a couple of other thefts—of jewelry, not art. Her former husband, one Don Dugan, is a suspect, as well."

"I suppose you have a security system?"

"Yes. I armed it when I left the house."

"Then it must have been bypassed. May I see the main box?"

Stone took the two detectives downstairs and showed them the panel. There was a light representing each sensor—door, window, motion—in the house. All the lights were off.

"I don't know how the hell they did that without setting off the alarm," Stone said.

"There are some very clever operators out there. When you came home from your dinner with Chief Bacchetti, did you enter the code, as usual?"

"Yes, and it made the right noises. I had no reason to suspect it had been tampered with."

"You'd better get your security guy here first thing in the morning and let him diagnose what was done to the equipment. We'd like to know in detail how they switched off the system."

"So would I," Stone said.

The two men asked more questions, then Connor said, "We'll be in touch."

Stone let them out, and he started to engage the security system. Then remembered he didn't have one.

37

Stone slept badly and awoke depressed. He had trouble getting out of bed. He called Bob Cantor, his electronics specialist.

"Good morning, Stone."

"Hello, Bob. My house was burgled last night and eleven paintings were stolen. The alarm system had somehow been turned off while I was out to dinner."

"I'm sorry to hear that, Stone, but if you remember, your current system was installed by your friends at the Agency last year at the same time they replaced all your windows."

"Oh, God, you're right, Bob." The Agency had done the work to protect his guest Marcel duBois.

"If I can be of any help to them, just call me."

"Thanks, Bob, I will." Stone hung up and called Holly.

"You're up early, Stone," she said.

"You remember last year when your people installed new windows and a new security system in my house?"

"Yes, I do."

"Last night, my house was entered while I was out to dinner, and all of my mother's paintings, eleven of them, were stolen."

"Oh, Stone, those beautiful pictures of New York?"

"Yes, those. Can you get somebody over here to find out why their system failed?"

"I'll make some calls immediately and get back to you."

"Thank you." They both hung up.

Stone ate half his breakfast, showered, shaved, and went downstairs. The phone on his desk was buzzing as he entered his office. "Yes?"

"Holly Barker on one."

"Holly?"

"Stone, a technician will be there in an hour or less."

He thanked her and hung up.

Joan came into the office. "You look terrible,"

she said. "Are you ill? Do you want me to call your doctor?"

Stone told her what had happened.

"That seems impossible," she said "Those Agency people said it was beyond state-of-the-art!"

"So they said. They'll be here in an hour. Try not to yell at them until they've diagnosed the problem and fixed it."

"I'll do my best," Joan said, then went back to her desk.

A moment later, she buzzed. "Mike Freeman on one."

"Hello, Mike."

"Good morning, Stone. You sound a little down. Something wrong?"

Stone told him.

"That's very disturbing. Would you like me to send some people over there to look at it?"

"No, the Agency is sending the people who installed it."

"If they don't resolve this to your satisfaction, let me know, and I'll send over a team."

"Thanks, that's comforting to know."

"I called to see if you'd like to have lunch."

"Thanks, Mike, but I've got my hands full here, How about tomorrow?"

"Usual place, usual time?"

"See you then." Stone hung up and noted the date on his iPhone calendar.

The Agency had sent a team of three, and they looked grim. "This doesn't happen to our equipment," their leader said. "We'll take a look at the panel." The man knew where it was, so Stone kept his seat. An hour and a half later the leader returned.

"Here's what happened," he said. "While you were out last night, someone snipped a wire to the outside alarm speakers, then picked your front door lock, entered the house, found the main panel, and cut the alarm and phone wires."

"Why didn't that set off the alarm?" Stone asked.

"By that time, you didn't have an audible alarm, but the system should have notified your monitoring service. That's where the problem is, I think. We've made repairs and reconnected everything. We've also installed front and rear outside alarms, two stories up, where no one could reach them without attracting attention. We've also installed backup circuits that will turn on the alarms if the same thing should be tried again."

"So what do I do now?"

"Call the police, tell them that you suspect someone at your monitoring service of ignoring the alarm last night, and ask them to investigate.

It's likely that there was only one person on duty after hours. I've spoken with Assistant Director Barker, and she has authorized us to route your monitoring directly to our station. We're fully staffed twenty-four/seven."

"So I'm back in business here?"

"You are. The system is up and running, and the monitoring has been rerouted. You should call this number and give them a new cancel code, in case of false alarm." He wrote down a number and gave it to Stone.

Stone thanked the man, and he and his team left. Stone called in his new cancel code, then found Detective Jim Connor's number and called him.

"Connor."

"It's Stone Barrington. The people who installed my security system were here and repaired everything. They suspect someone at my monitoring service of ignoring last night's alarm." Stone gave him the name and address of the service.

"We'll get over there and investigate," Connor said. "Are they still monitoring your system?"

"No, the system has been rerouted to a different monitor, a more secure one."

"I'll get back to you," Connor said.

Later in the day, Dino called. "How you doing?"

"Better."

"You're not going to believe who owns your security monitoring service."

"You don't mean . . ."

"Dugan bought the service less than a month ago."

"Then he has a license to steal," Stone said.

"Just about. I sent two men to see Crane Hart today. They spent two hours with her in a conference room."

"And?"

"And nothing. The woman has ice in her veins. She knows nothing, she did nothing, she has no idea what Dugan does when he's out of the house. My guys swear she could pass a polygraph without blinking."

"I thought she'd crumble under questioning," Stone said.

"Frankly, so did I. She seemed so delicate."

"What now?"

"The guy on duty last night at the monitoring service quit this morning at the end of his shift, and we haven't been able to locate him. Turns out, that service also monitored the apartment systems of the Coulters and Quincy, the guy who lost all the gold."

"Anything yet on Jake Sutton? I'll bet he fenced the Quincy property, too. And maybe he handles art."

"We're working Sutton flat-out. If we can connect him to some robberies, then there's a chance he'll roll on Dugan."

"Who do you want more, Dugan or Sutton?"

"That'll be up to the DA on the case. Did the Agency fix your security system?"

"Yes, and they installed backup equipment."

"I'm amazed that Dugan's people could get past your system, even owning the monitoring service."

"It seems that everybody who works for Dugan is the best in the business. They've pulled off three big jobs now, flawlessly and without hurting anybody."

"The older guys around here say this is the slickest work they've seen since Eddie Buono and his crew knocked over that currency outfit at Kennedy more than twenty years ago."

"Dino, can you get a search warrant for Crane's building? She has a duplex and rents two apartments. She liked my mother's paintings so much, I think she might have kept at least one."

"We don't have enough for a warrant, Stone, you ought to know that."

"You don't have a tame judge on tap?"

"Not that tame."

"What are you doing to find the paintings?"

"The art squad has a routine. You're getting the same attention that you would if the pictures were van Goghs and Picassos."

"Thanks, Dino. You want to join Mike Freeman and me for lunch tomorrow?"

"Sure."

"Usual time and place."

"I'll be there. Maybe I'll have more for you by then."

38

Mike and Dino were already at Mike's regular table at the Four Seasons Grill. Stone sat down, and a waiter poured him a glass of Chardonnay from a bottle in a cooler.

"How you feeling?" Dino asked.

"Better and angrier."

"I want you to know our art investigation team is all over this. They're checking shippers to stop the pictures from being sent abroad, they're harassing dealers who've been known to handle hot art, they're doing everything they can."

"Are you satisfied with what your techs did with your system yesterday?" Mike asked.

"I am. They did a great job, and they've switched my monitoring to an Agency office. Mike, did Dino tell you that Dugan bought my monitoring service?"

"No."

"Not yet," Dino said.

"And the guy on duty that night ignored the alarm, then left his job the next morning. How many of your clients use that service?" Stone asked.

"I don't know, but I'll find out."

"I should think you'd be better off with in-house monitoring," Stone said. "Have you considered that?"

"I'm considering it as we speak."

"There's something else, Mike," Dino said.

"Are you talking about Crane Hart? Your people spent two hours with her yesterday."

"Yes. Did she talk to you about it?"

"No, she left the office immediately afterward, and she called in sick this morning. What's going on?"

Stone was glad that he wasn't conveying this information.

Dino went on. "We suspect that Crane and Dugan may be involved in a series of robberies, of which Stone's is the third."

"Go on," Mike said.

"Turns out Crane had access to a lot of wealthy clients' records when she was with Steele, and it's possible she may have helped Dugan select victims. Stone recognized the voice of one of Dugan's people in the robbery last weekend at the Coulter apartment."

Stone brought Mike up to date on that.

"Mike, you might give some thought to the work that Crane is doing for you now."

"Right now, she's working on planning security for a private jewelry show in a couple of weeks." Mike took a large sip of his wine.

Dino and Stone exchanged glances.

"Just the sort of thing Dugan might like to know about," Dino said.

"I just can't believe Crane would be involved in something like this."

"Can you believe that Dugan might be?" Stone asked.

Mike drank some more wine and nodded. "Yes, I can."

"Did you know that they're back together?" Stone asked.

"No, I didn't."

"Immediately after their divorce decree came down."

Mike looked grim, but he didn't reply.

"It turns out," Dino said gently, "that Crane has a history of sleeping with people who can give her the kind of information that Dugan would need to pull off these jobs. Is there someone at Strategic Services who might fit that bill?"

"Yes, there is," Mike said. "Me."

Everyone got very quiet.

"Have you talked to her about anything you're working on that Dugan might be interested in?"

"Yes, the jewelry show she's working on. A dozen dealers will be exhibiting high-end pieces to an invited audience from the trade. There'll be more than a hundred million dollars in jewelry there."

"Where and when is the show to be held?" Dino asked.

Mike gave him the date. "It's at a new hotel, the Creighton Arms, that's opening that day. The jewelry dealers have taken the top floor. We're providing armed guards and a temporary, wireless alarm system. Each dealer will have a remote device with a panic button."

"And what part of this is Crane working on?" Stone asked.

"Overview. She knows the whole setup."

A waiter appeared, and they took a moment to order lunch, then they were alone again.

"May I make a suggestion, Mike?" Dino asked.

"I would be very grateful if you would."

"I suggest you assign someone to work as a kind of shadow to Crane. Change everything about your arrangements—guard numbers and positions, panic codes, everything. But keep Crane in the old loop. Let her think that she still has the whole layout."

"Good idea," Mike said.

"I also think you should have plainclothes armed guards with each dealer."

"Another good idea."

"My detectives will work with the hotel's security to handle everything outside the floor they've taken—elevators, parking garage, exterior access, and roof, including the helicopter pad, if there is one."

"There is one. It's already in service. That would make the most sense for a robbery team to get out fast."

"Then we'll have NYPD choppers overflying."

Their food came, and they ate quietly.

"Who was Crane sleeping with at Steele?" Mike asked finally.

"Jeb Barnes," Stone replied. "He kept the top client records in his office suite, and they spent nights there. Jeb says he's a heavy sleeper."

Mike nodded. "And you?" he asked Stone.

Stone shrugged. "That's how Crane saw the pictures—four of them were in my bedroom."

"That woman is something else," Mike said.

"She certainly is," Dino agreed. "And you're going to have to be very careful not to let her know about our conversation. When she comes back to work, ask her about the interrogation. Believe me, she'll have a plausible story ready."

"Should I keep sleeping with her?" Mike asked.

"I don't know," Dino said. "Can you do that without her sensing that something is wrong?"

"I honestly don't know," Mike said. "I'll have to think about it."

"If you're going to break it off, you should have a story ready for her. Tell her you've met someone else, something like that."

"I don't know how to bring that up," Mike said.

"Let her take the lead," Stone suggested. "She's good at that."

"That," Mike said, "is a new high in understatement."

39

Stone had hardly gotten back to his desk when Joan buzzed him. "There's an Alistair Tremont on line one for you."

"Remind me," Stone said.

"Tremont Gallery, he says."

"Oh, yes, I remember." He pressed the button. "This is Stone Barrington."

"Mr. Barrington, you may remember that I sold you a picture a few years back? A Matilda Stone?"

"Yes, of course."

"I didn't realize you'd sold it."

"Sold it?"

"If you'd come to me I'm sure I could have gotten you a far better price."

"I'm sorry, I don't understand."

"A young woman came in this morning with some slides. She's a kind of walking gallery—she buys things at estate sales and junk shops, then cleans them up and sells them to galleries or at antique shows. I thought perhaps you had engaged her to sell some of your works."

"Alistair, I've never sold any of the art I've bought. Are you telling me that the picture I bought from you—the Washington Square Arch scene—was among the things she was trying to sell you?"

"Exactly."

"Do you have her address and phone number?"

"No, just an e-mail address."

"Can you give me that, please?"

"Mr. Barrington, if you wish to repurchase the picture, I can do that for you."

Of course, Stone thought; he wants to make another profit from the picture. "Alistair, that picture and ten other Matilda Stones were stolen from my home the night before last."

There was a quick intake of breath on the other end of the line. "Good God!"

"Well, yes. And if she's offering you one stolen item, she may have others in her inventory. This is a matter for the police art theft squad."

"Well, I certainly don't want to deal with them," Tremont said. "I wouldn't want them in my shop. Word gets around about that sort of thing—it's not good for business."

"Stolen art is not good for business, either."

Tremont seemed indecisive about what to do.

"Alistair, was there anything else in what she showed you that you were interested in buying?"

"There was one other thing: a John Singer Sargent print from around 1910."

"And if you wanted to buy them from her, how would you proceed?"

"I'd e-mail her that I'd like her to bring the two pictures to my gallery, and if they were in satisfactory condition, I'd make an offer for them."

"Then do that," Stone said, "and when you've made an appointment with her, call me, and I'll be there. I won't bring the police, and there won't be any trouble."

"All right, I guess I can do that."

"Insist on a specific time for the appointment. I don't want to wait around all day for her to show up. Tell her you're busy, but you'll squeeze her in."

"All right, I'll e-mail her now."

"What is her name?"

"Anita Mays."

"I'll look forward to hearing from you." They both hung up, and Stone called Dino, who turned out to be at a meeting at the mayor's office for the rest of the afternoon. Stone called Detective Jim Connor and got voice mail. He left a message.

Then he realized that there was another call he should make. He dialed the Steele company and asked for Jeb Barnes.

"This is Mr. Barnes."

"It's Stone Barrington, Jeb."

"Oh, hello, Stone." He didn't sound happy to hear from him.

"There's been another robbery," Stone said.

"Oh, dear. Who is it this time?"

"Me."

"You? What was stolen?"

"Eleven of my mother's pictures."

"Your mother is a photographer?"

"No, she was a painter. Her name was Matilda Stone."

"Oh, yes, indeed. I didn't know there was a connection. Let me get your file." He put Stone on hold and came back a couple of minutes later. "Here we are: those pictures are insured for a total of one-point-eight million."

"That's an old figure—they've appreciated greatly over the past few years."

"I'll fax you a claims form to fill out, and we'll get right on it," Barnes said.

"There's something else: the dealer who sold me one of the pictures was visited by someone wanting to sell it to him."

"Well, we'd better get the police involved immediately."

"The dealer is being very shy about that, so I'm going to look into it myself."

"Yourself?"

"Perhaps you aren't aware that I'm a former police officer."

"No."

"Here's my point: we might be able to get this picture back, and perhaps others, too. Would Steele be willing to offer a significant reward for its return?"

"Return from whom?"

"Does it matter?"

"Well, we wouldn't want to reward a thief."

"I'm thinking of the dealer who called me about this."

"Oh, well, surely. What sort of reward, do you think?"

"Well, the picture is probably worth something over two million dollars."

"Then we'll offer a reward of a hundred thousand dollars for information leading to the recovery of *all eleven* pictures, or ten thousand dollars for the recovery of this one."

"That seems rather mean, considering their value."

"Anything more than that, and I'd have to go to the board, which doesn't meet until next month."

"All right, it's a start. I'll get back to you." Stone hung up. Connor still hadn't called back.

Joan buzzed. "Alistair Tremont on one."

Stone pressed the button. "Yes, Alistair?"

"She'll be here in half an hour," Tremont said.

"I'm on my way. If she arrives before I do, find a way to keep her there."

"How would I do that?"

"Ask her to show you some more slides—the same ones again, if necessary. Take a while to look them over."

"All right." They hung up.

Stone went into Joan's office. "How much cash do we have in the safe?"

She opened the safe and checked. "Thirty-five thousand."

"Give me all of it." He went and got his brief-case and put the money inside, then he went looking for a cab.

40

Stone arrived at the gallery, a small shop in the East Sixties, went inside, and found Alistair Tremont showing an elderly woman some watercolors. The gallery owner waved him to a chair, and Stone sat down and put his briefcase beside him.

He looked around the gallery as Alistair droned on about color saturation and perspective, and eventually the woman bought two pictures. As they were being rung up, Stone glanced outside and saw a sleek black motorcycle pull up and a woman get off and begin unlashing a portfolio from the rear luggage rack.

The motorcycle was black, and the woman was dressed in black leather and a black helmet; the portfolio in her hands was black, too. As she came through the door she took off the helmet, releasing a cascade of long black hair. She was nothing if not color-coordinated. And she was quite beautiful.

"Be right with you, Anita," Alistair called.

Stone kept his seat, but she was looking suspiciously at him, and she hovered near the door, as if to be ready for a quick getaway. Stone rested his head on the back of his chair, as if to appear uninterested.

Finally, Alistair had wrapped his customer's pictures and escorted her to the door. Then he turned back into the gallery. "Anita, meet my client . . ."

"Jim," Stone said, getting to his feet. "Nice to meet you."

Anita nodded, but still was watching him with suspicion.

"Come on back, Anita," Alistair said. "I've got an easel set up."

"I like your bike," Stone said, looking out the window. "What is it, a BMW F-800?"

"Right," she said.

"Have you put a lot of miles on it?"

"More than a few. It gets me around town."

"I don't know how you survive on that thing in this city," Alistair said as he smoothly took the portfolio from her and set it on his counter.

"I used to ride bikes around town," Stone said. "I found that other drivers gave me a wide berth, as if they were afraid they might kill me."

"Except taxi drivers," Anita said. "They couldn't care less."

"I'll tell you how to handle them," Stone said. "After one of them has nearly killed you, you sneak up on him from behind, on the driver's side—they always have their window open—and you scream at them as loud as you can."

The woman managed a smile; she was relaxing. "That might work, you know."

Alistair was opening the portfolio and taking out a print. "Let's see what we've got here."

"John Singer Sargent, 1910," Anita said. "In excellent condition."

"Can we have the wrapper off?" Stone asked, and Alistair took a craft knife and removed the clear plastic.

"A magnifying glass, Alistair?"

Stone took the glass and went over the picture, corner to corner, paying particular attention to the signature. "Mmm, it's all right," he said noncommittally. "What are you asking?"

"Eighteen hundred," Anita replied.

"Mmmm. The next one?"

Alistair removed the Sargent, lifted the oil from the portfolio, and set it on the easel.

Stone knew the painting intimately, but he made a show of examining it closely. The beautiful frame, for which he had paid $1,500, was missing. He turned it over and found, written in a childish hand, *Stone*. He had signed it when he was nine. "Mmmm. How much?"

"Twelve thousand," Anita replied with assurance. "Cheap at the price."

Stone agreed. He wondered if she knew how cheap. "Tell you what," he said, "I'll give you twelve thousand for the two of them. Cash. Right now."

She didn't hesitate. "Thirteen," she said.

Stone turned and offered her his hand. She shook it. "Done," he said, "with a good provenance, of course." He held on to her hand and looked her in the eye.

"Jim," she said, "I have a small shop. People come in and sell me things. I don't inquire." She removed her hand from his. "Thirteen thousand. As you see them."

"Who'd you buy the oil from?"

"A fella who comes in now and then."

"Do you think he might have anything else by the same artist?"

"Could be," she said.

Stone went to his briefcase, got $13,000, and returned. "A bill of sale, please?"

She took a sheet of paper from the portfolio, wrote out the document, and handed it to him. "There you are."

Stone handed her the money and glanced at

her letterhead: "Anita's Artfest, Barrow Street."
"I'd like to visit your shop and see what else
you've got," he said. "I'm always in the market."

"Sure." She was closing up the folio.

"You open weekends?"

"By appointment."

"How about noon on Saturday? Find me some
more like the oil, and I'll throw in a good lunch."

"You're on," she said. "Phone?"

Stone gave her his cell number and she wrote
it down.

"And your number?" He jotted it down. "I'll
bring cash," he said.

"See you noon Saturday," she said. "I'll give
the guy a call."

And then she was out, on the bike and gone.

"Well," Alistair said, "that was interesting.
And I think I'm owed a commission on the sale.
Say, twenty-five hundred?"

Stone returned to his briefcase and picked up
a banded bunch of bills. "Here's ten thousand,"
he said, handing the man the money. "Help me
get the rest of my pictures back, and there'll be
more. A lot more."

Alistair grinned. "Always happy to be of service," he said, wrapping the two pictures.

Stone shook his hand and left the gallery, the
pictures under his arm. "One down, ten to go,"
he said.

———

Back in his office, Joan came in. "Did you spend all that money?"

"Thirteen thousand," Stone replied, "but I got a two-million-dollar painting for it." He opened his parcel and showed her.

"Beautiful," she said. "And this is nice, too." She fingered the Sargent.

"Get that framed, will you? Something gilt, simple—you know what I like."

"Will do."

"And get me another quarter-million in cash from the bank. Used hundreds and fifties, banded."

"My, you're in an art-shopping mood, aren't you?"

"You bet your sweet ass I am."

41

Stone had still not heard from either Dino or Jim Connor, and he called Dino on his cell.

"Bacchetti."

"Hi, can you talk?"

"Sure, I'm walking back to my office."

"I got lucky today. The dealer who sold me one of my mother's paintings several years ago called me and said someone had offered it to him. He got the seller back into his shop, and I bought it from her, along with a Sargent print she had, for thirteen grand."

"A bargain. Where'd she get it?"

"I'm working on that. She has a shop in Barrow Street, in the Village, and she says the guy she bought it from may have others. I've made a date to go down there Saturday at noon."

"Mind if I come along?"

"I was hoping you would. I'm going to take a lot of cash with me, just in case."

"Should I set up a bust?"

"No, I don't want the neighborhood swarming with cops. I have a better idea. At least, I hope I do."

"Okay, we'll do it your way."

"Meet me here at eleven. We'll have Fred drive us."

"You're taking the Bentley to the Village?"

"We'll get out a couple of blocks away and walk. I'm taking a lot of cash, so come armed."

"Okay."

"Listen, I need a favor."

"Shoot."

"I want to get Fred Flicker a carry license. Can you manage that?"

"Let me see if I can think of a way of doing it without my fingerprints all over it. You can download the application online. Have him list his job as personal assistant and security guard."

"Got it." They hung up. His phone rang; Joan was gone for the day, so he picked it up. "Stone Barrington."

"Hi, it's Ann."

"Hi, there."

"You good for dinner on short notice?"

"As short as you like. We talking about tonight?"

"We're talking about in an hour."

"Bring your toothbrush?"

"See you in an hour."

Ann looked freshly showered when she arrived; her hair was still wet. She gave him a big kiss. "Sorry for the short notice, but I found myself without half a dozen people wanting something from me. I thought we could order a pizza and watch the debate."

"God, I forgot about the debate. What time?"

"Seven on PBS."

Stone phoned for a pizza, then hung up. "Let's have a drink while we're waiting for it."

"Good thinking. Have you had a good week?"

"No, but it's getting better." He told her about the theft of his paintings and his effort to recover them.

"This sounds like an art-theft-caper movie," she said.

"I hope it has a happy ending."

"Why wouldn't it?"

"Because I can't control what happens—all I can do is react, and hope nobody gets hurt."

"Why do you think somebody might get hurt?"

"The total value of the paintings is probably at least twenty million dollars."

"Holy shit!"

"I didn't pay that for them. They've appreciated

markedly over the years. Anyway, with that at stake, anything can happen."

"Obviously the woman you bought the one painting from didn't have any idea of its value."

"And the person she bought it from doesn't, either. If he did, we'd be in a very different ball game."

"Do you think he's the guy who stole them from you?"

"No. Whoever did that knew who I was, where I live, and where the pictures were. And the pictures were all that was taken."

"Do you have any idea who was behind it?"

"Yes, but I can't prove it."

Shortly, the pizza arrived, and Stone met the deliveryman at the door and paid him. They took the pizza and a bottle of wine upstairs, put the electric beds up, and settled in to watch the debate. Jim Lehrer introduced the vice president, Martin Stanton, Kate Lee, Senator Mark Willingham, of Virginia, and the governor of New Mexico, Peter Ortega, and each of them had a two-minute opening statement.

"Thank you," Lehrer said, then began the questioning.

"Vice President Stanton, you were recently involved in an incident at your La Jolla, California, home that has received a great deal of coverage in the press. Do you have anything new to add to what you've already said?"

Stanton looked unperturbed. "I think that's been fully addressed elsewhere," he replied. "I have nothing whatever to add."

"Director Lee, any comment?"

"Jim, as Johnny Carson used to say, 'I wouldn't touch that one with a fork,'" she replied.

"Good one," Stone said.

"Well planned," Ann said.

"Both of them."

The senator and the governor declined the opportunity, as well, and the questioning moved on to more mundane subjects, such as foreign and domestic policy.

"This is turning out to be a yawner," Stone said.

"That's how we'd like it. Kate sounds smart and knowledgeable, and that's all we need to convey at this point."

The pizza and the wine were half gone.

"Have you ever made love to the sounds of a political debate?"

"No, I think I would remember."

Stone set down their wineglasses, put the pizza box on the floor, and came for her. They finished about the same time as the debate did.

"I think we did better than the debaters," Ann said.

"Oh, we did a *lot* better than the debaters. We touched on every available point."

They awoke early and skipped around the morning shows for comments on the debate.

"Perfect," Ann said. "This weekend, things change."

"What happens this weekend?" Stone asked.

"There is a very large piece on Stanton's personal history coming in the *Times*, with particular attention to his conduct in La Jolla. It should be fun."

"Spend the weekend with me."

"I'd like that, but I'll be on the phone a lot."

"I'll entertain you while you're talking."

"Oh, no, I have to sound serious, and I can't do that while being 'entertained,' as you put it."

"I'll save myself for the evenings," Stone said. "I'll be out in the afternoon, anyway, Dino and I."

"Then I'll hold the fort here."

42

After Ann had left the house, Stone called Bob Cantor. Bob, in addition to being his go-to guy for tech work, was a PI, and a good one.

"Get your security system fixed?" Bob asked.

"Yes, and with new backups and a new monitoring service."

"Something wrong with the monitoring service?"

"Yes, it's now owned by the wrong guy, and when the alarm went off, everything stopped at their office—never got to the police."

"I've got a dozen or more clients using that service," Bob said.

"You might want to rethink that."

"Right."

"Bob, I've got something else for you, if you have some time today."

"I'll make time for you, Stone."

"Thank you. After the paintings were stolen I got word that someone was trying to sell one of them. Her name is Anita Mays, and she has some sort of shop or gallery on Barrow Street, in the Village. I've got a noon date with her tomorrow to look at other things, and I hope she might come up with some more of my pictures."

"Okay, got that."

"Before tomorrow, I want to know everything I can about her. I Googled her, but there wasn't much. I get the impression that she flies under the radar."

"Okay, I'll make a run at her, starting this morning."

"Be careful, if you visit her neighborhood. I don't want the neighbors warning her that some-one is asking questions."

"Okay."

"If you visit her shop, you might buy some-thing, just to seem genuine."

"Who knows, maybe I'll see something I like."

"If you do, it's on me."

"I'll get back to you late this afternoon and let you know what I've found out."

"I'll look forward to hearing from you." The two men hung up.

Bob Cantor equipped himself with a notebook and a pen and some cash, then, since he lived not too far from Barrow Street, got out his bicycle and rode down there. He turned into the street and rode slowly past Anita Mays's shop, then farther down the block. Finally, he stopped and locked his bike to a utility pole, using a heavy chain. It was all too easy to lose an expensive bicycle in New York.

He started at the opposite end of the street from Mays's shop and did some window-shopping, then went into a gallery and bought an old watercolor of Barrow Street, probably from the thirties. The picture was wrapped and put into a shopping bag from Barneys, which served as camouflage for Bob as he wandered among the other shops.

He made stops in two others and in each, after he had bought something, asked for recommendations of other neighborhood places.

"You might try Anita's shop, down the end of the street," a woman told him. "She gets interesting things." She paused. "If you're not too choosy about where they come from. She's got a boyfriend who comes home with a lot of stuff on a regular basis."

Bob nodded sagely. "Thanks a lot." He continued up the street, not missing a shop, until he came to Anita's Artfest. The shop was at stoop level, and he climbed the steps to get a better look in the window. It was crammed with tchotchkes, clocks, pictures, small statuary, old wristwatches, and jewelry. Then, down at the end of the window, Bob spotted something familiar. He went to the door and found a card hung on the knob. *Back in a minute*, it read. He sat down on the steps and waited.

Five minutes later he saw her coming down the street with a bag of groceries: fairly tall, slim, dark hair, wearing tight leather trousers and filling out a sweater very nicely. She started up the stairs.

"Morning," he said.

"Hi. Something on your mind?" She seemed wary.

"There's a Rolex in your window I'd like to see." He got up and pointed at the watch. "Oh, and could I have a look at that picture on the far right?"

"Okay," she said. She unlocked the door, set down her groceries, and let him in. "Let me get the key to the window." She disappeared into the rear of the shop, and Bob followed her for a few feet, taking in the place. It was crowded but orderly and seemed to be filled with the fruits of many auctions.

She reappeared from a little office at the rear, unlocked the access door to the shopwindow, fished out the Rolex, and handed it to him. "It's a nice one, a Submariner."

"Any idea how old?" he asked.

"Probably from the sixties," she said.

He wound the watch, and it began to run, always a good sign. The steel case was scratched from wear, but that would polish out. "How much are you asking?"

"Three thousand," she said.

"A new one is only five grand," he said. He wasn't sure that was still true.

"I might go twenty-five hundred."

He handed back the watch. "Can I see the picture?"

She unlocked another door at the end of the window and removed the painting.

"Mind if I get some sunlight on it?" he asked, nodding toward the stoop.

She went first, as if to block him if he ran with it.

He stepped onto the stoop and looked the painting over, front and back. He saw the name "Stone" on the back of the canvas; he had seen the picture in Stone's study. "Nice," he said. "What are you asking?"

"Fifteen thousand," she replied.

He affected shock. "Oh, that's way beyond

my budget." He handed back the painting. "I'll offer you fifteen hundred for the Rolex, though."

"I might do seventeen-fifty."

"I've got cash, no tax to pay."

"Sixteen hundred, and it's yours."

"Done." He followed her back into the shop. "Have you got the box?"

"You're in luck," she said, opening a cabinet and coming out with a Rolex box.

Bob took a wad of bills from his pocket and counted out sixteen hundred in hundreds. "You're just about cleaning me out," he said, handing her the money.

She got a pad and began writing out a receipt.

"Where do you get all this stuff?" he asked.

"Estate sales, auctions, places in the country. I'm not telling you where."

He laughed. "I don't have the energy to visit them. I'd rather let you do my shopping for me." He pocketed the receipt. "Would you take seven thousand for the picture?"

She laughed. "Not a hope. It's fifteen, firm."

"Oh, well, maybe in some other lifetime." He put the Rolex into its box and dropped it into the Barneys bag with his picture. "Thanks," he said.

"Come back next week," she said. "We're getting new stuff all the time."

"I'll do that," Bob said, and walked back up

the block toward his bicycle. He strapped his purchases to the rear rack, unlocked it, and started back up the street. As he approached Anita's Artfest, a battered gray van pulled up front, and a young man—six feet, 170, sandy hair and short beard—got out and began unloading items that Anita carried into the shop.

Bob smiled all the way home.

43

S tone was wrapping up his Friday when Bob Cantor called.

"What did you learn?" Stone asked.

"You're right, Anita Mays likes to fly under the radar. She doesn't advertise, doesn't use eBay. One of the local shopkeepers implied that her boyfriend is a burglar, and I think she might very well be right."

"Did you go into the shop?"

"Yep, bought myself a nice Rolex for sixteen hundred. She didn't know that it was one of a limited edition, celebrating the watch's fiftieth anniversary. It has a green bezel and larger numerals and is probably worth ten grand used, if you can find one. It was issued about ten years ago. And get this: one of your pictures was in the shopwindow."

"You're kidding me."

"I kid you not. The shop is full of very nice stuff, so the boyfriend has good taste in stolen goods. He arrived as I was leaving the block, and unloaded some stuff from an old van. The vehicle is registered to a William Murphy, of the Barrow Street address. I think the two of them live in the basement of the building."

"That's all very interesting, especially the part about my picture."

"She was asking fifteen grand for it, and she wouldn't budge on the price."

"Well, I guess I'd better get down there before they get any smarter. Any other observations?"

"The girl is very wary. I think she suspects everybody of being a cop, and given the sort of stuff they're dealing in, she should be wary. I didn't talk to the guy, but he's pretty well built, and I'd guess he probably knows how to throw a punch, so watch yourself."

"I'll do that."

"Tell you the truth, I wouldn't be surprised if the girl knows how to throw a punch, too, or maybe kick you in the balls."

"Then I'll *certainly* watch myself. What do I owe you?"

"Reimburse me for the Rolex, and we're square."

"The check is nearly in the mail. Thanks, Bob."

Stone hung up and buzzed Joan and asked her to send Cantor the check, then buzzed Fred Flicker on the intercom.

"Yes, sir?"

"Fred, I'm going to need you to drive Dino Bacchetti and me down to the Village tomorrow morning, shortly after eleven o'clock."

"I'll have the car ready, sir."

"And I have some papers for you to fill out."

"Papers, sir?"

"An application for a license to carry a firearm. Chief Bacchetti is going to be of help."

"I'll come right over, sir."

Fred was there in two minutes, and Stone gave him the license application. "You'll have to be fingerprinted at police headquarters, too. Any problem with that, Fred?"

"Not a bit of it, sir. If they investigate me they'll just find my service record." Fred was ex–Royal Marines.

"Good. Here's a pen, fill that out, and I'll give it to Dino tomorrow."

Fred sat down and began filling out the form. "Any word on my application for a green card, sir?"

"An immigration specialist at my law firm is handling that," Stone replied. "He expects a favorable outcome in a matter of weeks. Oh, on the application list your work as 'personal assistant and security guard.'"

"Righto, sir."

"Fred, did you ever carry a weapon out of uniform?"

"Only in Northern Ireland, sir."

"You served there?"

"That was our war, until the Falklands came along."

"You were there, too?"

"It was where the shooting was, sir. Royal Marines always run toward the sound of gunfire."

"Was it rough down there?"

"Not as rough as a Belfast pub on a Saturday night, sir, but I was aboard HMS *Sheffield* when she took an Exocet missile from an Argentine fighter jet. I had just delivered some documents to the captain and was getting ready to board our rigid inflatable for the return trip, when I saw the thing coming. I yelled, 'Hit the deck!' and did so myself. I got bounced around a bit, but I wasn't really hurt. Twenty of the poor sods in the crew bought it, though."

"I don't envy you the experience," Stone said.

Fred went back to filling out the form, then signed it and gave it to Stone.

"I'll get Joan to notarize it," Stone said, leaving it on his desk. "See you at eleven tomorrow."

Fred left, and Stone took the document to

Joan. "Notarize this, please, then pack two hundred thousand in hundreds in my briefcase and put it in your safe. I'll get it out tomorrow."

"You know the combination?"

"Unless you've changed it."

"Nope, it's the same."

"Then I'll be able to get at it."

44

Stone was on his second cup of coffee in his study when Dino let himself into the house. Stone poured him a cup. Stone's briefcase was open on the coffee table, displaying the cash.

"So," Dino said when he had settled into a comfortable chair, "what's your plan?"

Stone gave him the substance of his conversation with Bob Cantor the day before. "Fred will let us out a block or so from the shop, and we'll walk to it, with you remaining well back. I'll leave my briefcase containing the cash with Fred, and I'll call you when I need it." Stone slipped his little Colt Government .380 under the banded hundreds. "Just in case." He handed Dino a beeperlike black box and showed him his own. "Call this a panic button. If I signal you, come in fast, gun first."

"Okay. You sure you don't want some backup?"

"I don't think we'll need it, you're scary enough, if it comes to that."

"I'm flattered you think so."

Stone gave him Fred's completed carry application, complete with notary's stamp and a photo Joan had taken. "I'd appreciate anything you can do."

Dino looked over the form. "Royal Marines, pistol champion, et cetera, et cetera. Very impressive. His qualifications won't be an issue."

"What might be?"

"He's a foreigner. Has he got a green card?"

"Soon, our immigration lawyer says. Should we wait?"

"Nah, I think I can manage this without being seen to manage it. Tell me, what are you going to do when you get in that shop on Barrow Street?"

"Improvise," Stone replied.

"Oh, shit."

"Don't worry, I'll stay out of trouble. I'm just an art lover, shopping for pictures."

"If you say so."

Stone produced his little wallet that held his honorary badge and tossed that into the briefcase with the Colt, then he took one stack of hundreds and put it into his inside jacket pocket. "Shall we do this?"

"You betcha."

"Fred's waiting out front with the car."

Stone snapped the briefcase shut; they left the house and got into the Bentley Flying Spur. He gave Fred the address, and Fred entered it into the car's navigation system, not being a New Yorker and unfamiliar with Greenwich Village's eccentric street plan.

"Something I don't get," Dino said.

"What's that?"

"These pictures are auctioning for north of two million a pop, and this burglar is selling them for fifteen grand each?"

"Yeah, I wondered about that, too. This guy couldn't have stolen them from my house—he wouldn't know where they were, and I doubt if he could have defeated the alarm system."

"Maybe Crane or Dugan hired him, told him where to find the pictures."

"Then why would he have them and be selling them? He obviously has no idea of their value. They'd have paid him off and kissed him good-bye and sold the paintings somewhere else. Or Crane might have kept them, maybe in their Hamptons house. She loved the pictures."

"Well, I guess all that doesn't affect what you're doing today."

"No, this will be a quick in and out, I think—fifteen minutes, tops."

"If you say so."

"Fred," Stone said, "pull over right before the corner, then drive around the block and see if you can find a parking spot on Barrow Street. If not, double-park. I may need this briefcase later." He set it on the front passenger seat. "If so, I'll call Dino and he can bring it to the door of the shop."

"Yes, sir. And Chief Bacchetti, may I say how grateful I am for your help with the gun license?"

"Don't mention it," Dino said. "It's better that way."

"Okay," Stone said, "stay well back of me. Here we go."

They got out of the car and Stone strolled down to the corner of Barrow Street and turned the corner. It was noon sharp. He spotted the sign for Anita's Artfest and checked out the window before entering. The picture was no longer on display. The door was locked, and he rapped on the glass with his signet ring. He could see Anita coming from the rear of the shop.

She opened the door. "You're on time—good."

"I'm pathologically punctual," he said. He followed her to the rear of the shop. "Have a seat," she said, pointing to a velvet-covered straight-backed chair. "I'll show you what I've got."

Stone took the chair and waited. She began

bringing out pictures and lining them up on easels and an antique sideboard. Stone spotted his picture among them. "That one," he said. "May I see it up close?"

She handed him the picture, and he held it so the light struck it and examined it closely, finding his signature on the back of the canvas.

"You said you'd have others," Stone said. "Where are they?"

A young man stepped from behind a mirror, surprising Stone. He must have been in the rear office, he thought. "We have some," he said, "but first, let's have a chat."

45

Stone looked him over; Bob had described him perfectly, even to the attitude of potential violence.

"I came here to buy, not chat," Stone said.

"We're going to chat anyway."

"Then be quick about it."

"Who are you?"

"I'm Jim. Who are you?"

"He's Bill," Anita said, "and he's just being careful."

"Are you a cop?"

"I am not a cop, I'm an art lover."

"Why do you want these pictures?"

"That's the dumbest question I ever heard a seller ask a buyer."

"I mean, why these particular pictures? By this artist?"

"Lots of collectors collect artists. Aren't you aware of that? I like this one."

"He bought the little Sargent, too," Anita said. She seemed to be careful of her boyfriend, as if she thought he might have a short fuse.

"How many of this artist have you got?" Stone asked.

The two exchanged a glance.

"I might be able to put together ten of them."

"Then let's get started. Trot them out."

Anita nodded slightly to him.

"Just a minute," he said. He went back into the office and began bringing out Matilda Stones, setting them up for viewing.

Stone examined each of them carefully.

"They're fifteen grand each," Bill said.

Stone finished his examination. "Just a minute, I'll get some cash." He took out his phone and speed-dialed Dino's number.

"You still alive?" Dino asked.

"Yeah. You can bring me the briefcase. I'll meet you at the door." He hung up. "He'll just be a minute," he said to Bill.

"Who's the guy outside?" Bill asked.

"My boyfriend. We're thinking of getting married."

"He's not coming in here."

"He doesn't need to, he's just bringing me my briefcase. I don't walk around with that much money." There was a rap on the door, and Stone went to it and slipped the lock. He stuck a hand through the door and took the briefcase. "Thanks." He went back and resumed his seat.

"Let me tell you how this is going to go," Stone said, setting the briefcase on his lap and starting to stack bundles of hundreds on the footstool next to him.

"What do you mean, *you're* going to tell *me*?" Bill pulled back his jacket a little, exposing a semiautomatic pistol tucked into his belt.

"Bill, that's unnecessary," Anita said. "Just listen. I want to hear what he says."

"Thank you," Stone said. "Here is how it's going to go: I'm going to give you a hundred thousand dollars in cash, and you're going to give me the ten pictures. In their original frames. Then I'm going to leave, and you won't be hearing from me again. Is that clear?" He slipped his hand into the briefcase and took hold of the Colt .380, flipping off the safety with his thumb.

"I told you the pictures are fifteen grand each," Bill said. "Now it's twenty grand apiece." His hand crept toward his pistol.

"Hold it right there," Stone said, "or I'll shoot you in the knee, and you'll spend the next three months in a prison hospital. They don't do very good knee work in those places, so you'll limp for the rest of your life."

Bill's hand went back into his jacket pocket.

"May I continue?" Stone asked.

"Please do," Anita replied.

"That's my plan," Stone said, "all of it. Call it the carrot, but there's an alternative plan: after I shoot you in the knee, I can press a button and flood this place with police officers. After they've had a chance to compare your inventory to their list of stolen art, I'd guess you'd be answering at least a hundred charges of burglary, maybe a lot more. Call that the stick. Now, which is it going to be?"

Bill started to move toward Stone, but Anita put out a hand and grabbed his jacket. "Bill," she said, "go get the frames. We're taking the carrot."

"He's bluffing," Bill said.

Stone removed the .380 from his briefcase and pointed it at Bill's right knee. He thumbed the hammer back; it made a satisfying noise.

Anita held up a hand. "That won't be necessary. Bill, go get the frames." Bill vanished behind the mirror again, and Stone could hear him rummaging around in the back office.

"There's a little more," Stone said. "While Bill is busy, you can tell me how you came into possession of these pictures. And don't leave anything out."

Anita thought about it, then shrugged. "We

were cruising, casing houses for jobs, on my motorcycle," Anita said. "We were in Turtle Bay, in the East Forties, and we came upon what was obviously a burglary in progress. There were two guys, dressed in black, carrying the pictures out of a house and putting them in the van."

"Describe the two men," Stone said.

"Both big, Italian or Hispanic. They looked enough alike to be brothers."

"Go on."

"They drove away, and we followed them. They drove uptown into the East Sixties and turned down a street. They double-parked and left the engine running, then they got out and went into a town house."

"Give me the exact address." She did and described the house.

"And you stole the pictures from the van?"

"No," she said. "We stole the van. Bill just hopped in and drove away, and I followed him back here. We unloaded the pictures, then he got rid of the van. We were disappointed—we thought there'd be a lot more than just the pictures."

Stone laughed in spite of himself. "I love it," he said. "It's almost too good."

"How's that?"

Bill began fitting the pictures into their frames and tacking them in place.

"I love it that the people who stole my pictures

got robbed, and I love it that you and Bill hadn't the slightest idea what they are worth."

"What are they worth?" she asked.

"You don't want to know. If you'd tried to sell them to anybody else you'd have been arrested immediately. But you got lucky, you sold them back to the owner."

"Come on, what are they worth?"

"Please believe me, you don't want to know. But all this worked out very well for you: you've got a hundred and twelve thousand dollars of my insurance company's money, Bill hasn't been shot in the knee, and neither of you is going to prison."

"Well, I guess it didn't turn out too badly after all."

"If you're smart, you'll use the money to shut down this place and walk away from it. The police know about it now, and they'll come calling, sooner rather than later. You should be in another state by then, maybe in another country." He used his cell phone again. "Fred, bring the car," he said.

Bill tied the pictures with twine, making bundles of them, and he and Anita carried them outside and put them into the trunk of the Bentley.

Stone started to get into the car with Dino.

"See you around," Anita said.

"Better not," Stone replied, then closed the door. Fred drove them away.

"Everything went as planned?" Dino asked.

"I told you, I just improvised. By the way, wait until tomorrow before you send the art squad around here. It was part of the deal."

46

Stone called the house and asked Helene to make them some lunch. When they arrived Fred brought the pictures into the house and hung them in their original locations while they had lunch, and Stone related to Dino his conversation with Anita Mays and Bill Murphy.

"So we've got a witness to the burglary and a description of the burglars?"

"Not really. The burglars were the Drago brothers, and they took the pictures to Crane's house on East Sixty-first—until they were restolen—but Anita and Bill aren't going to be around to testify against them. They'll clear out before dawn tomorrow. Your art squad will recover a hell of a lot of stolen stuff, and the previous owners will be happy about that, but the thieves will be gone."

"So why didn't I just arrest them today?"

"Because they wouldn't have told us anything, and now we know for sure that Crane and Dugan were behind the theft."

"A lot of good that will do us."

"Wrong. Now you can eliminate all other suspects and concentrate your investigation on the two of them."

"Well, that's something, I guess."

"And you may bag Jake Sutton, as well."

"The jewelry squad is all over him."

"I wonder if he's smart enough to know that?"

"He's been getting away with it for so long that he's probably overconfident by now." Dino's phone rang. "Bacchetti. What do you mean? How did that happen?" He listened some more. "All right, get warrants for his house and business, and let's see what we can find. If we're lucky, we can go for extradition." Dino hung up. "Jacob Sutton and his wife left their Brooklyn home before dawn this morning and took a nonstop flight to Tel Aviv. They're probably halfway there by now."

"What happened?"

"He must have sniffed out our surveillance. I thought we were better than that."

Stone thought for a minute. "Dino, don't search his house and business."

"Why not?"

"Because the Suttons might just be going on a little vacation, and if they don't get a call from someone telling them that your people are ransacking his house and office, they might just come back. People do take trips abroad, you know."

Dino got out his phone and made the call. "Cancel the warrant requests and sit on the investigation until further word from me." He hung up.

"Even if Sutton suspects you're after him, if nothing happens here while he's in Tel Aviv, he might think he's being paranoid and come home."

"You're right," Dino said. "We'll just wait for him to make a decision. We've got a guy in the diamond center. We'll know if he returns to work."

"Would what Anita told me about the burglary here and the stealing of the van constitute probable cause for a search warrant of Crane's house?"

"Well, it's thirdhand information, and that isn't good. And the pictures never made it into Crane's house, so we can't place stolen goods there. That's a tough one."

"That's why you've got the top job," Stone said, "to handle the tough ones."

"Yeah, yeah."

"You know," Stone said, "I think we've given

Anita Mays and Bill Murphy enough time to bolt. Why don't you send some people down there and wait for them to load up and run, then bust them?"

"Why wait until then?"

"Because they'll have all the best stuff in the van, so you won't have to figure that out. Also, I gave them fair warning. One more thing: if there's anything they didn't tell me, they might give it up to make a deal."

"That's a thought," Dino said. They finished lunch in the kitchen and went up to Stone's study. Dino used the landline to issue his orders for the Barrow Street location. "Don't let them drive away," he told his people. "Take them when they look loaded up." He hung up. "You want to go to a movie?"

"Sure, why not, it's Saturday afternoon."

They took a cab up to Third Avenue and Fifty-ninth Street, where there was a cluster of theaters, and found a movie, then after that, found another one.

Viv met them at P.J. Clarke's, and they were having dinner when Dino got the call on his cell. He listened quietly, then said, "Good job," and hung up.

"What?" Viv asked.

"The art squad busted Anita Mays and Bill Murphy," he said. "They had a stolen motorcycle in their van and a lot of antique jewelry." He paused for effect. "And a little more than four hundred thousand dollars in cash."

Viv and Stone applauded.

"The boys are cataloging the shop's inventory now, and they say it looks like running into the millions."

"Good bust!" Viv said.

"And all because Stone had his mother's pictures stolen," Dino said.

"And they're back on my walls."

"You'll get your hundred grand back," Dino said.

"My insurance company will be delighted to hear that, since they won't have to reimburse me."

"So everybody's happy," Viv said.

"Only thing wrong with that is Dugan and Crane are still happy," Stone pointed out.

"I'll see that there's nothing released about your pictures," Dino said, "so they still won't know what happened to them and their van."

"I hope it drives them crazy," Stone said. "Go ahead and report their van stolen, Dino. If you recover it, I'd like to see the expressions on their faces when they get the call."

47

Ann arrived at Stone's house in a state of excitement. She kissed him and threw her bag into the elevator. "Come on," she said, "we've got to change."

"Are we going out?"

"We're having dinner at the Carlyle apartment with the president and Kate."

"What's the occasion?"

"The *Times* story—the big one on Marty Stanton—is going to break tonight, and she wants to be incommunicado when it does, but they don't want to be alone, so we're company."

They took a shower together and used the tiled seat in the stall to good advantage, then Ann spent the better part of an hour doing her hair and makeup, while Stone watched the news.

"There won't be anything on the air about it yet," Ann said, "unless there's a leak, and the paper has gone to some lengths to see that there isn't. The story goes into the early Sunday edition, which won't hit the newsstands until the middle of the evening."

"Tell me again why we're excited about this?"

"All I've got is a rumor that there's something big in the story."

"Suppose it's something big about Kate?" Stone shouted over her hair dryer.

Ann turned off the hair dryer and faced him. "What?"

"If they had big news about Kate, wouldn't this be a good place for it—in a story about Stanton?"

Ann thought about it. "No, if they had something on Kate, it would be its own story." She turned the hair dryer back on.

"If you say so."

She turned it off again. "What did you say?"

"I said if you say so."

She turned it back on.

They arrived at the Carlyle on time and rode up in the elevator with two Secret Service agents, who escorted them to the apartment's door, where the butler greeted them and took their drink orders. They sat in the living room and waited.

"I don't think I've ever seen you nervous before," Stone said.

"I'm not nervous."

"Then why are you tapping your glass with your fingernails? You never do that."

"All right, I'm a little nervous. I just have the feeling that something's about to change in the campaign. Call it a premonition."

"A premonition about what?" Kate said as she swept into the living room, a half-finished martini in one hand. She administered kisses and sat down. "Will's on the phone about something," she said. "He'll join us in a few minutes. Now, what premonition?"

"I was just telling Stone that I have a feeling that the campaign is going to change when this story hits the streets."

"You know, I have the same feeling," Kate said. "That's why I'm drinking martinis. I know I'm not going to make any statements tonight, no matter what it says, so I can relax."

A man came into the living room. "Excuse me for a moment," he said. He went to a computer set up on a table next to the big flat-screen TV and typed in some keystrokes.

Will Lee came into the room. "Have you got it?"

"Five seconds," the man said. He hit ENTER, and the TV came to life.

Will didn't bother to greet anyone; he sat down. "Watch this," he said.

The screen was pretty dark, except for some pinpoints of light.

"We'll bring up the light level," the technician said.

There were two clicks, and the screen became brighter, then brighter again.

"It's the middle of the night over there," Will said.

The lights were strung out in a line now, and it became apparent that they were looking at four vehicles, all of them black, racing along a desert road.

"Which car are they in?" Kate said. "I'm counting four."

"All of them," Will replied, his eyes glued to the screen.

"This is being shot from a drone," Kate said by way of explanation.

"They were inside a house in a village until twenty minutes ago," Will said. "Some kind of high-level meeting."

Then streaks of light appeared on the screen, and they converged on the convoy. All four cars exploded, no more than a second apart.

"Jesus Christ," the technician muttered. "That's four dead-on hits with Hellfire missiles from two drones."

"Who is—was—in the cars?" Stone asked.

"Six or seven top al-Qaeda leaders," Will said. "I've seen a bunch of these strikes, but this is the most incredible of all of them."

The butler brought him a drink, and they raised their glasses. Kate gave the toast: "To drones and Hellfire missiles," she said.

The Lees were as excited as Ann and talked nonstop all through dinner. As they were finishing dessert a young man came into the apartment bearing a stack of newspapers. "Hot off the presses!" he said as he distributed them to the diners.

Stone got his and immediately was drawn to a headline stretching halfway across the front page:

MRS. STANTON WON'T BE
VOTING FOR MR. STANTON

Will began to read the accompanying article, which was short and in a front-page box: "Mrs. Barbara Stanton, wife of the vice president, Martin Stanton, who is the leading candidate for the Democratic nomination for president, sat in her La Jolla, California, living room and heard this question from our reporter:

"'Why should the Democratic Party choose your husband as its presidential nominee?'

"Her answer seemed spontaneous and unrehearsed: 'I won't be voting for my husband, either for the nomination or in the general election. I've given this a great deal of thought, and I have decided that I will not be the first lady in a Stanton administration.

"'I have lived with Marty's infidelities since the first year of our marriage, more than a dozen of them—that I knew about. Each time this happened, he begged my forgiveness and I forgave him each time. I forgive him this time. But I won't live with him anymore, and I won't go back to Washington. I'm going to live here in California, in this house that I love, paint the pictures and take the photographs that I love, and maybe I'll even write a book. If I do, it won't be published before the election.

"'But to address your question: Martin Stanton is, arguably, one of the two candidates in both parties best qualified to run the country, but to elect him is to start the clock running for his next affair to be exposed, embarrassing himself, his party, and the country. I won't sit in the White House and wait for that to happen, and I won't vote for him. From this moment I will give my vote and all my support to Katherine Lee.'"

"Wow," Ann Keaton said.

48

S tone leafed quickly through the first section of the *Times*.

"The story on Stanton runs for more than four full pages," he said, "but nobody is going to get beyond that box on the front page."

"I believe you're right, Stone," Will Lee said.

"Kate," said Ann, "you haven't said a word."

Kate placed a hand on her chest and took a deep breath. "Speechless," she said.

"Nothing like this has ever happened before," Will pointed out. "This is a political nuclear bomb."

Suddenly, a phone rang, startling all of them. Then a second phone began ringing, then Ann's cell phone rang.

"Ann, will you take these calls, please?" Kate asked. "No comment, but be nice."

Ann started with her cell phone. "Ann Keaton. Director Lee will have no comment on Mrs. Stanton's statement, now or later. She sends her sympathy to both of the Stantons during this difficult time for them." She hung up, went to a landline, and repeated the same words. This went on for half an hour, until Will asked a Secret Service agent to call the switchboard and stop all calls from being put through.

Will switched on the TV and was greeted with a banner slide: BREAKING NEWS!

MSNBC had already assembled a panel of reporters to discuss the news. Everybody watched in silence as they each sounded the death knell of the Stanton campaign.

"Put it on Fox News," Kate said to Will. Unaccustomed to tuning it in, Will took a moment to find the channel. A beautiful blond commentator faced the camera. "The battleship that is Martin Stanton has just received a successful kamikaze attack from his wife. The battleship is sinking."

Kate spoke up. "I want to call Barbara Stanton," she said. "She must be feeling so alone right now."

"I'll get her for you," Ann said. She went to her iPhone contacts and pressed a number. "Kate Lee for Mrs. Stanton," she said to whoever answered. Ann handed the phone to Kate. "She's on the line."

Kate took the phone, walked across the living room, and sat down in a chair. She remained there for a minute or so, then hung up and came back. "Barbara was perfectly composed," she said. "I commiserated briefly and asked her to call me if she needed anything."

"I hope you thanked her for her support," Will said.

"I did not," Kate replied. "The call wasn't about me."

"Any predictions about the political fallout?" Stone asked the group.

"Who knows?" Will said. "Thirty years ago, Marty would have had to get out of the race, but after the Clinton years, anything could happen. Marty is already only a dozen votes short of the nomination. I don't think he's going to gain any new supporters after this, but if his usual supporters stick, then he could still pull it out at the convention."

"How about the general election?" Stone asked.

"Two of the four remaining Republican candidates have infidelities in their pasts," Will said, "and Marty is demonstrably a better man than any of the four. He could win."

"Then we'd have an unmarried man in the White house for the first time since Woodrow Wilson," Ann said, "during the period between his first wife's death and his remarriage. Women will be lining up to sleep with Marty, and he's not noted for saying no."

"The mind boggles," Kate said.

They watched various television channels for the next hour. Martin Stanton was surrounded by reporters at a political dinner in Kansas and made a brief statement, saying that he had no statement.

Ann's cell rang again. "Good evening, Senator," she said, then covered her phone. "Mark Willingham," she whispered. Kate shook her head. "I'm sorry, but Director Lee isn't taking any calls tonight. I'm sure you can understand why. Of course, I'll give her a message." She listened at some length, then thanked him and hung up.

"What was that about?" Kate asked.

"Can't you guess?" Will said.

"He didn't come right out and say it," Ann said, "but he intimated that he might throw his support and his delegates behind you in return for the vice presidential nomination."

"He didn't!" Kate said.

"Oh, yes he did," Will said. "And he meant it."

Kate stared blankly at the coffee table.

"Something wrong, Kate?" Ann asked. "This could throw the nomination to you, if Marty doesn't get it on the first ballot."

"This is what's wrong," Kate said. "I don't want Mark Willingham for my vice presidential candidate. I just don't trust the man."

"How would you feel about Pedro Otero?" Will asked.

"I like him. I think he'd be a great running mate."

"And the Hispanic vote would be all yours," Ann pointed out.

"She'll win the Hispanic vote big, in any case," Will said.

"Otero is young, he's smart, he has a great record as governor and congressman, and he gives a great speech."

"He sounds perfect," Stone said.

"He is," Ann interjected. "But he won't call and offer us that deal. That kind of backroom dealing is not in his blood."

"I won't offer it to him before the convention," Kate said, "and not at the convention, either, unless I have the nomination first."

"Then you will lessen your chances of winning the presidency," Will said. "But I love you for saying that."

49

Stone sat up in bed, watching television and reading the *Times* and the *Daily News*. The Barbara Stanton story was at the top of the front page of both papers, and the *Times* ran her statement in a box for the second time. The morning television shows could talk of nothing else for the first hour. Practically every Washington journalist appeared on one show or another, sometimes on three or four.

Ann was in charge of the remote control and changed channels every time a commercial came on. "I don't see how Marty Stanton can stand up under this barrage," she said.

"Well, so far he's done nothing but issue a bland statement through his press secretary," Stone said. "He doesn't seem to be at work in his office in the Executive Office Building, and he hasn't appeared outside the vice president's residence. It's as if he's taking an artillery barrage and chooses just to go underground until it stops."

"How can he do anything else?" Ann asked. "If he sticks his head up, he takes another bullet."

The cuckolded husband of Stanton's paramour seemed to be the only participant in the story who was enjoying it. He announced that he had filed for divorce from his wife and moved out of their home.

Ann picked up her cell phone and listened to her voice mails. "That's weird," she said. "I have a voice mail from Don Dugan, asking me to call him. What could he possibly want?"

"Maybe he's still annoyed about being barred from the campaign and wants to try again. I'd ignore the call."

"Done," Ann said, erasing it. She called back three of her favorite reporters and gave them just a little more information. "Director Lee spoke with Mrs. Stanton briefly Saturday night but did not discuss her endorsement. She has written Mrs. Stanton a letter thanking her for her support. No, the director will have no further comment on the matter." Finally, she hung up and got her feet on the floor. "Whew! I'd better get to the office early today. It's going to be chaos."

"If you need to hide, come here," Stone said.

"That's exactly what I'll do."

The phone rang, and Stone picked it up.

"It's Dino."

"Hi, there. How'd the interrogation of Anita Mays and Bill Murphy go?"

"Well, there's kind of a problem about that," Dino said.

"What kind of problem? They lawyer up?"

"Yes, but there's more. Ms. Mays was on her way in from Rikers Island this morning on a prison bus, when the bus was broadsided by a heavily loaded beer truck. Mays got out through a broken window and disappeared into the rush hour crowd."

"Was she handcuffed?"

"Yes, she was cuffed to a chain that ran the length of the bus, but the chain was broken in the impact."

"Any reports of her?"

"Not a one, and we don't know who her friends are."

"Does Bill Murphy know about her break?"

"No, we've kept the escapees' names off the news. There were two others. We're going to start in on Murphy in a few minutes. We're waiting for his lawyer to arrive."

"Good luck!"

Anita Mays sat on a rooftop overlooking Barrow Street and spotted the two cops in an unmarked car parked outside her shop. Satisfied there was no one inside the place, she climbed off the roof and down a ladder to the fire escape, then down to the ground. The plot of land behind the shop was filled with odd pieces of statuary that were too big to display inside, and she found the spare key under some dirt inside a concrete planter and let herself into her apartment through the rear entrance. She paused inside and listened for footsteps from upstairs but heard none. She was alone in the building, and she knew exactly what she wanted.

She and Bill had been loading the van when the cops took them, and they hadn't finished. Her backpack still lay on the bed where she had left it, hidden under the pulled-back duvet. She had her wallet in there, and the thirteen thousand dollars that the guy Jim had paid her for the two pictures. She also had three sets of fake IDs—driver's licenses, birth certificates—and her own passport.

She showered and changed into motorcycle leather, then packed a bag and left the apartment the way she had come in. She emerged into the block behind the shop and walked to the garage where she kept her motorcycle. There she exchanged the license plate with one from another bike parked nearby. She strapped her bag to the luggage rack and got into her helmet. Five minutes later she was headed north on the West Side

Highway and thence to Connecticut, where her older sister lived in a village called Roxbury. Halfway there, she found a mall with an electronics store and bought herself a prepaid, throwaway cell phone and called her sister.

"Hey, Berta," she said.

"Hey, Nita."

"Is your garage apartment available for a couple of weeks?"

"Sure. I had an ad in the paper to rent it, but no takers. When are you coming?"

"In about an hour and a half," Anita said.

"I'll have some lunch ready. I'm not going to work until early afternoon." Alberta was a real estate agent.

"See you then."

Anita got back on her motorcycle and onto the Sawmill River Parkway. She made a point of sticking to the speed limit.

Dino sat in an observation booth behind an interrogation room and watched through a one-way mirror as Bill Murphy came into the room with his attorney, a woman named Beth Cutter, a smart lawyer whom Dino knew from other cases. Detectives Connor and Cohn were the interrogating officers.

Connor read Murphy his rights again, and

Murphy signed a document saying that he under-
stood them and had an attorney.

"All right," Cutter said, "Bill is willing to talk
to you and maybe answer some questions, if what
you're offering is good enough."

"Right now, we're not offering anything,"
Connor replied. "This is just a friendly little chat."

"Then, in the absence of an offer, my client
will have nothing to say."

"Where's Nita?" Bill said. "She should be here."

"You two won't be seeing each other for a
while," Connor said, "but Anita is talking to some
other detectives, and she's being very cooperative."

"The fuck she is," Murphy said.

"We're prepared to be lenient on some of the
burglary charges against you, Bill, if you're willing to help us with another case."

"Another case?" Murphy asked.

"I'm talking about the people who stole the
pictures that you stole from them."

"Oh, those guys. I don't know them."

"How about the people who live at the East
Sixty-first Street address where you stole the van
and the pictures?"

"I don't know them, either."

"Do you know somebody named Don Dugan?"

Murphy's eyes opened a little wider. "I've
heard the name."

"In what connection have you heard the name?" Connor asked.

"Tell you what," Murphy said, "I'll tell you everything I know about Dugan if you'll drop the burglary charges."

"I can't promise you that, Bill, because I don't know what you know. Now, you tell me all about Dugan, and then we'll see what we can do."

The attorney, Cutter, nodded to him.

"I can give you enough to help you solve a major robbery," Murphy said.

"What robbery is that?"

"A lot of big-time jewelry was stolen."

"We might be able to deal, but you're going to have to give us names and dates, and what you give us is going to have to lead to convictions. And you'll have to testify. Why don't you start by describing the crime, and we'll see if it matches up with anything we've got on our books."

Dino picked up a phone and called an assistant district attorney. "Come down to interrogation room two," Dino said. "Something interesting is going on."

"Be right there," was the reply.

50

B ill Murphy whispered with his attorney for a
couple of minutes. The door to the observation booth opened, and the ADA, Shirley Kravitz,
came in and sat by Dino.

"What?" she asked.

"This guy is facing dozens of burglary charges,"
Dino said, "but he says he can give us information
about a major crime, if he walks."

"Anybody promise him anything?"

"Jim Connor is too smart an interrogator to do
that, but let's listen and see what he has to say."

Murphy finished talking with his attorney.
"Okay, I'll tell you this much. The crime I'm talking about was committed in a fancy apartment
building on Fifth Avenue in the Sixties. There was

a big dinner party, and some people came in with guns and stole all their jewelry."

"And who was behind this robbery?"

"That's it, until we have a deal," Murphy said.

Dino turned to Kravitz. "You know about this robbery?"

"Everybody knows about it," she said.

"Is clearing it worth bouncing this guy from the burglary charges?"

"You got his charge sheet?"

Dino handed her a file folder. "He has a record for burglary, did eight months at Rikers while trying to strike a deal, and finally got time served."

"What's the value of the stolen jewelry?" Kravitz asked.

"Upwards of twenty million," Dino said. "And the victims were some very important people."

"Okay, I'll bite, if we can get a conviction out of what he says and if he testifies."

"How about bail?"

"A hundred grand."

Dino pressed the intercom button, and Connor picked up the phone. "Yeah?"

"Kravitz is here. She'll drop the charges and give him a hundred thousand bail if he gives us the whole ball of wax and testifies."

"Okay." Connor hung up. "You're in luck, Bill. The DA will deal if you give us the whole thing."

"Bail?" his attorney asked.

"A hundred thousand."

"He had more than that in the van when you busted him."

"That's the proceeds of stolen goods," Connor pointed out.

"It's genuine U.S. currency, and as of right now, he's guilty of nothing. He needs his money back. And he needs his girlfriend out, too."

"I'll do what I can," Connor said.

"Tell him, Bill," Cutter said to her client.

"Okay," Murphy said, "I had a cell mate at Rikers I got to be buddies with. He called me three weeks, a month ago, and asked me if I wanted into a big-money job."

"What did he tell you about the job?"

"He said that the boss had somebody on the inside at the building, and that getting access would be easy. The alarm system would fail to work, and nobody there would be armed. We'd walk in with shotguns, get everybody on the floor and strip them of every piece of jewelry, including the men's wristwatches, and get out in a waiting vehicle. The best part was that we'd be paid within five days."

"How much?"

"He didn't know, but he said it would be big for a couple of hours' work."

"What's your buddy's name?"

"Jerry Kowalski."

"With a *J* or a *G*?"

"Jerome."

Connor made a note, and Dino, next door, called for Kowalski's record.

"And who were the other guys?"

"I didn't get any names, but two of them were brothers, and they were Kowalski's cousins."

"And who was the big guy?"

"I was told I'd have to go see him if I wanted the work. I was to meet him on a street corner at a certain time."

"What corner?"

"Forty-second and Third Avenue."

"Did you meet him?"

"They drove up in a black van with dark windows. Jerry was driving, and I got in the front passenger seat. The big guy was sitting directly behind me, and he had a hat over his face when I got in."

"Go on."

"He told me the pay would be fifty grand each. And that we'd be paid in five days. I asked how he would guarantee payment. He said if I didn't get paid in five days, I could kill Jerry."

Connor and Cohn both laughed.

"I told him I'd do it, and he said Jerry would be in touch. I got out of the van at Fifty-seventh and Third. I couldn't exactly see the guy, but I could see in my peripheral vision that he was not just the big guy, but a *really* big guy."

"How big?"

"Tall, broad shoulders. His head was about touching the headliner."

"Anything else? An accent?"

"No accent. He sounded like one of those radio announcers, big, deep voice."

"What happened next?"

"Jerry called me a couple of hours later and told me they had a full team so wouldn't need me, but he said the big guy had liked me, and that there'd be another job soon, something even bigger, and a lot of money."

"Anything else? Anything at all?"

"He said he'd call me about the big job. He can't call me in here."

"Excuse us a minute," Connor said. He and Cohn got up, left the room, then let themselves into the observation booth.

"What do you think?" he asked Dino.

"I think I know what the big job is going to be," Dino replied. "It's something that Dugan's woman is working on at Strategic Services, a private jewelry show at a new hotel uptown."

"What's your recommendation?" Kravitz asked him.

"I think you should spring him, give him his money, then let him make contact with Kowalski."

"When is the jewelry show?"

"A week, ten days. If Murphy is on the inside, we could bag the whole team and put away Dugan and the woman, Crane Hart."

"Okay," Kravitz said, "I'll buy into that, but I'm going to have to go to the deputy DA with it, and he's out this morning."

"What are we going to do about the girl, Anita Mays? She's his brain. I think he'd be lost without her."

"Well, we can't spring her, because we haven't got her," Dino said. "We can offer to drop her charges and pull the APB that's out on her. You game?" he asked Kravitz.

"I'll take it to the DDA," she said. "I'll beg, if I have to."

51

Stone was having a sandwich at his desk when Dino called.

"Hey."

"Hey. We had a good morning with Bill Murphy."

"Anything new on the girl?"

"Let me tell you the whole story: Murphy was nearly in on the jewelry robbery at the Coulters' apartment, but they didn't use him. However, there's a good chance they'll use him on the hotel jewelry show robbery. We sprung him and pulled the APB on the girl, so that he can make contact with his connection to Dugan."

"Did he identify Dugan?"

"He met with him, but couldn't see him. He even described his voice, like a radio announcer."

"So we still don't have him?"

"Be patient. If Murphy gets asked along on the picnic, then we'll spray all the ants, and one of them will give us Dugan."

"And Crane?"

"Yeah, I guess. If we get Dugan, I think he'll roll on her."

"Right, he's that kind of gentleman."

"Now, what you and I have to do is meet with Mike Freeman and figure out how we're going to cover the hotel robbery. And we don't want Crane to know about the meeting, so let's do it at your office."

"When?"

"Anytime you're both free, I'll shake loose."

"What have you got in mind for covering the robbery?"

"My idea is to throw everything we've got at it, but I expect Mike is going to have some ideas, too."

"Well, I don't have any ideas, so I'll listen to you two."

"First time I ever knew you not to have any ideas."

"Tell you the truth, this one is so big that it seems more like a military operation than a bust, and I'm out of my depth there."

"Set the meeting with Mike, and we'll see. I'm betting that you'll be talking your head off."

"Whatever you say."

"I wish you'd say that more often."

Bill Murphy stood in front of a desk in a judge's chambers and stared forlornly at the pile of his money on the judge's desk.

"I don't have nearly enough meetings like this," the judge said, fingering a stack.

"Thank you for meeting us in chambers, Your Honor," ADA Kravitz said. "It's important that word doesn't filter out about this deal, because Mr. Murphy will be assisting us in preventing a major crime."

"I got that," the judge said. "So all this cash is mine to keep?"

Beth Cutter spoke up. "Judge, you can do with it as you will, as long as my client gets a bail receipt in that amount." She handed him the document; he looked it over and signed it, then he opened a desk drawer and raked the cash into it.

"Detective Connor," the judge said, "I want two armed, uniformed officers to take possession of these funds and give *me* a receipt."

"They're waiting outside, Judge. I'll send them in."

"Okay, Mr. Murphy, you're free on bail."

"Unhook him," Cutter said to Connor, and Connor did.

"Here are the keys to your van," Connor said,

handing them over to Murphy. "Everything that was in it is now in a police custody locker, except your motorcycle, which actually seems to be registered to you, instead of being stolen." He handed Murphy an envelope. "You can have some walking-around money from your stash." Murphy didn't thank him.

"Let's get out of here," Cutter said. "Oh, and here's your cell phone." She handed it over, then led him out of the building and down the street to the police compound, where the van was waiting. "Now, listen to me, Bill," Cutter said. "You've gotten a once-in-a-lifetime, get-out-of-jail-free card, and now you're going to have to earn it, so don't get any ideas about leaving or skipping out."

"Don't worry," Murphy said.

"And you're going to have to make this robbery setup happen. If you don't get the job, you're going to find yourself back inside, and with everything they've got on you, you'll do a *lot* of time."

"I get it."

"Another thing—all the stolen stuff that was in your shop is still in your shop. *Don't try to sell any of it.* It's not yours. If you need more cash, sell your motorcycle."

"All right, all right, Beth. I appreciate the deal you got me, and I won't blow it, I promise."

"And you owe me three grand," she said.

Reluctantly, he produced the envelope with his walking-around money and paid her.

"Okay, get out of here." She walked away.

Murphy got into the van and started it. Cutter had a word with the guard at the gate, and he was waved through. He was so happy, he was nearly in tears.

52

Murphy found that his apartment under the shop had been tossed, but not destroyed. The contents of the office desk upstairs had been emptied onto the floor, and he rummaged among the detritus until he found Nita's address book and her sister's number.

"Hello?"

"Berta, it's Bill. Let me speak to Nita."

Berta was wary; she had never approved of Murphy. "Who says she's here?"

"She does."

Berta didn't bother to cover the phone. "Nita!" she yelled. "The idiot is on the phone!"

Nita picked up an extension. "Okay, Berta, I've got it. *I said, I've got it!*" Berta hung up. "Bill?"

"I'm here, baby."

"Are you on a jail phone?"

"Nope, I'm in the office, sitting at the desk."

"Take down this number," she said. She gave him her throwaway cell number. "Now, go buy a throwaway, then call me back."

Murphy let himself out of the shop and found a RadioShack on Sixth Avenue, then he went home and called the number.

"Bill?"

"It's me."

"What the hell happened?"

"Beth Cutter cut a deal, and I got sprung. So did you."

"Me? I'm not in jail."

"They yanked the APB as part of the deal. I'm free on bail, and you're just plain free."

Anita took a deep breath and let it out with a whoosh. "Wow! I thought I'd be on the run forever."

"We're going to walk away clean, don't worry about it."

"And who do we have to kill to pull that off?"

"It's not as hard as it sounds. Jerry Kowalski is going to call me about a big job that's coming off soon. All I have to do is tell the cops where, when, and who and testify. No more charges! And I think I'll get all the money back, too.

They let me use a hundred grand of it to make bail and gave me another ten of it to live on. I had to give Beth three grand."

"Cheap at the price. What do we do now?"

"Come on home, and we'll live as usual, except we can't pull any jobs, and we can't sell any of the stuff still in the shop. It's been inventoried and tagged, so we can't sneak anything out."

"Bill, this sounds almost too good to be true. Are you sure it's real?"

"I'm out, aren't I? Come on home."

"I'll stay the night and come home in the morning. I don't want to have to deal with rush hour traffic."

"Oh, I got my bike back. It's still in the van. We can sell it if we need cash."

"I've got the thirteen grand that that guy Jim paid me for the two pictures, so we're afloat for a while."

"Yeah, after we get clear of this thing, we'll relocate and start over."

"Where do you think?"

"Somewhere out of the tristate area, I guess. L.A.? San Francisco?"

"That sounds inviting. How long do you think it will take to get clear?"

"The bust will be real soon. I'll have to testify, of course, but if they bag the big guy, they won't need me. We could be out of here before the end of the month, and with our money!"

"Okay, baby, I'll be there by noon tomorrow. Berta sends love and kisses."

"Yeah, sure!" They both hung up.

Murphy went to the van and drove around the corner to their garage. He parked it, then unloaded his motorcycle.

"Hey, Murphy!"

He turned around and saw another bike owner coming.

"Yeah?"

"Something funny happened. Suddenly, my license place is gone and my bike is wearing your girlfriend's plate. She must be wearing mine!"

"I'm sorry, we had a little thing, and she must have panicked. She'll be home midday tomorrow, and I'll see that the plates are switched back."

"Do that, or I'll call the cops on her."

"Don't worry."

Murphy went back to the shop and began to go through the inventory, looking for something that didn't have a tag on it. He found three pretty good pieces that could bring a buck at the weekend flea market and set them aside.

San Francisco, he was thinking. Maybe even Carmel or Santa Barbara. That would be rich pickings, and they could sell the stuff in Frisco!

53

Stone, Dino, and Mike Freeman sat in Stone's study and sipped their drinks.

"Okay, Mike," Dino said, "tell us what the setup is for your jewelry show."

Mike unrolled a set of plans for the floor where the show would be held, spread them on the coffee table, and began pointing out things. "Sellers are in the suites around the exterior of the building. They wanted privacy to make their sales, instead of a large showroom. There's a central lounge on the north side of the building, where there's a bar set up. That takes up about a third of the floor. The rest are suites. We'll have a plain-clothes guard in each suite, and there'll also be a uniformed policeman with body armor and a shotgun concealed in the entryway closet. There'll be guards downstairs at the elevator banks and upstairs outside the elevator. To secure the roof and helicopter pad we'll have twelve men with full body armor and shotguns, hidden in the building on the roof, here, that houses the heating, air-conditioning, and telephone systems. It's a tight fit, but it will work.

"If the robbers arrive by helicopter, as we think they will, we'll allow them to get down the stairwell, where they'll be confronted by our people on the floor. The team on the roof will follow them down very quickly for backup. We'll round them all up, cuff them, read them their rights, then take them down in elevators to the garage, where there will be three paddy wagons waiting for them."

"That looks pretty much like the same plan that Crane Hart was overseeing," Dino said.

"It's exactly the same plan," Mike replied.

"So what's the real plan?"

"The real plan is this plan, but it happens a day earlier. The organizers have brought forward the show date by a day, and sworn both sellers and buyers to secrecy, and Crane doesn't know that. I'll send her out on a different job that will occupy her all day on the day. The next day is when the robbers will arrive, and there won't be any sellers or buyers there to get hurt, if there's shooting. And we don't have to make a new plan.

Even if we did, it would look a hell of a lot like this one."

Dino and Stone sat quietly and thought about it.

"I can't think of any reason that wouldn't work," Dino said finally.

"Neither can I," Stone said.

"Oh," Dino said, "something new. Mr. and Mrs. Jacob Sutton are back from Israel. They got in last night, and Jake is back at work at the diamond center today."

"Suppose Sutton hears about the sale and calls Don Dugan," Stone said.

"Jake isn't invited to participate. He'll know about it, but, like Crane, he won't know the new date," Dino said.

"Have you heard anything from Bill Murphy about doing the job?" Stone asked.

"Who's Bill Murphy?" Mike asked.

Dino explained it to him. "We're talking to Murphy every day. We'll know as soon as he knows. Anyway, he's just backup, in case we don't bag everybody on the day."

"It would be nice to know who we're dealing with," Mike said.

"It's Don Dugan, the Drago brothers, and their cousin Jerry Kowalski—on his mother's side," Dino said. "Probably plus two or three other guys. We know all that, we just can't prove it until they're either busted on the day, or until Murphy is in a position to rat them out."

"It would be nice if you could bag Jake Sutton on the same day," Stone said.

"We'll have four guys on him," Dino replied. "If he makes a move, we'll be all over him. We've tapped his phone lines at home, in his booth, and in his office, too. And don't worry, we have the warrants."

"We're listening to Crane's office extension, too," Mike said. "We don't need a warrant to tap our own phones or wire our own offices."

"What about Bill Murphy and Anita Mays's shop and apartment?" Stone asked.

"Everything's wired. We can listen to their cell phones when they're on the premises, too. When Murphy got home, the first thing he did was to buy a throwaway and call her. Turns out she's at her sister's house in Connecticut. She's coming back tomorrow."

"You think Anita's on board with this?"

"She bought everything he had to say in their phone conversation," Dino said. "They're already talking about moving their operation to California when he's clear here."

"Will he get his money back?" Stone asked.

"I'm a little unclear on that," Dino said. "If we drop the charges, do we have a basis for confiscating the money? I mean, confiscating all the stolen goods, sure, but the money? Without charges? What's your legal opinion, Stone?"

"My opinion is that I'm glad the DA's office will have to make that distinction and that decision."

Dino snorted. "You can never get a legal opinion out of a lawyer when you need one," he said.

54

Bill Murphy walked into the bar on Bleecker Street and spotted Jerry Kowalski. He bought two beers at the bar and took them over to the table where Jerry was waiting.

"How's it going?" Murphy asked.

"It's going just great," Kowalski replied. "You still up for the job?"

"I sure am. Tell me all."

"First thing is, we need one more guy to cover the ground. You know somebody who can handle it?"

"I know just the guy, but it's not a guy. It's my girl, Anita. You've met her."

"Well, she's a looker, but how is she with a shotgun in her hand?"

"She's smart as a whip, tough as nails, and she

has ice water in her veins. You want to talk to her? I'll call her now."

Kowalski nodded.

Murphy called Anita's new cell number and got her. "Where are you?"

"I just got to the house," she said.

"You know that bar where we heard the guitarist?"

"Yeah."

"I'm there now with a buddy, and he's got something for us. Come straight over."

"I'm on my way."

"How long you know her?" Kowalski asked.

"Going on five years. We've done very well together, and she's never once dropped the ball."

"The big guy has a girl in on this, too, so maybe he'll go for it."

They sipped their beer and waited for Anita. She spotted them immediately, picked up three beers at the bar, and came over.

"Nita, you remember Jerry."

"Sure."

"I'm helping to set up a job, and Bill tells me you can handle yourself."

"I beat him up all the time," she said.

"You think she's kidding?" Murphy laughed.

"Okay, here's the deal: we're hitting a jewelry show at a big hotel. The big guy has all the inside info, and he's got the scene tapped, plans and everything. It's going to run like clockwork."

"When?" Nita asked.

"Pretty soon. You won't get any notice. I'll come get you, we'll go to a place where everything is set up. Everything's provided: clothes, weapons, masks, transportation. You sit down with the big guy, he runs us through it, we do some practicing. We sleep over, next day we walk in, point guns at people, take out the security, and walk out with a couple of duffels full of high-end diamond jewelry."

"Anybody going to get hurt?" Murphy asked.

"Only if there's opposition. The plan is so good they won't see us coming. We're in, we're out."

"Nita and I are in," Murphy said.

"Lemme make a call," Kowalski said. He went outside for five minutes, then came back, tucking his cell phone into his pocket. "Okay," he said, "the big guy has bought you both."

"What's the money?"

"Fifty grand five days after the job, another fifty after the stuff is fenced—couple of weeks."

"That's a hundred grand each?"

"Right. We all get the same."

Murphy and Anita looked at each other and nodded. "We're up for it." Murphy gave him their new cell numbers.

Kowalski made notes about their clothing and shoe sizes. "Here's how it will go," he said. "I'll call you and say, 'We're on.' No conversation. Exactly one hour after the call you're standing in front of Washington Square Arch, and I'll pick you up in a black van. Bring a small overnight bag and a change of clothes. No guns, knives, or other weapons. And no cell phones. You'll be thoroughly searched, then equipped. We rehearse that day. The next day the job goes down. You'll be delivered well away from the job, you go home and wait. Five days later you'll get a call from me again. I meet you at Washington Square, you get your money, I drop you off. Any questions?"

"Who's the big guy?" Anita asked.

"You'll meet him. You won't know his name. You don't want to know his name or anything about him, believe me. You perform, you get paid, that's it."

"So we're trusting you," Murphy said.

"Remember what the big guy said? You don't get paid, you can kill me?"

"So that's how it is."

"That's how it is. You still in?"

"We are," they both said simultaneously.

Kowalski got up and left, and Murphy and Anita ordered a burger.

"You really think it's going to go the way he says?" she asked.

"Kowalski is a standup guy. If it's good enough for him, it's good enough for me."

"Well," she said, "if it's good enough for you, it's good enough for me."

"After lunch, we need to call the cops," Murphy said.

"Do we?" she asked. "Do we really need to?"

55

Mike Freeman was at his desk, his office door open, then there was a soft rap on the jamb. He looked up to find Crane Hart, fetching in a white dress that was fitted tightly across her breasts. His breath quickened a little, and he felt himself growing tumescent. "Hi," he breathed.

"Good afternoon," she said.

"Come in."

Mike worked in a soft chair at a coffee table, and she took a chair across from him and crossed her legs. He didn't see much, but he knew she only rarely wore underwear, so his carnal tension went up a notch. "What's up?"

"I came to protest," she said.

"Really? About what?"

"You're shipping me off to Atlanta just when the big event I planned comes off. I want to be here for that."

Mike shook his head. "There would be nothing for you to do," he said. "The plan and the date are fixed. You've done your work, now it gets turned over to operations and they make it happen. They don't need you to hold a shotgun and look threatening."

"I know, I know, it's just that this is the first operation I've planned, and I want to see it work."

"You'd be a liability to operations. They'd be worried about protecting you, and they have more than enough to protect."

"Come on, Mike," she said, in that inviting way she had. "Please."

"Nope."

"How about if I come around this coffee table, kneel in front of you, unzip your trousers, and take you in my mouth?"

Mike's heart skipped a beat. "People might talk," he said.

"I know, but I want to do it so much."

"As soon as you get back from Atlanta," he said, "it will be all yours."

"Yum," she said, getting to her feet. "You certainly know how to turn a girl on."

"You're not so bad at that yourself," he said.

"At turning a girl on? I didn't know you were interested in a threesome. Perhaps I can arrange one for us."

Jesus, he thought. She could make me come right now, without even moving.

"*Immediately* after Atlanta," he said. If he had his way, she'd have plenty of girls to choose from at Rikers Island's Singer Center, the women's jail.

She made a disappointed face. "All right," she said, "I'll let you make it up to me. You'll have to do all the work."

"Love to," Mike replied.

Murphy and Anita rode their separate bikes back to the garage and parked them.

"Just a minute," he said, taking a screwdriver from his saddlebag and handing it to her. "The guy next door would like his license plate back."

"He noticed?"

"He certainly did, and I don't want to have to look him in the eye until he has his plate back."

She knelt, unscrewed and exchanged the plates, and tightened the screws. "There," she said.

He put away the screwdriver, and they started back toward the shop.

"What did you mean?" he asked.

"About what?"

"You asked if we really needed to call the cops."

"Did I?"

"You did. Let me tell you something here, because we can't talk about it at home."

"Why not?"

"I think the whole fucking building is wired for sound. I think they can hear a pin drop in the shop or in the apartment."

"You're paranoid. They wouldn't waste that much effort on a couple of burglars—or rather, one burglar and one antiques reseller."

"Is that your job description?"

"Yes, and it's way down the totem pole for the art squad at the NYPD."

"Maybe so, but this job that Jerry wants us for is way up at the top. They were cagey when they brought it up, but I could tell they had the hots for it, and I don't see how in the hell we could help pull it off, collect a hundred grand each, and get away with it."

"You always lacked imagination, Bill."

"Okay, enlighten me."

"I won't be able to figure that out until we know the job and all the details."

"Remember, Nita, we don't get the first half of the money until five days after the job. If we pull it and don't warn the cops ahead of time, we'd get up again, and the DA would start piling on the charges."

"What if we don't come home after the job? What if we nest somewhere else, get a hotel room, maybe, and wait for the delivery of the money?"

"You're not thinking clearly," he said. "They've got a hundred grand of our money right now."

"And you think they'll give it back to us if we tip them off about the job?"

"Beth says that if they drop the charges, as promised, they'll have to give us the money back. They get our stock, but not the money. It's a legal thing."

"I don't see them giving it back to us."

"Well, it's a dead certainty that they won't give it back if we don't tip them off, go through with the robbery, and then disappear. Then all we'll have is our two hundred grand from the job, and what if they fuck us? Or just shoot us in the head?"

"You have a point, kind of."

"You need to rein in your imagination and play the odds on this thing. We'll have a much better outcome if we hold up our end of the deal."

"Maybe."

"Even if we got our two hundred grand from the job—"

"I wasn't thinking about the two hundred grand. I was thinking about all of it."

"*All of it*? You mean the jewelry?"

"That's what I mean."

"Then we'd have the cops *and* the big guy

looking for us, and we don't have a fence who could handle that much."

"I know about a fence in Tijuana," she said.

"Nita, this isn't a caper movie. We're not going to end up in Mexico with fifty million dollars in big-time jewelry. You're thinking about that Steve McQueen thing, aren't you? What was it?"

"The Getaway," she said. "I think we could pull it off."

"What's really scary about this conversation is that you actually have the balls to try it."

"That's right, and you don't."

"That's why I have a deal with the cops," he said. "Because I'm cautious and careful, and I go for the sure thing instead of the long odds."

They were back at the shop now, and he let them in the front door. She started to speak, but he held a finger to his lips, and she shut up.

He knew he hadn't heard the last of this, though.

56

Crane Hart poured the coffee and called out to Don, "Breakfast is ready!"

He came into the kitchen, tucking his shirt in and with wet hair. He said nothing, which was unusual for him.

"What's wrong?" she asked.

"I don't know," Dugan replied. "Something, though."

"Oh, come on, Don, what's set you off? I mean, I know you think you have this sixth sense, but . . ."

"My 'sixth sense,' as you call it, has worked pretty well for us, hasn't it?"

"Come on, what set you off?"

"I don't like it that you're being sent to Atlanta

right before the job, that's what. I want you to talk to Freeman and get out of it."

"I'm way ahead of you," she said. "I tried that yesterday, and he gave me perfectly good reasons for sending me to Atlanta."

"What reasons?"

"He said that my job as a planner is over, and now operations will take charge, and they won't want me in the way. I asked him repeatedly to let me be there, and he wouldn't."

"The job is set for Thursday. Why would he send you to Atlanta on Tuesday?"

"Because that's when they need me in Atlanta, I guess."

"You guess? Why do you believe that?"

"Why would Mike lie to me? I've got him in the palm of my hand, believe me."

"You mean, you've got his dick in the palm of your hand."

"Same thing." She smiled.

"Call in sick on Tuesday," Dugan said.

"For what purpose? You don't need me here to do the job, do you?"

"If something goes wrong, we may have to run."

"I can run from Atlanta, can't I?"

"I guess."

"Don, I'm getting the distinct feeling that you

don't trust me, that you think I'm somehow in cahoots with Mike to blow up this thing."

"It crossed my mind," he said.

She grabbed the plate of scrambled eggs and bacon from in front of him, took it to the sink, and washed it down the garbage disposal. "Have breakfast somewhere else," she said.

"Oh, come on, you know I'd trust you with my life."

"Then start doing it, or just pack up and get out."

He stood up and drew her to him.

"What's that I feel down there?" she asked, pushing her belly into his crotch.

"You know what it is," he said.

"Let's go take a look at it," she replied, taking him by the hand and leading him toward the bedroom.

Jacob Sutton was at his desk when he got a call from his booth, downstairs at the diamond center. "Yes?"

"There's a gentleman named Mario Carnavale down here who says he wants to see you."

"The cop from the jewelry squad?"

"That's the one."

"Tell him I'll be right down."

Sutton slipped into his jacket and straightened his tie. This was not unusual; a lot of cops came to him to buy. He walked down the stairs and across the open floor, nodding to friends at other booths. Carnavale was standing next to his counter, looking at things on display. "Mario, how are you?" he asked, shaking the man's hand warmly.

"Hiya, Jake," the cop replied. "I came to see you last week, but they said you were out of town."

"Yes, my wife and I went to Israel for a week. We have a condo on the beach at Haifa."

"And you got some sun, too."

"A little. Now, what can I do for you today?"

"I'm going to ask my girl to marry me, and I want a ring for her. I'm going to need the best possible price. I haven't got all that much saved up."

"I'll tell you what, Mario, you tell me what you want to spend, and I'll get you the best possible ring for that price."

"I was thinking about three thousand."

"And what sort of size?"

"Maybe five carats?"

"Mario, I'm going to be honest with you, that's an unrealistic size of stone for that kind of money. For something that size, something nice, it's going to run you six to eight thousand, best price."

Carnavale gulped. "Suppose I can come up with five thousand?"

Sutton thought about it. It would be good business to please this policeman. After all, you never knew when you might need the friendship of someone in law enforcement. "I'll tell you what," he said, "I've bought some rings from an estate. They should be here Friday, Monday at the latest. There just might be something suitable in that lot, and I don't have to worry about paying wholesale market prices for a loose stone."

"That sounds good," Carnavale said.

"Come back and see me this time Monday, and I'll have something nice for you, I promise."

"Okay, Jake, I'll do that. And thanks!" The cop left.

Sutton went back upstairs to his desk. He'd send the cop away happy.

Mario Carnavale was happier than Sutton knew. He got into his waiting car and called Jim Connor, who was the lead on this case. "I saw Jake Sutton," he said, "and he told me he has some new stuff coming in from an estate purchase, and he'd have something for me on Monday."

"Well, that dovetails nicely, doesn't it?" Connor replied.

57

D on Dugan was in his office when a call came in from his contact at the Creighton Arms hotel, a desk clerk.

"Something's going on," the woman said.

"Tell me, Kristie," Dugan said. This was the woman who had given him the first alert on the jewelry show, and he was intensely interested to hear what she had to say.

"I overheard a conversation between two assistant managers a couple of minutes ago. I went into the reservations file for the show, and all the overnight rooms have been rebooked for Tuesday night, instead of Wednesday."

"What about checkouts?" Don asked.

"Most of the Thursday departures are now checking out on Wednesday afternoon."

"Do me a favor, will you? Check catering to see if they've moved their lunch and bar setup."

"I'll call you right back."

Don hung up. His mind was reeling; he was already making a mental checklist of what had to be done. A few minutes later Kristie returned his call.

"Yes," she said, "catering has now scheduled for Wednesday, instead of Thursday."

"Change my bookings to Tuesday night," he said.

"Certainly," she replied.

"I owe you, baby. You get a bonus."

"I can live with that. You want me to drop off new cards?"

"Sure, and we'll have a drink."

"I'll look forward to it."

Dugan hung up and started making calls.

The Bacchettis, Mike Freeman, and Stone sat down for dinner Monday evening at Patroon; Ann Keaton had called and said she'd be late.

"A toast," Stone said. Everybody raised a glass. "To gangbusting," he said.

Everybody laughed and drank.

"There isn't as much gangbusting as there used to be," Dino said. "La Cosa Nostra isn't much of a problem today. Even the meaning of 'gang' has changed. This one is going to be satisfying."

"Not to mention the publicity," Stone said. "You're going to be the department's new hero, and when the time comes—"

Dino held up a hand. "Stop right there," he said. "I don't want to hear any more of that."

"Superstitious?" Stone asked.

"Cautious," Dino replied.

"You don't mind if we talk among ourselves about this, do you?" Stone asked him, impishly.

"I certainly do," Dino said. "Shut up about it, all of you!"

"I guess I'd better change the subject, then. Mike, you all ready for the jewelry show?"

"I've been all over the thing half a dozen times, using my finest-toothed comb, and I think we're ready for anything."

"Oh, yes," Dino said. "Good news on the Jake Sutton front. We dangled a little bait, and he says he's got a new shipment coming in the next few days, ready to sell."

"Any nerves about this, Mike?"

"Just the usual ones."

"Dino, are Bill Murphy and Anita Mays behaving themselves?"

"Yep. They've signed on for the job and are waiting for the call."

"Will you know when the call comes?"

"We'd damned well better know," Dino said. "I'm not going to be caught on the wrong foot when this goes down."

Stone looked across the dining room and saw Ann coming. "Okay, now we can switch the conversation to politics," he said.

Stone got up and greeted Ann with a kiss, and she joined the table. A waiter swiftly brought her a martini.

"Tell us the news from the political front," Stone said.

"The good news is that we're seeing some cracks in the California delegation," she said. "It looks as though at least a few are rethinking their vote for Stanton on the first ballot. This is good, because we didn't think we'd get any California votes until the second ballot."

"That's wonderful," Stone said. "I haven't mentioned this until now, but you're going to have some company at the convention. Strategic Services' L.A. operation is handling security at the Coliseum and at The Arrington. I'm going out so that I can see Peter, and Dino and Viv want to see Ben, so we'll all be there."

"I don't suppose I have to ask where you'll be staying," Ann said.

"We'll be at The Arrington, of course. I have a four-bedroom house on the grounds, and Peter and Ben have bought houses of their own in Brentwood, so I'll have room for everybody. Will you join us?"

"That's a lovely invitation," Ann said, "but the Lees will be at The Arrington, too, in the presidential cottage, and they've hinted that they'd like me to stay with them. But we'll see. Can I let you know a little later?"

"Certainly," Stone said. "If you stay with the Lees, then I'll have to have them over for dinner, just so I can see you."

"Well, I am going to be pretty busy," Ann said. "Surprising how much time it takes to count votes, especially when the tally is always changing."

Stone sipped his Knob Creek and looked around the table at his friends, feeling lucky to have them all, and all at the table. They would make L.A. and the convention more fun, too. All, he reflected, was right with the world.

Crane Hart got home from the office early, and surprised Don Dugan with a woman in the living room. There were half-finished drinks on the coffee table, and there was the smell of sex in the air. There was a thong on the floor, and the woman tried to push it under the sofa.

"Hey, baby," Dugan said, sounding nervous. "This is Kristie. We're doing a little business."

"Oh, is that what you call it these days?" Crane stalked out of the living room and went to the bedroom, where she got out her suitcase and started packing.

Ten minutes later, Dugan came into the room. "What are you so hot about?" he demanded.

Crane said nothing, just continued throwing things at her suitcase.

"Kristie is my contact at the Creighton Arms. I couldn't pull this off without her help."

"You don't seem to need any help pulling things off," Crane said.

Dugan went to the chest of drawers and came back with an envelope and handed it to her. "This is a ticket from Atlanta to Mexico City, and the name of our hotel there. After the job I'll meet you there."

"Oh, you've already decided to run?"

"Just think of it as a vacation," Dugan said. "When the dust settles and we've banked our new funds, we'll be back."

"And how am I supposed to explain a trip to Mexico to Mike Freeman?"

"Tell him you have a sick aunt."

"Or something else as lame? When I've finished my business in Atlanta, I'm coming back here. It will be Friday afternoon. Be gone, if you like, and don't come back, if you like."

Dugan threw up his hands. "I can't talk to you anymore."

"Please don't," she said. She went into the bathroom, locked the door, sat down on the toilet lid, and cried a little. When she came out, he was gone.

58

Dugan didn't come back to her house that night. Crane fumed for a while and finally fell asleep. She woke up Tuesday morning to a ringing telephone, and she grabbed it. "Don?"

"Hello, Ms. Hart, this is Mac, your Strategic Services driver. I'll be picking you up in half an hour for the trip to the airport."

"Right, Mac, see you then." She hung up, took a quick shower, and put on some makeup. Looking in the mirror, she saw her hand trembling as it held the lipstick.

She had allowed Don to suck her into this, and now she was terrified. He was talking about walking away from everything in New York, and everything she had was in New York—house, job, friends, everything. He had said it might come to this, but she hadn't believed him until now, and she was beginning to panic. She dressed, closed her suitcase, and sat down on the bed, trying to gain control of herself.

The doorbell buzzed, making her jump. The car was waiting. She picked up the phone and called a number she still remembered.

Stone was in bed, reading the papers and watching Ann towel herself off, when the phone rang. "Hello?"

"Stone, it's Crane."

Stone put his hand over the phone. "I'm sorry, I have to take this," he said to Ann. "What is it, Crane?"

"I'll be there in fifteen minutes, and then I'll tell you everything. It would be good if you get Dino over there, too." She hung up.

"Something wrong?" Ann asked, slipping into her dress. "You look funny."

"I'm sorry, an old client insists on coming over here immediately. I'd better get dressed."

She allowed him to zip her up, then got into her shoes and kissed him. "I'm off. See you tonight?"

"You certainly will. Don't let them work you too late."

Ann left, and Stone got dressed. He was in his

office when Crane arrived. Joan wasn't downstairs yet—too early—so he let Crane in the street door and took her into his office.

"Did you call Dino?" she asked.

"Not until I know what this is about."

She sat down on the sofa and took a deep breath. "Don is pulling off some kind of robbery."

"When?"

"Tomorrow or Thursday—tomorrow, I think. I don't know all the details."

Stone picked up the phone and dialed Dino's cell phone.

"Bacchetti."

"Where are you?"

"Park Avenue and Fifty-second Street, headed to the office."

"Come here instead."

"What's up?"

"I'll save it for when you get here," Stone said, then hung up.

Joan came into the office, then stopped when she saw Crane. "I'm sorry, I didn't know you had a visitor."

"Dino's on the way over. Let him in, will you?"

"Of course. Coffee?"

"Crane?"

"Yes, please."

"For three."

Joan went out the back door toward the kitchen

and came back with a thermos carafe. She poured two cups and set one on the coffee table and the other on Stone's desk. The front doorbell rang, and Joan went to answer it. She came back with Dino and poured him a cup of coffee, then left.

"Hi, Crane," Dino said. "What's up, Stone?"

"Start again," Stone said to Crane.

"Dino, Don Dugan is going to pull off a big robbery."

"When and where?"

"At the new Creighton Arms hotel. It was supposed to be Thursday, but I think it's been moved up."

"Up to when?"

"Probably tomorrow. I did the security planning for the event, and I brought the plans and the file home to work on a couple of weeks ago. I think Don got into it when I was asleep."

"Does Mike Freeman know about Don's interest in the event?"

"He may," she replied. "He's sending me to Atlanta today. I think he moved up the jewelry show a day to throw Don off, but Don has a contact at the hotel who must have tipped him off."

"So you know some of this, but not all of it?" Dino asked.

Crane tossed off the rest of her coffee and set the cup down. "I guess you want to know everything."

"Yes, I do," Dino said.

"I'm going to need immunity."

"Immunity from what?"

"From any crime Don may have committed."

"With your help?"

"I'm going to need immunity before I can answer any more questions. Stone, you can represent me in this."

"I'll advise you, but I won't represent you."

"What's the difference?"

"There's a difference, trust me."

"All right, advise me."

"I advise you to get immunity, then tell Dino everything you know."

Dino said, "Excuse me for a minute, I have to make a call." He left Stone's office and walked down the hall to where Joan sat, then pulled out his cell phone.

Stone looked at Crane, who was a nervous wreck. "Don't tell me anything you don't tell Dino," he said. "I won't be held to attorney-client privilege on this."

"I understand," she said.

Dino came back and sat down. "I asked Joan to call Mike Freeman and get him over here," he said. "Crane, I've spoken to the DA, and you've got immunity on any crimes of Don's that you may have known about or taken part in. But I have to know absolutely everything you know, and if you lie to me once, the deal is off. Do you understand me?"

Crane nodded.

"Say, 'Yes, I understand you.'"

"Yes, I understand you."

"Stone, you're my witness," Dino said.

"I am." Stone took a small recorder from his desk, pressed a button, and put it on the coffee table. "Go ahead," he said to her.

Crane took a deep breath and began to talk.

Stone listened as she confirmed everything he had suspected Dugan of, and with a lot of detail he hadn't imagined. As she was wrapping up her story, Mike Freeman arrived.

"What's going on?" he asked. "Crane, why aren't you on the way to Atlanta?"

"I don't think I'll be going to Atlanta," she said.

"Somebody tell me what's going on," Mike said.

Stone picked up the recorder and pressed the PLAYBACK button, and Mike listened. His face betrayed nothing.

After the playback finished, Stone turned off the recorder and gave the memory cartridge to Dino, who slipped it into a pocket.

"Stone," Dino said, "I have a lot of calls to make, and I don't have time to go down to my office to make them."

"Take the office next to Joan's," Stone said. "Call anybody you like."

Stone looked at Mike and Crane. "Shall I leave you alone?"

"Please don't," Mike said.

59

Bill Murphy and Anita Mays were having a late breakfast when the call came. Murphy opened the cell phone. "Yeah?"

"It's now," Jerry Kowalski said, then hung up.

"We've got an hour," Murphy said to Anita, checking his watch. "Pack some things." He opened the phone again.

She put her hand on his. "Don't call them," she said. "Let's play it by ear."

"Get packed," Murphy said, and punched in Detective Connor's number.

"This is Connor."

"It's Bill Murphy. I just got the call."

"Where's the pickup?"

"Washington Square Arch, one hour. A black van."

"We're on it. Go."

Murphy closed the phone and went to get packed.

Anita was angrily stuffing underwear into a duffel.

"Don't start," Murphy said. "Don't ever bring it up again. I'm not going to prison for you or anybody else."

She didn't say a word, just kept packing.

Jim Connor and Aaron Cohn sat in a battered Honda supplied by the police compound a block from Washington Square Arch and watched, occasionally through binoculars.

"Why am I nervous?" Cohn said.

"You shouldn't be, we've got this taped."

"Listen, Jimmy, anything could happen here. The Hart woman could be doing this to throw us off."

"You and I weren't there to hear her story, but Bacchetti bought it. It's going down a day early," Connor said, "and there won't be any helicopters involved. Dugan booked rooms on the floor below the jewelry show, and they'll come up the stairs. Bacchetti believes it."

"I hope to God he's right. Did Bacchetti cancel our choppers over the scene?"

"All but one—he's being cautious."

Cohn pointed. "Look, there are the kids."

Murphy and Anita got out of a cab at the Arch; they were five minutes early. Murphy looked around for a cop car and couldn't find one. There was nobody on a motorcycle, either. "We're good," he said.

Anita still wasn't talking.

"Did you leave your cell phone at home?"

She nodded.

"Good. They'll search us anyway."

"This guy Dugan . . ." she started to say.

"Don't ever mention that name again. We're not supposed to know it. We'll call him the big guy."

She nodded again.

Murphy saw the black van coming down Fifth Avenue a block away. "Here we go," he said. The van made a right turn and stopped. Murphy and Anita trotted across the street and got into the open sliding door, which closed automatically.

"You leave your guns and your phones at home?" Jerry asked.

"Yes, we're clean," Anita said. "I can't see any cops, either."

"Neither can I." Murphy turned toward Sixth Avenue.

Jerry handed Murphy two plastic cards. "The keys to your room," he said, "which is 3625." Then he handed them two pairs of latex gloves. "Put these on now, and don't take them off again until we're done tomorrow. Not even in the shower." He handed them hairnets. "These, too. We're not leaving any traces. If you smoke, take your butts with you in your pocket when you leave the hotel."

Down the block, Connor spoke into a hand-held radio. "The van is on time. It turned right toward Sixth. Somebody pick it up." He drove off slowly, so as not to crowd his quarry.

The black van turned right on Sixth Avenue and started uptown. Connor kept well back and two lanes over. "This car is a piece of shit," he said absently.

"I hope we'll never see it again after today," Cohn replied.

They were up to Rockefeller Center when Connor saw an identical black van pull away from the curb and fall in behind the van he had been following. "You see that?" Connor asked.

"I sure do. Which one are we going to follow?"

"The first one, if we can, but I have a feeling they're going to the same place."

A block farther north, yet another black van joined the little convoy.

"Jesus, how many people are on this job?" Cohn asked.

Connor spoke into his radio. "We have a total of three identical black vans now. They appear to be sticking together."

The three vans turned right on West Fifty-seventh Street and proceeded east. "Anybody in the garage?" Connor asked.

"It's staked," somebody replied.

"Coming your way."

A block short of the hotel, Dino sat in his black SUV and listened to the radio channel. "This is looking good," he said.

The three vans passed his car and he watched as they turned into the hotel garage.

Connor spotted Dino's car and stopped. "You take the wheel and wait here," he said to his partner.

"Right."

Connor got out of the car, trotted over to Dino's SUV, and tapped on a black window. The window slid down a couple of inches. "Get in," Dino said. Connor got into the car and closed the door. "Let's just listen."

The radio crackled. "The three vans are unloading half a dozen big canvas suitcases on wheels. They've waved off the bellhops and are headed for the garage elevator. They're getting into the elevator—six people and the bags. Doors closing, headed up. I'll watch for where they get off."

"Thirty-sixth floor," Dino predicted. "Dugan came in the front door of the hotel half an hour ago and headed upstairs. Our guy spotted his contact at the front desk. We've got a detective on her."

The radio came to life again. "They got out on thirty-six. The car is on the way down again."

Dino picked up the microphone. "Okay, everybody's aboard the ship. Maintain your stations, in case anybody tries to leave. If anyone does, follow him."

Murphy and Anita got off the elevator with the others and, towing their luggage, walked down the hall until they came to 3625. He slipped the card into the slot, opened the door, and walked in, holding the door for Anita.

She looked around. "Hey, not bad," she said. "Big room."

Murphy picked up his bag, laid it on the bed, and unzipped it. "Holy shit," he said, holding up a black nylon jacket with the NYPD badge embroidered on the chest and the letters SWAT on the back. "It's like Halloween. We've got the whole costume—flak jacket, cap, boots." He checked the sizes.

Anita had her bag open now. She put everything on the bed, then brought out a stubby shotgun from the bottom of the bag and racked the slide. A shell popped out onto the bed. "Riot gun," she said. "NYPD issue, I'll bet. Where do they get this stuff?"

"Who cares?" Murphy said. The phone at bedside rang, and he picked it up. "Yeah?"

"Meeting in five in the corner suite," Jerry's voice said.

Murphy hung up. "Class is about to begin," he said to Anita.

"I'm up for it," she replied, "but if I don't like the plan, I'm walking."

"Do you think they're going to let you walk out of here now? Do you want a bullet in the head? We're in. Get used to it."

"In until the cops come," Anita said.

"That's right, until the cops come."

60

Stone's iPhone rang, and he answered it.

"It's Dino."

"How's the thing going?"

"Everybody showed up at the hotel. They're in their rooms on the thirty-sixth floor, and we're sitting on them. We don't expect movement until tomorrow morning. The show starts at ten. I expect we'll see them soon after that."

"Sounds right."

"You want a ticket to the party?"

"Yeah, I think so. Ann has a birthday coming up—maybe I'll buy her a bauble."

"Don't think of this as a shopping excursion, pal. You could end up with a shotgun stuck in your ear."

"Don't worry about me," Stone said.

"I'll pick you up at eight tonight," Dino said.

"Dinner?"

"We'll be dining at the hotel, in our room."
Dino dug into a pocket and came up with a plastic key. "Corner suite, thirty-fifth floor. Bring your jammies. No women."

Murphy and Anita listened as the big guy, who was wearing a very creepy plastic mask, walked them through the plan.

"We enter the stairwell at nine o'clock, climb to thirty-seven, and take the rooms. There are four of them that will have goods on display. We'll take one at a time, then leave a man in place and move on to the next. As you enter the room, there will be a coat closet on your left, just as in your rooms. That will contain a cop with a shotgun, but they won't be in the closets until ten, when the show opens. You'll each have a plastic garbage bag with a drawstring. You'll empty each tray into the bag. When you hear this whistle"— he showed them a referee's silver one and blew it for them—"you head back to the stairwell where we entered. No hesitation, no exceptions. We walk back down a flight, where an elevator will be locked open for us. The elevators on the thirty-seventh floor will be locked shut at nine, so nobody will be joining us unexpectedly.

"You'll keep your police uniforms on until

we're in the vans and out of the building. As you get into a van, you'll be relieved of your plastic bags. When you're dropped off, leave your uniforms in the vans and take at least two cabs to your destination to be sure you aren't followed.

"There won't be a full complement of cops on the show floor until nearly ten, so we shouldn't have a lot of opposition. Your shotguns are loaded with number nine birdshot—no double ought. We don't want to kill anybody. If you have to shoot an armed man, aim at his gun shoulder. You'll knock him down, don't worry. Any questions?"

"Will any of the jewelry sellers be armed?" Anita asked.

"Good question. Probably not, but maybe. Everybody will be frisked and, if necessary, disarmed. Check for ankle holsters, too. Remember, you're wearing full-body armor, so you'll be well protected. The cops and security people will be in plainclothes, and they'll be wearing lapel buttons for ID. The only SWAT team will be on the roof. They're expecting a chopper, and they won't be expecting us to come up the stairs. The door to the staircase to the roof will be locked from the inside. We want to be off the floor in five minutes, so move your asses."

"Have you considered what traffic will be like?" Murphy asked.

"Just past rush hour, so not as bad as it could be. The vans are equipped with police lighting and whoopers, so that will help us move along."

"Where will we be dropped?"

"You'll see when it happens. You won't be far from a cab. When you leave the vans, take nothing with you but your own luggage, which will be taken from your rooms and placed in the vans."

"When do we get paid?" Anita asked.

"On Monday," the big guy replied. "You'll be contacted, and you'll meet to get your cash. The next payment will come in a couple of weeks. You'll be paid in used hundreds, fifties, and twenties. Live your lives as usual. It would be very unwise of you to start making expensive purchases or paying off your bookies or other debts. Wait a few months. With your second payment you'll get written instructions on how to open an offshore bank account. You'd be very smart to do that. They'll give you a credit card you can use anywhere in the world, and the purchases deducted from your account."

He looked around. "No more questions. Everybody back to your rooms, and stay there until we come and get you at eight forty-five tomorrow morning. Be fully dressed and armed, and leave your luggage on your bed. You may already have noticed that you can't make outside calls on your phones. The only call you can make is to room service. Tell them to leave the food outside your door. Everything will be already paid for, and the waiter tipped. Don't be seen by anybody."

He held up a black mask. "There's one of these with every uniform. Don't leave your room without it tomorrow morning, and keep it on until your van has left the hotel garage. See you in the morning."

The big guy walked into the bedroom of his suite and closed the door, and Jerry Kowalski shooed everybody out.

Back in their room, Murphy sank into a chair. "So? What do you think?"

"I think it's going to work," she said. "When do we get out?"

"Unless the cops interrupt us, we're out when we get out of the van."

"That works for me," she said.

61

Stone tossed his duffel into Dino's black SUV, and they were off. "I'm hungry," he said, "and I want a drink."

"You haven't already had one?" Dino asked.

"I wanted your company. I hate drinking alone."

Ten minutes later they were in the hotel's garage and waiting for the elevator. Three minutes after that they were in their suite. "Very nice," Dino said.

"Do we have any of the rooms upstairs wired?" Stone asked.

"Yes, but they only got up and running an hour ago. We may have missed a lot."

Stone tossed Dino a room service menu. "What would you like?"

"Steak, rare, onion rings, green beans, double

Johnnie Walker Black first, then a bottle of your choice."

Stone ordered the same and a bottle of the Mondavi Napa Cabernet. The drinks came almost immediately. "Long time since I was on a stakeout," he said.

"Me, too. Not since I made lieutenant, except for that one thing at the Carlyle that time." That was when Dino had gotten shot, and Viv had saved his life.

"I don't recall ever doing a stakeout as comfortable as this," Stone said, flipping on the huge flat-screen TV. He stretched out on one of the two beds. "What did you do with Crane?"

"She's at home, with two cops all over her."

"She'll like that," Stone said, laughing.

Don Dugan picked up his cell phone and called Crane's cell.

"Hello?" Sounded like she was in the room.

"How's Atlanta?"

"It's Atlanta."

"Good flight?"

"Passable."

"Still mad at me?"

"A little less so. Is everything all right?"

"Everything's going like clockwork. It's going to be a masterpiece. If everything clicks, I won't leave for Mexico. I'll come to your place."

"I won't be back until Friday," she said.

"Oh, right."

"There's a TV show starting I want to watch," she said. "Good night and good luck."

"Thanks." They both hung up.

A floor below Dugan's suite, Stone and Dino were into their steaks. Dino's cell rang and he answered. "Bacchetti."

"Crane Hart just had a cell call from Don Dugan," Connor said. "He thinks she's in Atlanta."

"Good."

"By the way, his suite is directly over yours."

"Swell. Did you hear anything about his plan for the robbery?"

"No, I think we were too late for that."

"Rats."

"Yeah."

"How many people have we got for tomorrow?"

"Two dozen. All the sellers will be either cops or Strategic Services people. The jewelry will be real."

"Good. I'll be up there in good time. Barrington is with me."

"We won't shoot you."

"Good night."

"Good night." Dino hung up.

"You nervous?" Stone asked.

"Not until I wake up tomorrow."

"You'll sleep?"

"I always sleep, and I wake up when I want to. On the dot."

"Wake me when you wake," Stone said.

Dino pointed up. "Dugan is right up there."

"In this same suite, up one floor?"

"Right."

"Why don't we put a few rounds through the ceiling?" Stone suggested.

"Lovely idea, but noisy. Anyway, I'd rather take him than kill him."

"I'd enjoy it either way," Stone said.

"You're bloodthirstier than I am."

"Only where Dugan is concerned." Stone brushed his teeth and got into his nightshirt.

"I always forget you wear those things," Dino said. "I don't get it."

"Well, if you're sleeping with a woman, there are no bottoms to take off. She can get at you."

"That's something, I guess."

"I'm turning in," Stone said.

"Me, too."

Stone switched off the TV, and the room was dark, curtains closed against the light from the New York skyline.

"Happy dreams," Stone said.

"You bet your ass."

62

Stone and Dino were having a fine room-service breakfast in their suite. Dino checked his watch. Simultaneously, his phone rang. "Bacchetti."

"They're up and around upstairs," a cop said.

"Good." Dino hung up.

"What's the plan?"

"We're going to let them come up the staircase and take the jewelry," he said. "I want it in their hands—and the real thing in their hands—before we bust them. When they come back and head down the stairs, they'll be met by a SWAT team coming the other way, and we'll be right behind them."

"Smooth. What about helicopters?"

"We know that Dugan canceled his, but we

still have a team of four guys on the roof, in case they're needed."

"You have your own choppers?"

"I did have four, then I cut it to one, then I cut that."

"Why?"

"I was being too cautious. They can't get out that way."

"What would you like me to do?" Stone asked.

Dino handed him a lapel pin. "Put this on, and go up there unarmed. They'd just frisk you anyway. Take it all in and be a witness. We can use the testimony of a cool head in court, and you don't need to bust anybody."

"Whatever you say."

"And don't get brave—we've got it covered."

"Fear not," Stone said. "I'm not feeling brave."

Just short of nine o'clock, the team leader on the roof heard a helicopter coming. "Everybody quiet," he said. The chopper set down on the roof, and the rear door opened.

"Get set."

A tall Hasidic Jew in a black suit and hat, with beard and ringlets, got out of the machine and unloaded a suitcase on wheels.

The cop stepped out to meet him.

"I'm delivering," the man said. "I'll be leaving again shortly, so my helicopter will wait for me."

"Go ahead," the team leader said. He went back to the shed. "Stand down," he said. "We've got a seller here, that's all."

The man in black went to the rooftop door and started downstairs. The helicopter pilot cut his engines, and the rotors came to a halt.

"What's that guy doing?" one of the men asked.

"He's waiting for his man," the team leader said, then radioed downstairs. "They say it's okay—nobody else can land while that chopper is sitting there."

Dugan walked down the stairs to the thirty-sixth floor and let himself through the fire door. His group was standing in the hall, waiting, their uniforms on. "Surprise," Dugan said to them. He checked his watch: "Two minutes and we go upstairs. Nobody makes a sound or says an unnecessary word. Rack your shotguns, safeties on."

Stone and Dino arrived two floors up from their suite by elevator and stepped into the hallway. There was considerable bustle as sellers found their rooms and arrayed their wares on tables already set up.

"You go in there," Dino said to Stone, pointing at an open door. "Look like you're selling or buying—you choose."

"Gotcha," Stone said.

"Are you still packing?"

"No, I left it in the room, unloaded."

"I'll be around," Dino said.

Stone watched as a detective with a shotgun went into a coat closet and closed the door behind him. Another detective, pretending to be a seller, buttoned his jacket to conceal his weapon.

Then suddenly, and very quietly, the room was flooded with SWAT members, armed and wearing masks. The occupants of the room were covered, and two men went to the closet door, yanked it open, and roused the surprised detective, then everybody was frisked and disarmed. Nobody said a word. Two of the SWAT team raked jewelry into a bag, then they left the room, leaving one man to cover the room. He was enough.

Stone stood there and listened but heard nothing except the breathing of the people around him. Three or four minutes passed, then the man covering them stepped into the hall. "Nobody move," he said, then closed the door behind him.

Stone tried the phone: dead. His cell phone had no signal.

Dugan received the jewelry bag, then made a cell call. "Start your engines," he said. "Okay, everybody, back down the stairs and move according to plan. Don't shoot anybody, if you can avoid it." He watched them go, then walked slowly down the hallway, feigning a limp, to the fire door and walked upstairs to the roof. He could hear the helicopter engines turning.

Dino watched from the cracked door of a linen

closet as the fake SWAT team assembled and headed for the stairs. As soon as they were through the door, he ran over and locked it behind them. Out of the corner of an eye he saw a tall but stooped Hasid limping slowly down the hall, carrying a bag. He was about to call to him when Stone burst out of the room where he had been held. "Got 'em?" he asked Dino.

"All of them. They're trapped in the stairwell being disarmed."

"What's that noise?" Stone asked, looking up.

"Sounds like a helicopter arriving," Dino said. "Don't worry, we've got it covered."

Dugan walked across the roof, set his bag inside the helicopter, and got inside. He took off his hat and ringlets and put on a headset. "Go," he said to the pilot over the intercom. The chopper rose, then banked and headed west.

A minute later, Dino burst onto the roof, followed closely by Stone. "SWAT team!" he yelled.

A cop stuck his head out the utility shack on the roof. "Yes, Chief?"

"Who's in that helicopter?" Dino demanded, pointing at the fast-disappearing aircraft.

"One Hasidic guy," the team leader said.

"Why was he leaving? The sale hasn't even started!"

"When he landed he said he was delivering, and I called it in," the team leader said.

Dino's radio crackled. "This is Bacchetti."

"We bagged them all," a voice said. "They're stripped of the uniforms and cuffed."

"Did you get the jewelry bag?"

There was a brief silence. "Negative, Chief. No bag."

Dino turned to the team leader. "Did the guy in the chopper take a bag with him?"

"Yes, Chief, one of those things on wheels."

"Oh, shit," Dino said.

63

Dino pressed a button on his cell phone.

"This is Monte."

"Have you got Jake Sutton covered?"

"Yes, Chief, he arrived at eight a.m. and hasn't left his office."

"Is there another way out of his office?"

"There's a staircase to the roof—nowhere to go from there."

"Dugan just left the hotel in a chopper, and he has the loot with him. Get up on that roof and make sure Sutton doesn't join him!"

"Got it, Chief! Stand by!"

Dino waited patiently until the man came back.

"Chief?"

"Yeah?"

"Jake is still in his office. I've got a man posted to keep him off the roof."

"Call me if a chopper shows up."

"Yes, sir."

Dino had a sudden thought. "Monte, does Jake have any kids?"

"Yeah, Chief, he's got a son, Isaac, called Ike. He works in an office across the street."

"Get a couple of men over there, and don't let him leave the building! He may be meeting Dugan! And call me back when you have him contained!" Dino hung up.

"What's happening?" Stone asked.

"Our only shot at Dugan now is if he meets Jacob Sutton with the jewelry." Dino barked into his radio. "Chopper, chopper, you there?"

"Yes, Chief," the pilot replied.

"Pick me up on the Creighton roof, now!"

"Yes, sir! Coming in."

Dugan watched the city slide beneath him as he headed west. He took out his cell phone and pressed a button. It rang three times before being answered.

"Hello?"

"It's Don."

"Where are you?"

"In a helicopter, headed for the meet with Sutton."

"Where?"

"West Side Heliport. Listen, baby, if you want to be with me, use that ticket for Mexico tomorrow. I'm headed for Fort Lauderdale after the meet, and then to the Bahamas. I'll do some banking in the Caymans tomorrow, then head for Mexico City. I want you there when I arrive."

"Okay, I'll be there."

"See you then. Gotta go!" He hung up. "How long?" he asked the pilot.

"Air Traffic Control is holding us off—too much traffic on the West Side."

"How long?"

"Five, six minutes."

"Shit!"

As Dino and Stone watched the helicopter's approach, both their cell phones went off.

"Yeah?" Dino shouted.

"Chief, it's Monte. Ike Sutton didn't show up at his office this morning."

Stone answered his phone. "Yes?"

"It's Crane."

"What do you want?"

"Don just called from a helicopter. He's meeting somebody at the West Side Heliport, then he's headed for Fort Lauderdale and the Bahamas, then the Caymans. He wants me to meet him in Mexico City tomorrow."

"Thanks!" Stone hung up at the same time Dino did. The chopper was setting down, and Dino was starting to move toward it. Stone grabbed his sleeve. "Crane just called me. Dugan is headed for the West Side Heliport to meet Sutton, then he's headed south."

Dino nodded and jumped into the chopper, and Stone followed. "West Side Heliport!" he yelled at the pilot, then he put on a headset. "Did you hear me?"

"Yes, sir, on our way." The machine lifted off to the south, then banked west.

Dino got on his radio and asked for four patrol cars at the heliport. "Nobody leaves that place until I say so!"

Stone spoke up. "Crane says Dugan's plan is to get to the Bahamas, then the Caymans, then to Mexico City tomorrow."

Dino nodded. The pilot came on. "There are delays getting into the West Side Heliport," he said. "Heavy traffic."

"Fuck that!" Dino said. "You tell ATC we're going straight in on a police emergency and to get everybody else the hell out of the way!"

"Yes, Chief!" The pilot began a descent.

"We're cleared in," Dugan's pilot said.

"There'll be a black Lincoln Town Car waiting for me," he said. "Can he pull up to the chopper?"

"No, sir, he'll have to wait outside the gate. How long will you be?"

"Five minutes. I'll pick up one piece of luggage, then we'll head for Teterboro, to Atlantic Aviation. There'll be a Citation CJ-4 on the ramp, November one, two, three, Tango Foxtrot, so set down as close to it as you can."

"Yes, sir!"

The nose was low as they approached, and Dugan could see another helicopter on the ramp, its blades turning. "Can we land?" he asked the pilot.

"Yes, sir, the pad will take two. We'll be landing on the downtown side. The gate's only about thirty yards away, and I see a black Lincoln just outside the gate." He pointed.

"Great! Get us on the ground!"

"Thirty seconds, sir!"

Dugan sat back as the machine slowed, then settled lightly onto the tarmac. "Keep the engines running!" he shouted.

"Yes, sir!"

Dugan picked up his bag and opened the door, then went out, bag first. Somebody reached for the handle. "Let me get that for you!" a man shouted over the noise.

Dugan tried to snatch it back, but the man already had it. Then he noticed something in the man's other hand: a black pistol pointed at Dugan's chest.

"You're under arrest, Dugan!" Dino shouted as he handed the bag to Stone Barrington. "Get on the ground right now!" Stone held the bag and the gun while Dino cuffed him, then got him on his feet and started for the gate. There were cops everywhere, and two of them were taking a man out of the rear seat of a Town Car. They ordered the driver to pop the trunk, then took a large suitcase out of it.

"It was almost payday, wasn't it, Dugan?"

"I haven't done anything," Dugan said. "What are the charges against me?"

"A list as long as your arm," Dino said as he stuffed the big man into the backseat of a patrol car. "Don't worry, we've got your luggage."

64

They were all at the Four Seasons—the Bacchettis, Stone and Ann Keaton, and Mike Freeman. It was a celebratory dinner, and they were in the beautiful pool room.

Stone raised his champagne flute. "I give you Chief of Detectives Dino Bacchetti, soon to be—"

"Stop it," Dino said. "I told you, I'm cautious."

Their first course arrived.

"I have news," Ann said. "I'm not staying with the Lees during the convention, so I'll stay with you."

"Great news," Stone said. "Are you traveling on Air Force One with them?"

"No, they're leaving from Washington. I'll take the campaign plane."

"Don't bother," Stone said. "Strategic Services

has a very nice Gulfstream 650, so all of us will ride with Mike."

"Sounds wonderful."

"For an airplane, it's as good as it gets."

"Dino," Mike said, "what did you do with Crane Hart?"

"She's confined to her apartment until we figure it all out," Dino said.

Stone spoke up. "And what did you do with Bill Murphy and Anita Mays?"

"We cut them loose until the trial," Dino said. "Don't worry, I'll see that you get your hundred grand back. You won't have to make another insurance claim."

"Now that I think about it, it was an insurance claim that started all this," Stone said. "I'll think twice before I file another one."

AUTHOR'S NOTE

I am happy to hear from readers, but you should know that if you write to me in care of my publisher, three to six months will pass before I receive your letter, and when it finally arrives it will be one among many, and I will not be able to reply.

However, if you have access to the Internet, you may visit my Web site, at www.stuartwoods .com, where there is a button for sending me e-mail. So far, I have been able to reply to all my e-mail, and I will continue to try to do so.

If you send me an e-mail and do not receive a reply, it is probably because you are among an alarming number of people who have entered their e-mail address incorrectly in their mail software. I have many of my replies returned as undeliverable.

AUTHOR'S NOTE

Remember: e-mail, reply; snail mail, no reply.

When you e-mail, please do not send attachments, as I never open these. They can take twenty minutes to download, and they often contain viruses.

Please do not place me on your mailing lists for funny stories, prayers, political causes, charitable fund-raising, petitions, or sentimental claptrap. I get enough of that from people I already know. Generally speaking, when I get e-mail addressed to a large number of people, I immediately delete it without reading it.

Please do not send me your ideas for a book, as I have a policy of writing only what I myself invent. If you send me story ideas, I will immediately delete them without reading them. If you have a good idea for a book, write it yourself, but I will not be able to advise you on how to get it published. Buy a copy of Writer's Market at any bookstore; that will tell you how.

Anyone with a request concerning events or appearances may e-mail it to me or send it to: Publicity Department, Penguin Group (USA) LLC, 375 Hudson Street, New York, NY 10014.

Those ambitious folk who wish to buy film, dramatic, or television rights to my books should contact Matthew Snyder, Creative Artists Agency, 9830 Wilshire Boulevard, Beverly Hills, CA 98212-1825.

AUTHOR'S NOTE

Those who wish to make offers for rights of a literary nature should contact Anne Sibbald, Janklow & Nesbit, 445 Park Avenue, New York, NY 10022. (Note: This is not an invitation for you to send her your manuscript or to solicit her to be your agent.)

If you want to know if I will be signing books in your city, please visit my Web site, www.stuartwoods.com, where the tour schedule will be published a month or so in advance. If you wish me to do a book signing in your locality, ask your favorite bookseller to contact his Penguin representative or the Penguin publicity department with the request.

If you find typographical or editorial errors in my book and feel an irresistible urge to tell someone, please write to Sara Minnich at Penguin's address above. Do not e-mail your discoveries to me, as I will already have learned about them from others.

A list of my published works appears in the front of this book and on my Web site. All the novels are still in print in paperback and can be found at or ordered from any bookstore. If you wish to obtain hardcover copies of earlier novels or of the two nonfiction books, a good used-book store or one of the online bookstores can help you find them. Otherwise, you will have to go to a great many garage sales.

Read on for a sneak peek of
the next heart-pounding novel
from #1 *New York Times*
bestselling author Stuart Woods,

INSATIABLE APPETITES

Available from Putnam
in January 2015

1

Election night, late.

Stone Barrington sat on a sofa in the family quarters of the White House, watching the presidential race unfold on television. Things were not going as he had hoped. The race, between Katharine Lee, First Lady of the United States, and Senator Henry Carson of Virginia, seemed to be a dead heat.

Kate Lee and her husband, President Will Lee, were Stone's friends, and he had looked forward to their invitation to spend election night in the family quarters with a couple of dozen good friends. He had not looked forward to seeing her lose the race to a cardboard cutout of a Republican senator, which was how he saw Henry

Carson, known in the Lee campaign as Honk due to a failed attempt to get the nation to think of him as a Hank instead of a Henry. A mispronunciation by a French official had rechristened him.

Ann Keaton, deputy manager for the Lee campaign, to whom Stone was very, very close, came and sat beside him.

"How do you feel about all this?" he asked Ann.

"Nauseous," she replied.

"What's going wrong?"

"We're not getting the turnout our pollsters told us to expect," she said. "Young people and independents are not voting in the numbers we had hoped. At least, that's what our exit polling is telling us. Also, Florida is taking a hell of a long time to count. They've got a Republican governor, and we're worried about hanky-panky. It could be Bush-Gore all over again. On top of that, Ohio is neck and neck."

"The West Coast polls close in ten minutes," Stone said. "Those states should give Kate a boost."

"They should, yes, but California can't put her over the top if Florida and Ohio go the other way. This could be a very big upset."

"Something's happening," Stone said, pointing at the TV. Chris Matthews and Tom Brokaw were on-screen.

"Based on our own exit polling and with eighty-nine percent of the precincts reporting," Brokaw was saying, "our desk is calling Florida for Senator Henry Carson."

"No!" came a shout from across the room. "Not possible!" Senator Sam Meriwether of Georgia, Kate's campaign manager, yelled.

"Easy, Sam," Will Lee said. "It's not necessarily over because a network has called it."

"CBS has called it that way, too, but ABC is holding out," a woman watching another TV set called.

"Fox called it for Honk half an hour ago," somebody said.

"I regard that as encouraging," Stone said, and everybody laughed, releasing some tension in the room.

Kate Lee emerged from the Presidential Bedroom with a coat over her shoulders. "I'd better get over to the armory," she said. "I'm going to have to make a statement soon."

"It's not over yet," her husband said.

"I hope you're right," Kate said, kissing him, "but I'd better be ready." She started for the door, two Secret Service agents in tow.

"Wait a minute!" Sam Meriwether shouted. "CBS is reconsidering their call."

Kate stopped. "Have they reversed themselves?"

"No, but they're saying that Florida is back in the undecided column."

"That has to be a good sign," Ann said to Stone.

"I hope so."

"New totals from Florida," Sam called out. "With ninety-six percent of precincts reporting, Kate leads by three thousand votes!"

Kate walked back toward the TV set. "That's too narrow a margin. What precincts haven't reported?"

Sam pointed at a north Florida county.

"That county is nearly all African-American," Kate said. "It should be ours by a big margin."

"I'm thinking hanky-panky," Sam said.

"Have we got anybody in the courthouse there?"

As they watched, cars pulled up in the courthouse square and men in suits got out.

"Republicans?" somebody asked.

"FBI agents! I see badges."

The men swept into the courthouse.

Will came and stood beside Kate. "You're right," he said. "You'd better get over to the armory. They've got a comfortable room for you to wait in there. Don't do anything precipitous."

Kate kissed him again and ran for the door.

"The West Coast has closed," somebody called.

"MSNBC is backing away from their call in Florida," somebody else said.

"What do they know that we don't?" Stone asked Ann.

"I don't know anymore," Ann said. "I'm through reading exit polls and guessing. We'll know soon anyway."

"One precinct in north Florida has reported and that alone has widened Katharine Lee's lead by another two thousand points," Chris Matthews said. "And we're hearing that they'll have a statewide count at any minute."

"Here's some good news for the Lee campaign," Brokaw said. "Now that the polls in the West have closed, we can tell you that our exit polls show Katharine Lee winning California by nearly thirty points."

A cheer went up around the room.

"We've got a report from Ohio," Brokaw said. "Let's go to Amy Roberts there. Amy?"

"Tom, this is official. All Ohio votes are in, and Kate Lee has won by less than twenty thousand votes!"

There was a roar of glee from the people present. Will Lee was on his cell phone, and everybody knew who he was calling.

Five minutes later, Florida came in with a final vote. "Katharine Lee has won Florida by thirty-one thousand votes!" Chris Matthew said. "We can now call the election. The next president of the United States will be Katharine Lee!"

"Will," Stone called, "did you reach Kate?"

"Yes, and she's hearing that Henry Carson is about to speak."

Carson came on camera before a big crowd and waved for silence. "Well," he said, "we haven't heard from Guam yet." His crowd both laughed and moaned. "But it's clear that our next president will be Kate Lee. I congratulate her for the campaign she ran and the victory she has won. I will do all I can to help her."

The TV switched now to the armory, where Kate was making her way to the podium. Will was not with her by design; he had wanted her to accept or concede on her own terms. She stood for nearly ten minutes, waving to the crowd and waiting for the noise to die down. Eventually, the floor was hers.

"Thank you all," she said, "and my thanks to every American who voted today, no matter for whom. Once again, we are on the brink of new leadership in our country, just the way the framers of the Constitution wanted it. I promise you the best government I can put together, and I invite our Republican friends to help us make this country better than ever!" Finally, when she could speak again, she said, "Will, I know you're watching. Unpack!"

Back at the family quarters, people were pounding Will Lee on the back and opening more champagne.

Stone sank into the sofa, relieved and grateful, happy to be in this room on this night.

2

Stone felt Ann ease from his bed, then heard her get into a robe and slip from the Lincoln Bedroom. He looked at the clock. Half past five.

Wide-awake now, he got out of bed and into some trousers and a shirt, then left the room, looking for coffee, following the scent. He walked into the big oval room and found a table of pastries and a coffee urn. He drew himself a mugful and turned to find a seat.

"Good morning," a female voice said.

Stone turned to find Kate Lee sunk into an armchair, coffee in her hand. "Good morning, Madam President-Elect," he said. "May I be the ten thousandth to congratulate you?" He took a chair facing hers.

"I couldn't sleep," she said. "Will is out like a light, but my mind is still racing."

"I'm not surprised."

"For years I couldn't let myself believe this could happen, and now it has, and I still can't believe it."

"Enjoy your disbelief," he said. "It will get real soon enough."

She checked her watch. "Right now, it's just another early morning at home. In a couple of hours, all hell will break loose. I must remember to find time to write in my journal today." She patted her belly. "He or she will want to read that someday."

"You still don't know?"

"I know I'm out of fashion, but I don't want to know until I can hold him/her in my arms. Neither does Will."

"Maybe this is callously political of me," he said, "but I think your being pregnant is going to be a material advantage to your presidency."

"I hadn't allowed myself to think of that," Kate replied. "How an advantage?"

"It's going to be hard for your opponents to criticize a pregnant woman," Stone said. "I've noticed that men are very delicate with women who are carrying a child."

"That's true in its way."

"I think you should try to get as much as possible accomplished before you give birth."

"After that, I'll just be another mom, huh?"

"Men aren't afraid to argue with their moms."

Kate laughed. "God knows I wasn't afraid to argue with mine. What about you?"

"I learned early on that my mother had an annoying tendency to be right. It was daunting, and I thought twice before I opposed her."

"You were a smart boy."

"That's what she used to tell me."

"Stone, I want to appoint you to something."

He held up a hand. "No, please, Kate."

"Shut up. This is your president-elect speaking. You are now officially the first member of my Kitchen Cabinet."

Stone laughed. "How could I not accept that post? I'm honored beyond words."

"And you will serve for the entire eight years."

"That's thinking ahead."

"A president can get things done in a first term, but she needs a second to keep her opponents from dismantling her accomplishments."

"You've got a narrow majority in both houses—that should help."

"The next congressional campaign starts today," she said, "and so does my charm offensive with Republican congresspeople and senators. They may vote against me a lot of the time, but I'm going to make their hearts break when they do."

"I believe you."

"I heard Ann sneak back to her room a few minutes ago."

"Oops."

"I'm happy that you two were able to get together for a while, and, believe me, I'm sorry that I'm going to be keeping you apart for a long time."

"Thank you. We've talked about that, and we know it has to be done."

"What is it the mafiosi say? This is the business we've chosen."

"Ann knows that."

"I'm glad she does." Kate got to her feet. "I hope you'll be around for a few days."

"No, I have to get back. I've been away from my desk for too long, what with the Paris trip, and I flew a borrowed airplane down here that has to be returned."

"I hear you bought a house in Paris."

"I did, and I have to be careful about doing that every time I get a little depressed. If you and Will ever need a hideaway, it will be waiting for you."

"That's sweet of you," Kate said, patting his cheek, "but the only hideaway we're going to have is the one we have now at Camp David. And that's sort of like a White House in the woods. We'll take you up on your Paris house when they kick us out of town." She kissed him on the forehead and padded out of the room.

Stone thought maybe he should start a journal of his own.

e. B.